老師天天在用

套用・替換 零失誤！
雙語教學萬用句

針對各科課室英語教學設計

作者 白善燁　譯者 許竹瑩

全音檔下載導向頁面

https://globalv.com.tw/mp3-download-9789864544059/

掃描QR碼進入網頁並註冊後，按「全書音檔下載請按此」連結，可一次性下載音檔壓縮檔，或點選檔名線上播放。
全MP3一次下載為ZIP壓縮檔，部分智慧型手機需安裝解壓縮程式方可開啟，iOS系統請升級至iOS 13以上。
此為大型檔案，建議使用WIFI連線下載，以免占用流量，並請確認連線狀況，以利下載順暢。

使 | 用 | 說 | 明

本書
第 1 部分

收錄校園相關單字

整理從校園、各學科到課堂上的各類單字，校園內所到之處都可用英文表達。

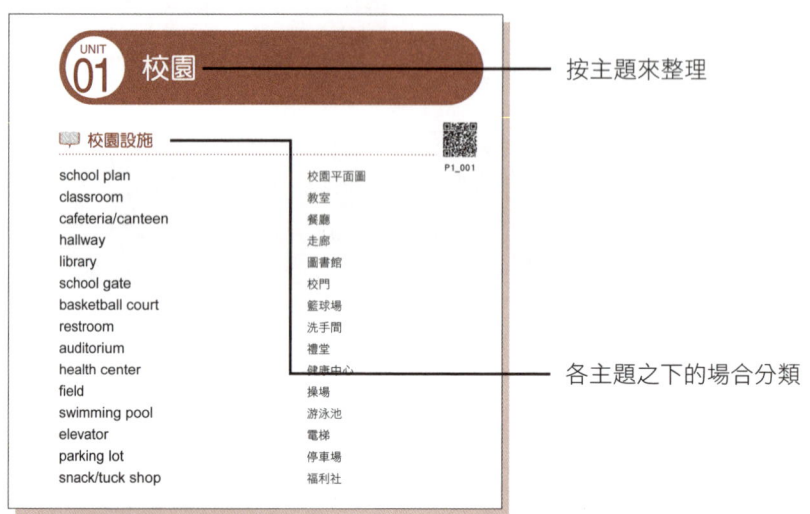

按主題來整理

各主題之下的場合分類

本書
第 2 部分

歸納學期間、課堂上的課室用語

收錄如「上課前」、「考試週」、「第一堂課」等學期間各場合適合的常用語，以及教室管理、班規等的用語。

各主題之下的課堂情境分類

英中對照的例句整理

★ 音檔錄製方式：
・先聽到英文。
・再聽到中文。

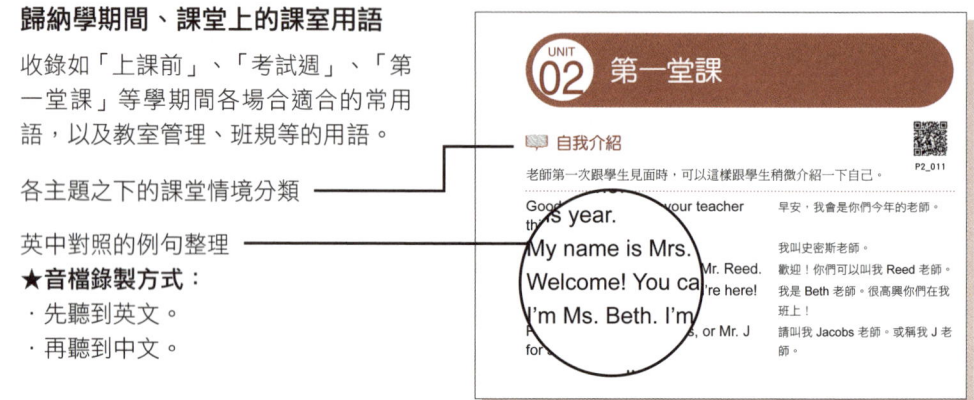

本書第 3 部分

嚴選實際課堂上的常用課室英語句型

依各主題、場合或目的整理出 200 多個句型公式,讓你一次學會如何靈活運用課室英語。

- 依課堂上各目的來分類
- 課室英語的常用句型
- 解說文字
- 套用句型的例句示範

★ 中英反應力訓練的音檔設計
· 先聽到中文。
· 接著聽 2 遍英文。
- 短對話

依各科分類的課室英語用語

依各科來分類的課室英語

英中對照的例句整理

★ 音檔錄製方式:
· 先聽到英文。
· 再聽到中文。

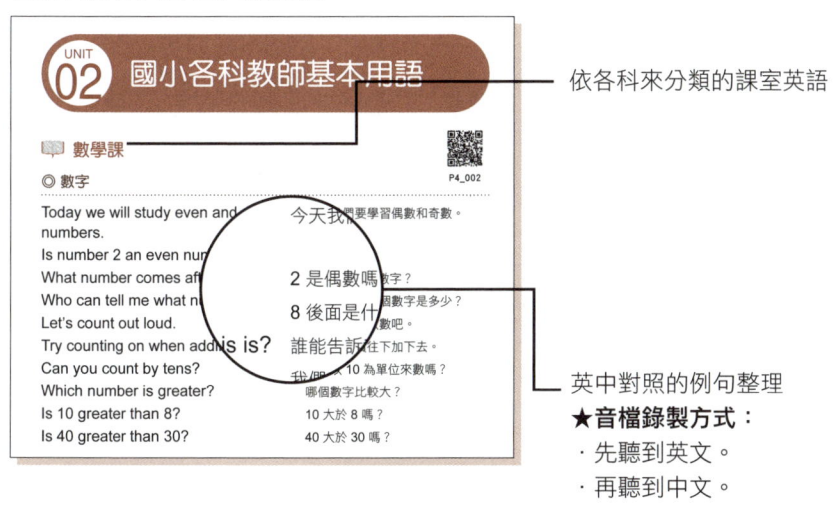

contents 目錄

PART 01 校園基本單字　21

Unit 01 校園　22

- 001　校園設施　22
- 002　校園設備　22
- 003　辦公室　23
- 004　教室　23
- 005　校園活動　23

Unit 02 學科　25

- 001　學科名稱　25
- 002　教職員　26

Unit 03 教室　27

- 001　設備　27
- 002　必備用品　28
- 003　文具（筆）　28
- 004　其他文具　28
- 005　上課時常做的事　29
- 006　使用設備時可用的表達　30
  黑板／投影機／麥克風／燈光、空調／掃描 QR 碼／網路

PART 02 教室基本用語　　　33

Unit 01 學期間的常用語　　　34

001　準備上課　　　34
002　確認今日課程　　　34
003　詢問課程主題　　　35
004　請拿出課本或文具　　　35
005　請翻開課本　　　35
006　是否翻到正確頁面　　　36
007　是否找到文字或圖片　　　36
008　描述單字在書上的位置　　　36
009　發教材或講義　　　37
010　請學生發東西　　　37
011　確認拿到的資料　　　37
012　確認是否理解　　　37
013　開始進行活動　　　38
014　分組　　　38
015　上台解題　　　38
016　表演或發言　　　39
017　是否同意某想法或建議　　　39
018　徵求意見與想法　　　40
019　放學前　　　40
020　考試　　　41
021　學期末放假前　　　42
022　開學第一天　　　42
023　關心用語　　　43
024　讚美用語　　　44

contents 目錄

Unit 02 第一堂課 *46*

- 001　自我介紹 *46*
- 002　課程介紹 *46*
- 003　班級介紹 *47*
- 004　選班長 *47*

Unit 03 教室管理 *48*

- 001　班規 *48*
- 002　課堂秩序管理 *49*
- 003　吸引注意力 *49*
- 004　要求仔細聽、仔細看 *50*
- 005　要求看某物或某人 *50*
- 006　請求幫助 *50*
- 007　離開一下、請假 *50*
- 008　同學間的衝突 *51*

PART 03 課室英語句型及用語　　53

Unit 01 準備上課 *54*

001　就座 *54*

001　Take your seats...　請坐，～

002　開始上課 *55*

002　Class will begin...　課程將～開始。

| **003** | 請拿出課本或文具 | 57 |

003　Everyone take out... 每個人都拿出～

| **004** | 請把東西準備好 | 58 |

004　Please have your... 請準備好～／請拿出～

| **005** | 翻頁 & 確認頁碼 | 59 |

005　Open your books... 把書翻開～
006　Turn to page... 翻到第～頁

| **006** | 教室管理 | 61 |

007　I want you guys to... 希望大家～／麻煩大家～
008　Everyone, calm down... 大家都冷靜下來～
009　Please quiet down... 請安靜～
010　Please stop... 請停止～／請別～
011　It's time to... 是時候～／該來～／～的時間到了
012　Raise your hand if... 如果～，請舉手

Unit 02 提醒、要求與關心 ─────────────── 67

| **007** | 提醒要做與不要做的事 | 67 |

013　Please avoid... 請避免～／請不要～
014　Try not to... 儘量不要～
015　Would everyone return...? 請大家回到～／交回～／歸還～
016　Don't neglect... 別疏於～／別忽視～
017　Don't forget... 別忘了～
018　Don't lose your... 別弄丟你的～

| **008** | 時間上的叮嚀 | 72 |

019　You have... minutes... 你們有～分鐘時間～／距離～還有～分鐘時間

contents 目錄

009 請注意這裡 — 74

020 Turn your attention to... 注意聽～／注意看～／專心～
021 Please give your attention to... 請注意～／請專心～
022 Listen up everyone... 各位，請認真聽～

010 要求 — 77

023 Everyone, please... 請各位～
024 Could you all please...? 請大家都～
025 Everyone needs to... 每個人都要～
026 Keep working... 繼續～
027 The last thing I want you to do is... 我希望你們做的最後一件事～
028 I need you to... 我需要你們～

011 關心與協助 — 83

029 The head teacher wants to see you... 班導師～要見你
030 Can I help you...? 我能幫你～嗎？
031 Would you care for...? 你想要～嗎？
032 You will need... 你們需要～
033 When in doubt, ... 如有疑問／不確定的話，～
034 Feel free to... 請隨時～／請自在～
035 Take a moment to... 花點時間～
036 Take your time... 慢慢來～／花點時間～
037 Does anyone need...? 有人需要～嗎？

012 確認狀況與進度 — 92

038 Is that what...? 這是～的嗎？
039 Are you done with...? ～完了嗎？
040 How many of you...? 你們之中有多少人～？
041 I'm still waiting for... 我還在等～
042 Which one of you...? 你們之中哪一位～？
043 Are there any...? 有～嗎？

8

013 強調 — 98

044 What I'm trying to say is that... 我想說的是～
045 In the meantime... 在此期間，～／與此同時，～
046 Can someone carry...? 有人能幫我搬一下～嗎？
047 Is that okay with...? ～可以嗎？／～同意嗎？
048 It's been... since... 自從～已經～了
049 The only thing that... is... …唯一的～是～
050 This is the last... 這是最後一次～
051 Without a doubt, ... 毫無疑問，～

014 徵求自願者 — 106

052 I need a volunteer to... 我需要一名自願者來～
053 Can someone...? 有誰能～嗎？
054 Who's going to...? 誰將～呢？／誰要～呢？

015 說明原因 — 109

055 That's because... 那是因為～

016 表達動機 — 110

056 I just wanted to... 我只是想～
057 I just wanted to let you guys... 我只是想讓你們～

Unit 03 課程與教材 — 112

017 確認上課主題 — 112

058 Let's review... 我們複習一下～
059 Let's go over... 我們來（仔細）看看～
060 Our English lesson today will cover... 今天的英文課，我們要來學～
061 This morning, we will... 今天早上我們要～
062 Let's begin by... 我們先～／我們先從～開始
063 Are we going to talk about...? 我們要來談談～嗎？
064 Let's look at... 我們來看看～

contents 目錄

018 說明主題特色 ——————————————————— 119
065 Our guest today is... 今天的嘉賓是～
066 This book is... 這本書～

019 提示接下來的主題 ——————————————— 121
067 After lunch, we will... 午餐後，我們將～

020 解說 ——————————————————————— 122
068 Let me tell you about... 我來告訴各位～／我來跟各位說～
069 Let me explain... 我來解釋一下～
070 That's the way... ～就是～／～正是～

021 請學生仔細聽（看） ————————————— 125
071 Watch closely... 注意看～／仔細觀察～
072 Listen carefully... 注意聽～

022 確認是否跟上進度 —————————————— 127
073 Can everyone see...? 大家都能看到～嗎？／大家都懂～嗎？

023 確認是否有問題 ——————————————— 128
074 Any questions...? 有什麼疑問嗎？
075 Do you see...? 你理解～嗎？／你有看到～嗎？

024 回到上一步 ————————————————— 129
076 Could we go back to...? 我們回到～好嗎？

025 進行下一步 ————————————————— 130
077 Let's move on to... 我們接著進行～／我們開始進行～

026 按順序說明 ————————————————— 131
078 First of all, ... 首先，～

079 Next, ... 接下來，～

027　詢問學生想法 ─── 133
080 What do you think about...? 你對～有什麼看法呢？
081 Does anyone have...? 有人（有）～嗎？／誰（有）～嗎？
082 Can anyone tell me...? 誰能告訴我～？
083 Please explain... 請解釋一下～
084 Which one do you...? 你～哪一個呢？

028　學習上的指示與建議 ─── 138
085 Please follow... 請按照～／請遵循～
086 If you get confused... 如果你感到困惑，～
087 Focus on.... 專注於～／注意～／把重點放在～
088 Notice... 請注意～
089 You should all... 你們都應該～
090 I recommend... 我推薦～／我建議～
091 If you have a question, ... 有任何疑問，～
092 As you listen... 邊聽～邊～／聽的時候，～
093 Take care to... 確保～／注意～

Unit 04 發講義或教具 ─── 147

029　發東西下去 ─── 147
094 Everyone, take a ... 請各位～／請大家各～
095 I'm handing out... 我要把～發下去
096 Take one and... 拿一張（個）～

030　多拿一張時 ─── 150
097 Who has an extra...? 誰有多的～嗎？

Unit 05 課堂練習、作業與考試 ─── 151

031　出作業 ─── 151
098 Tomorrow's assignment is... 明天的功課是～

11

contents 目錄

| 032 | 做課堂練習 | 152 |

099 This exercise requires you to... 這題練習題是要你～
100 Is this problem...? 這個問題～嗎？

| 033 | 寫考卷 | 154 |

101 Please put your name.... 請在～寫上你的名字
102 No cheating... ～不許作弊
103 The test will cover... 考試範圍為～
104 The test is... 測驗～

| 034 | 繳交作業或考卷 | 158 |

105 Pass forward your... 把你們的～往前傳
106 Turn in your... 請交～
107 The assignment is due... ～前要交功課
108 The highest score was... 最高分是～

Unit 06 進行活動 ——————————————— 162

| 035 | 徵求表現機會 | 162 |

109 Come up to the front and... 到前面來～
110 Who would like to...? 誰願意～呢？
111 Who wants to recite...? 誰想朗誦～？
112 Who can solve...? 誰能解決～？
113 Who knows...? 有誰知道～？

| 036 | 輪流進行 | 167 |

114 Let's take turns... 我們輪流～吧。
115 Whose turn is it to...? 輪到誰～了？

| 037 | 一起覆誦 | 169 |

116 Repeat after me... 跟著我唸～／跟我一起唸～

12

| 038 | 同學間倆倆做練習 ———————————————————— 170

117　Turn to your partner and... 請向你們的搭檔～／請～你們的搭檔～

| 039 | 動筆寫 ————————————————————————— 171

118　Write this down... 把它寫下來
119　Write your name... 在～寫上你的名字

Unit 07 進行討論 ————————————————————— 173

| 040 | 出題與開頭 —————————————————————— 173

120　Let's suppose... 假設～
121　Imagine what it was like... 想像一下～是什麼～
122　Let's discuss... 我們來討論～／我們來談談～
123　True or false: ...? ～，對還是錯？

| 041 | 集思廣益 ——————————————————————— 177

124　Can you think of...? 你們能想到～嗎？
125　Try to come up with... 試著想出～

| 042 | 針對議題探討 ————————————————————— 179

126　It's important to consider... 考慮～是很重要的。

| 043 | 回應對方觀點 ————————————————————— 180

127　There has never been... 從未有過～／沒有比～更～
128　Your theory is... 你的理論～
129　Can you be more...? 你能夠更～嗎？
130　This will be difficult... 這很難～
131　That's not my idea of... 我不認為～

| 044 | 宣布答案 ——————————————————————— 185

132　Grades are announced... 成績將於～公布
133　The correct answer is... 正確答案是～

13

contents 目錄

Unit 08 基本的回應與互動 ... 187

045 鼓勵 ... 187

134 There will be extra points... ～將獲得加分。
135 Let's try to... 我們試著～吧。
136 I'm sure that... 我確信～／我相信～
137 There's no time to... 沒時間～
138 If you try to... 如果你試著～／努力～，就～
139 Don't be afraid of... 不要害怕～
140 Do your best... 盡力～／盡你所能～
141 Don't give up... 不要放棄～

046 給予建議 ... 195

142 It doesn't mean... 這並不表示～
143 You should try to... 你應該試著～／你應該儘量～
144 May I suggest...? 我可以建議／提議～嗎？
145 The best way to... is... ～最好的方法是～
146 Let's put a little more effort into... 我們再加把勁～吧
147 It would be wise to... 最好～
148 You should have... 你早應該要～
149 Would you just...? 你能不能～呢？
150 Why don't we...? 我們何不～呢？
151 It's not enough to just... 僅僅～是不夠的／光～是不夠的。

047 引導 ... 205

152 Wouldn't you like...? 難道你不想～嗎？
153 There are so many reasons why... ～的理由有很多
154 Why do you always...? 為什麼你總是～？
155 If I were you, I'd... 如果我是你，我會～

048 讚美 ... 209

156 I like your... 我喜歡你的～
157 This is the best... 這是～最～的～

14

158　Good work...　～做得很好。
159　It's very... of you to...　你～真是太～了。
160　Congratulations on your...　恭喜你～

049　拒絕 ——————————————————— *214*

161　I'm sorry I can't...　抱歉，我無法～
162　I'm sorry to say that...　很遺憾，～

050　結論 ——————————————————— *216*

163　No wonder....　難怪～
164　The worst part is...　最糟糕的是～

051　責備 ——————————————————— *218*

165　There's no excuse for...　沒有任何理由～／～是沒有任何藉口的
166　I told you guys to...　我告訴過你們～了。

052　給予評論 —————————————————— *220*

167　I don't like the way...　我不喜歡～的方式。
168　That's not exactly...　那不完全是～
169　Don't underestimate...　不要低估／小看～

Unit 09 學生在課堂中的常用句 ——————————— *223*

053　心情的表達 —————————————————— *223*

170　I can't wait...　我迫不及待要～了。／我等不及要～了。
171　I'm so glad...　我很高興～
172　I can't believe...　真不敢相信～
173　There are so many...　～真的很多。

054　表達想法 —————————————————— *227*

174　Don't you think...?　你不覺得～嗎？／你不認為～嗎？
175　It's better for me to...　我最好還是～
176　I didn't mean to...　我不是故意～的。

15

contents 目錄

177 I don't mind... 我不介意～
178 That's all I... 這就是我所～的。
179 I didn't get... 我沒（獲得）～

055 準備要做的事 ——————————————————— 233

180 I'm planning to... 我打算～
181 I was just going to... 我（剛剛）正打算要～

056 建議 ——————————————————————— 235

182 We'd better... 我們最好～
183 How about...? ～如何？

057 必須 ——————————————————————— 237

184 I had no choice but... 我別無選擇，只能～／我不得不～
185 We all need to... 我們都需要～

058 堅決與肯定 ———————————————————— 239

186 I won't... 我不會～
187 I'm absolutely... 我絕對～／我真的～／我十分～

059 請求協助 ————————————————————— 241

188 Can you check...? 你能檢查一下～嗎？／你能看一下～嗎？
189 What is ... in English? ～用英語怎麼說？
190 I'm looking for... 我正在找～
191 We're out of... 我們～沒了。／我們～用完了。
192 There's no way... 沒辦法～／不可能～
193 Have you got...? 你有～嗎？
194 All I need is... 我只要～就好。／我所需要的是～。

060 感謝 ——————————————————————— 247

195 Thank you for... 謝謝你～

061　同儕合作 — 248

196 Let me see if...　讓我看看是否～

062　提出問題 — 249

197 I don't understand why...　我不明白為何～
198 I don't understand...　我不明白～
199 How often should we...?　我們應該要多久～一次～？
200 Is there anything...?　有什麼～嗎？／有～的嗎？
201 I'm not sure what...　我不確定～什麼
202 What was it like...?　～是什麼感覺？
203 What's the most efficient way...?　～最有效率的方法是什麼呢？
204 What if...?　如果～怎麼辦？
205 What I want to ask is...　我想問的（是）～
206 I don't know if...　我不知道～是否～
207 How come...?　怎麼會～？／為什麼～？
208 I have no idea...　我不知道～
209 I wonder why....　我想知道為什麼～

063　確認是否可以 — 262

210 Is it okay...?　可以～嗎？

064　做確認 — 263

211 Let me check...　讓我看一下／檢查～
212 There must be...　一定有～／肯定有～
213 It sounds like...　聽起來（好像）～
214 I never thought...　我從沒想過～
215 Did you know...?　你知道～嗎？
216 I have heard...　我聽說～
217 I'm afraid, but...　我有點害怕，但～
218 It's easy to...　很容易～

17

Unit 10 下課或放學 — 272

065 下課休息 — 272
219 When the bell rings, ... 打鐘時～
220 Let's take a break... ～我們休息一下吧！

066 待在原位 — 274
221 Stay seated... 請待在座位上，～

067 放學前提醒 — 275
222 By the way, ... 順帶一提，～
223 Like I said before... 正如我之前所說，～
224 Remember to... 要記得～
225 Remember to bring... 要記得帶～
226 Be sure to study... 務必要好好學習～

068 放學道別 — 280
227 We'll meet again... 我們～再見。
228 Have a terrific... 祝你有個愉快的～

PART 04 各科目上課基本用語　　287

Unit 01 幼兒園教師基本用語 — 288
001　日常對話 — 288
002　熱身與帶動唱 — 288
003　課堂互動 — 288

18

Unit 02 國小各科教師基本用語 —— *290*

- 001　數學課 ———————————————————————— *290*
　　　　數字／加減乘除／教學與解題／時間
- 002　自然科學課 ————————————————————— *292*
　　　　動植物／人體／氣候與天氣／地球科學／物理化學
- 003　體育課 ———————————————————————— *295*
　　　　暖身／籃球／足球／棒球／網球／游泳／體操／田徑
- 004　音樂課 ———————————————————————— *298*
　　　　節拍與韻律／音符／歌曲／表演與樂器
- 005　視覺藝術課 ————————————————————— *301*
　　　　色相環／色調／調色／繪畫

校園基本單字
Basic Vocabulary

UNIT 01 校園

📖 校園設施

P1_001

school plan	校園平面圖
classroom	教室
cafeteria/canteen	餐廳
hallway	走廊
library	圖書館
school gate	校門
basketball court	籃球場
restroom	洗手間
auditorium	禮堂
health center	健康中心
field	操場
swimming pool	游泳池
elevator	電梯
parking lot	停車場
snack/tuck shop	福利社

📖 校園設備

fire hydrant	消防栓
drinking fountain	飲水機
locker	置物櫃
public address(PA) system	廣播系統
school bell	學校打鈴鐘

📖 辦公室

P1_002

principal's office	校長室
academic affairs	教務處
student affairs	學務處
general affairs	總務處
teacher's and staff's office	教職員辦公室
special education office	特殊教育辦公室
counseling office	輔導室
personnel office	人事室
accounting office	會計室
security room	警衛室

📖 教室

language lab	語言教室
audiovisual room	視聽教室
music classroom	音樂教室
home economics room	家政教室
computer lab	電腦教室
fine arts room	美術教室
laboratory	實驗室

📖 校園活動

school anniversary	校慶
sports day	運動會
weekly assembly	週會
morning assembly	朝會

23

parent-teacher conference	家長會
new family orientation	新生家長說明會；新生訓練
class assembly	班會

補充說明

Snack/Tuck shop 福利社

合作社裡大多販賣一些簡單的零食（snacks）、飲料（beverage）、文具（stationery），方便學生在短暫下課時間快速購買與充飢。因此「合作社」的英文叫做（school）snack shop，或是英式說法的 tuck shop，前者的 snack 是指「零食；點心」，後者的 tuck 則有「填塞」的意思，這裡也就是指「能充飢的食物」，所以無論是前者或後者皆指「購買點心的地方」。

學科

 學科名稱

Mandarin/Chinese	國語
English	英文
Math/Mathematics	數學
Science	自然科學
Physics	物理
Chemistry	化學
History	歷史
Geography	地理
Biology	生物
Art	美術
Music	音樂
Physical Education (P.E.)	體育
Intergrated Activities	綜合活動
Civic and Social Education	公民與社會
Earth Science	地球科學
Home Economics	家政
Information Science	資訊
Health and Nursing	健康與護理
Living Technology	生活科技

📖 教職員

P1_004

principal	校長
homeroom teacher	班級導師
substitute teacher	代課老師
Chinese teacher	國語老師
English teacher	英文老師
math/mathematics teacher	數學老師
science teacher	自然老師
physics and chemistry teacher	理化老師
history teacher	歷史老師
geography teacher	地理老師
biology teacher	生物老師
art teacher	美術老師
music teacher	音樂老師
school physician	校醫
school nurse	護士
technician	技士
security guard	警衛

UNIT 03 教室

 設備

P1_005

whiteboard	白板
blackboard	黑板
teacher's desk	導師桌
desk	書桌
chair	椅子
magnet	磁鐵
eraser	板擦
chalk	粉筆
marker	白板筆
bulletin board	公告欄
class schedule	課表
suspended projector	懸掛式投影機
screen	螢幕
extension cord	延長線
blackboard eraser cleaner	板擦清潔器
chalk dust	粉筆屑
curtain	窗簾
microphone	麥克風
internet	網路
computer	電腦

📖 必備用品

P1_006

schoolbag	書包
backpack	後背包
textbook	課本
workbook	作業本
notebook	筆記本
pencil box	鉛筆盒
water bottle	水壺
uniform	制服
sports clothes	運動服
handkerchief	手帕
lunch box	便當盒
lunch bag	便當袋

📖 文具（筆）

pencil	鉛筆
crayon	蠟筆
marker	彩色筆；麥克筆
pen	原子筆
highlighter	螢光筆
mechanical/propelling pencil	自動鉛筆
fountain pen	鋼筆

📖 其他文具

eraser	橡皮擦
correction tape	修正帶

ruler	尺
white glue	白膠
binder	活頁資料夾
protractor	量角器
glue stick	口紅膠
loose-leaf paper	活頁紙
compasses	圓規
safety scissors	安全剪刀
box cutter	美工刀
stapler	釘書機
staples	釘書針
post-it	便利貼
calculator	計算機
plastic book cover	書套

 上課時常做的事

P1_007

have roll call; check attendance	點名
discuss	討論
answer	回答
erase the board	擦黑（白）板
pair up	（分組）配對
make a presentation	報告
hand in	繳交
dismiss the class	讓學生下課
raise your hand	舉手
write on the board	寫黑（白）板

29

📖 使用設備時可用的表達

◎黑板

Can you erase the board?	你可以擦黑板嗎？
Please erase the board for me.	請幫我擦黑板。
Who would like to show how to solve the problem on the blackboard?	誰願意上來解黑板上這道題？
Can someone take notes on the blackboard?	誰可以上來在黑板上做記錄嗎？
I'll write your homework on the blackboard.	我會把你們的作業寫在黑板上。

◎投影機

I'll show you on the projector.	我用投影機來呈現給你們看。
Eyes on the screen, please.	請看螢幕。
We'll be using the projector today.	今天我們會用投影機。
Follow along on the overhead projector.	跟著投影機上的內容。
I'll post the notes on the projector.	我會把筆記放在投影機上。

◎麥克風

Can you hear me?	你們聽得到我說話嗎？
I'll use the microphone.	我要使用麥克風。
Can you turn up the microphone?	你可以把麥克風的音量調大嗎？
It's easier to hear with the microphone.	使用麥克風比較聽得清楚。
Is the microphone loud enough?	麥克風的音量夠大嗎？

◎燈光 / 空調

Can we turn the lights off?	我們可以關燈嗎？
Are the lights too bright?	燈光會不會太亮？
Hit the lights, please!	請關燈！

I'm getting hot. 我覺得有點熱。
Let's turn on the AC. 我們來開空調吧。

◎掃描 QR 碼

Scan here for the link. 請掃描這裡取得連結。
If you scan the QR code, it will open the app you need. 如果掃描這個 QR 碼，它會打開你需要的應用程式。
Here's a QR code for the video. 這是影片的 QR 碼。
Scan this code for the book. 掃描這本書的這個 QR 碼。
Here's a QR code for you to use. 這裡有個 QR 碼讓你掃描。

◎網路

I don't think the Wi-Fi is on. 我覺得 Wi-Fi 沒有開。
Is anyone else's iPad not working? 還有誰的 iPad 不能用嗎？
Are you connected to the internet? 你有連上網路嗎？
What is the Wi-Fi password? Wi-Fi 密碼是什麼？
The internet is slow today. 今天的網路很慢。

31

教室基本用語

Classroom English Expressions

UNIT 01 學期間的常用語

📖 準備上課

學生剛進教室時可以這樣跟學生打招呼。

Welcome to school!	歡迎來到學校！
How are you today?	你今天好嗎？
It's good to see you.	很高興見到你。
Nice to see you!	很高興見到你！
I'm glad you're here.	很高興在這裡見到你。
Come on in!	請進！
Good morning, class.	同學們早安。
Happy Monday!	祝有個快樂的週一！
It's going to be a great day!	今天會是個美好的一天！
How's it going?	一切都好嗎？

Dialogue

T How are you today?	你今天好嗎？
S I'm doing well.	我很好。

📖 確認今日課程

Where did we leave off?	我們上次上在哪裡？
What page did we stop at last time?	我們上次上在第幾頁？
Did we end on section 14?	我們上次是結束在第 14 節嗎？
What page did we end on yesterday?	昨天我們結束在哪一頁？
What was the section we were on?	我們上次上到哪一節？

📖 詢問課程主題

P2_002

What's the topic for today?	今天的主題是什麼？
What will we be covering today?	我們今天要上什麼？
What is today's lesson about?	今天的課程是關於什麼？
What will we be learning about today?	我們今天要學什麼？
Do you know what the lesson is about?	你們知道今天的課程是關於什麼嗎？

📖 請拿出課本或文具

Please take out your reading book.	請拿出你們的閱讀課本。
Grab your math book.	拿出你們的數學課本。
Can everyone get their book out?	各位都可以把課本拿出來嗎？
It's time for reading. Get your book out.	現在是閱讀時間，把你們的課本拿出來。
Let's get started with science. Please take out your book.	我們開始上科學課了，請拿出你們的課本。

📖 請翻開課本

Turn to page 43.	請翻到第 43 頁。
We'll start on page 70.	我們從第 70 頁開始。
Looks like we left off on page 27.	看起來我們上次停在第 27 頁。
I'd like you to find page 34.	希望你們都找到第 34 頁。
Flip to page 55.	請翻到第 55 頁。

35

📖 是否翻到正確頁面

P2_003

Did everyone find the page?	各位都找到那一頁了嗎？
Do you need help finding the page?	需要我幫忙找到那一頁嗎？
Raise your hand if you need help finding the page.	需要幫忙找到那一頁的話，請舉手。
Are you on the right page?	你們在對的頁面上嗎？
Give me a thumbs up when you find the page.	找到那一頁時，請比個讚。

📖 是否找到文字或圖片

Do you see the bold word?	你們有看到那個粗體字嗎？
Does anyone need help finding the chart?	有人需要幫忙找圖表嗎？
Raise your hand if you don't see what I'm talking about.	如果沒看到我在講的內容，請舉手。
Put your hand up if you don't see the picture.	如果沒看到那張圖，請舉手。
Does everyone see the graph?	你們每個人都看到圖表了嗎？

📖 描述單字在書上的位置

It's on the second page.	它在第二頁。
You'll find it in the third paragraph.	你們會在第三段找到。
Look at the first line on page 40.	請看 40 頁的第一行。
It's near the end of the second sentence.	在第二句的後面。
Check out the 4th line of the second paragraph.	請看第二段的第 4 行。

📖 發教材或講義

Take a copy of each.	每人拿一份。
Take what you need.	拿各位需要的那一份。
Take a look at these materials.	看看這些教材。
Let's look over the materials.	我們一起來看這些教材。

📖 請學生發東西

Who is my paper passer?	誰是負責幫我發資料的人？
Who can help pass these out?	誰可以幫我發這些？
Jacob, can you pass out these papers?	雅各布，你能幫忙發這些資料嗎？
Will you return these tests, please.	你能幫我把這些考卷發還給大家嗎？
Please pass these out.	請幫忙發這些。

📖 確認拿到的資料

Did you get everything you need?	都拿到所有需要的東西了嗎？
Did everyone get these materials?	每個人都拿到教材了嗎？
Any questions for these?	關於這些有什麼問題嗎？

📖 確認是否理解

Do you understand?	你們理解了嗎？
Are there any questions?	有任何問題嗎？
Does anyone need help?	有人需要幫助嗎？

Should I go over it again?　　　　　我需要再講一遍嗎？
Does anybody need me to review　　有人需要我再重複一次嗎？
it again?

📖 開始進行活動

Let's get started!　　　　　　我們開始吧！
Who's ready?　　　　　　　　誰準備好了？
Time to get started!　　　　　是時候開始了！
Go ahead and start!　　　　　開始吧！
Is everyone ready?　　　　　大家都準備好了嗎？

📖 分組

We'll split up into groups of three.　　我們將分成三人一組。
I'm going to put you in pairs.　　　　我要把你們分成兩人一組。
I'll count off groups.　　　　　　　　我會按人數分組。
We'll be working in groups. I'll　　　我們分組進行，我來分配你們的組
assign you your team.　　　　　　　別。
Let's count off for groups of 4.　　　我們四人一組。

📖 上台解題

Jen, can you solve the problem on　　Jen，你能解黑板上這一題嗎？
the blackboard?

Ryan, will you show us your work　　Ryan，你能在黑板上示範一下你
on the blackboard?　　　　　　　　的解題過程嗎？

Who can show us how to solve the problem on the board?	誰能解黑板上這一題？
I need a volunteer to write the answers on the blackboard.	我需要一位自願者把答案寫到黑板上。
Lisa, can you write the answer on the board?	Lisa，你能在黑板上寫出答案嗎？

📖 表演或發言

Who would like to read out loud?	誰要來朗讀？
Andrew, can you read your speech to the class?	Andrew，你能在全班面前朗讀你的演講稿嗎？
Mary, would you show us how to play this part?	Mary，你可以飾演這個角色嗎？
Who can act out this part for everyone?	誰能為大家飾演這角色？
Will you show the class how you did that, Ryan?	Ryan，你能在全班面前示範一下你是怎麼做到的嗎？

📖 是否同意某想法或建議

Do you agree or disagree with the idea?	你同意還是不同意這個想法？
How do you feel about their opinion?	你對他們的觀點有什麼感覺？
What are your thoughts on the suggestions?	你對這些建議有什麼看法？
What part do you disagree with?	你不同意的是哪一部分？
Do you agree with her opinion?	你同意她的看法嗎？

📖 徵求意見與想法

P2_007

What are your thoughts?	你有什麼看法？
Who agrees with the writer?	誰同意作者的觀點？
Does anyone disagree with this statement?	有人不同意這個說法嗎？
How did you feel about the article?	你對這篇文章有什麼感受？
Did you agree with the decision they made?	你同意他們做的決定嗎？
What did you think of the story?	你覺得這個故事如何？
Did you like the film?	你喜歡這部影片嗎？
Raise your hand if you liked the story.	如果喜歡這個故事，請舉手。
Who disliked the film?	誰不喜歡這部影片？
What was your favorite part of the story?	你最喜歡故事的哪一部分？

📖 放學前

準備放學回家前，老師可以用英文提醒學生一些重要的事。

Put on your jacket.	請穿上外套。
Don't forget your book!	別忘了你的書！
Be sure to take your homework with you.	務必把作業帶回去。
Do you have everything?	所有東西都帶了嗎？
Whose sweatshirt is this?	這件運動衫是誰的？
Did you remember your lunchbox?	便當盒有記得帶吧？
Don't forget to take home your art project.	別忘了把美術作品帶回家。
Have a great afternoon!	祝你有個美好的下午！
Don't forget to pack your school bags before leaving.	離開前別忘了把書包收好。

Put your take-home folder in your bag. 請把要帶回家的資料夾放進書包。

Dialogue

- **T** Be sure to take your homework with you. 務必把作業帶回去。
- **S** I have it in my backpack. 我已經放在書包裡了。

📖 考試

準備考試前，老師可以用以下英文關心學生，並提醒要注意的事。

P2_008

Did you study?	你有念書嗎？
How are you feeling about the test?	要考試了，你感覺怎麼樣？
Are you nervous?	你會緊張嗎？
Why are you worried?	你為什麼擔心呢？
Did you eat a good breakfast this morning?	你今天早上有吃豐盛的早餐嗎？
Do you have any questions about the test?	你對考試有什麼問題嗎？
Do you feel prepared?	你準備好了嗎？
Did you do the practice test?	你做練習題了嗎？
Do you understand the instructions?	你明白指示說明嗎？
Are there any questions before we get started?	在開始之前有什麼問題嗎？

Dialogue

- **T** How are you feeling about the test? 要考試了，你感覺怎麼樣？
- **S** I think I'm going to do great. 我覺得我會考得很好。

41

📖 學期末放假前

學期末準備放寒暑假時，老師可以用以下英文來問候。

P2_009

I've enjoyed having you in class.	（這段時間）很高興你們在我班上。
I wish you the best!	我祝你們一切順利！
Enjoy your summer.	好好放暑假。
Have a good break.	假期愉快。
You're going to do great in 2nd grade!	你們在二年級會表現得很棒的！
It's been a great semester.	這學期很棒。
You did wonderful this term.	這學期你們表現得很棒。
Good luck next semester!	下學期加油！
I'll see you around!	再見！
Keep in touch!	保持聯絡！

Dialogue

T You're going to do great in 2nd grade!	你們在二年級會表現很棒的！
S Thank you! I can't wait!	謝謝！我等不及了！

📖 開學第一天

開學第一天見到學生，可以針對假期的部分跟學生寒暄一下。

How was your winter break?	寒假過得怎麼樣？
Did you have a good winter break?	寒假過得好嗎？
What did you do over the winter break?	你們寒假做了什麼？
What was the best part of your break?	假期中最棒的部分是什麼？
Did you go on a vacation over the winter break?	你們寒假時有去哪度假嗎？

Did you read over your summer break?	你們暑假有閱讀嗎？
Did you play outside a lot?	你們常去戶外玩嗎？
Was your break nice?	你們放假時過得好嗎？
Did you play baseball over the summer?	你們暑假時有去打棒球嗎？
Did you get to go swimming over summer break?	你們暑假時有去游泳嗎？

Dialogue

T Did you read over your summer break? 你們暑假有閱讀嗎？
S Yes! I read two Harry Potter books. 有！我看了兩本《哈利波特》。

關心用語

可以用以下一些表達來關心與鼓勵學生。

I missed you!	我很想念你！
I'm so glad you're in my class.	很高興你在我的班上。
I love having you in our class.	我喜歡你在我班上。
Are you doing okay?	你還好嗎？
You seem upset.	你看起來很不開心。
What's bothering you?	是什麼困擾著你？
Is something wrong?	怎麼了嗎？
You can talk to me about anything.	你可以和我聊聊。
I'm here for you if you need anything.	如果需要任何幫助，我都在這裡。
You're important to me.	你對我來說很重要。

Dialogue

T Is something wrong? 　　　　　　　怎麼了嗎？
S I don't feel good today. 　　　　　我今天不太舒服。

讚美用語

可以用以下一些表達來讚美學生。

Nice work!	做得好！
Awesome job!	太棒了！
Great job!	做得好！
Good job!	做得好！
You rocked this!	你做得太好了！
You're awesome!	你真厲害！
Well done!	很好！
Very good work.	表現得非常好。
You aced this!	你表現得很出色！
Keep up the good work!	繼續保持好表現！
You're doing a great job!	你做得很棒！
I can tell you worked hard on this.	我可以看出你很努力。
You're amazing!	你真了不起！
You're so smart!	你真聰明！
You did a terrific job!	你做得非常好！
Nicely done!	做得很好！
That's a job well done!	那真是一個出色的表現！
I'm proud of you!	我為你感到驕傲！
You should be proud of yourself.	你應該為自己感到驕傲。

MEMO

UNIT 02 第一堂課

📖 自我介紹

老師第一次跟學生見面時，可以這樣跟學生稍微介紹一下自己。

P2_011

Good morning, I'll be your teacher this year.	早安，我會是你們今年的老師。
My name is Mrs. Smith.	我叫史密斯老師。
Welcome! You can call me Mr. Reed.	歡迎！你們可以叫我 Reed 老師。
I'm Ms. Beth. I'm happy you're here!	我是 Beth 老師。很高興你們在我班上！
Please call me Mr. Jacobs, or Mr. J for short.	請叫我 Jacobs 老師。或稱我 J 老師。

📖 課程介紹

We have a lot to cover in this class.	我們這堂課要上很多東西。
We'll be learning addition and subtraction in math this year.	今年我們數學課要學加法和減法。
Let's go over what we'll be doing in science class.	我們來看看我們科學課會學些什麼。
I'd like to share a bit about this class.	我想跟你們分享一些關於這門課的一些內容。
Let me explain more about the class.	讓我再解釋一下這門課。

📖 班級介紹

We will have lunch at 11:30.	我們午餐時間是 11 點 30 分。
There are 18 kids in our class.	我們班上有 18 位學生。
We have assigned seats. Please look for your name tag.	我們有指定座位。請各位找出你們的名牌。
We take a break in the afternoon.	我們下午不上課。
We will study math, science, and reading in the morning.	我們早上會上數學、科學和閱讀課。

📖 選班長

The class president election is next week.	下週要選班長。
You have two classmates running for class president election.	你們有兩位同學要參選班長。
Let's review the class president nominations.	我們來看看班長提名。
Here's how you vote for the election.	這是選班長的投票方法。
Let's talk about what a class president does.	我們來說說班長的工作有哪些。

UNIT 03 教室管理

📖 班規

Turn up to class on time.	準時到課。
Obey the school rules.	遵守學校規則。
Please walk in the classroom.	教室裡請勿奔跑（請用走的）。
Everyone should be in their seat.	每個人都應該要坐在自己的座位上。
Raise your hand if you'd like to speak.	如果想發言請舉手。
Keep your desk tidy.	保持桌面乾淨整潔。
Listen to your teacher.	聽老師說話。
Listen to your classmates when they speak.	同學說話時要聆聽。
Always ask for help if you need it.	你們需要幫助時，請隨時尋求協助。
Help your classmates.	請幫助你們的同學。
Never use hurtful words.	話語不傷人。
Be quiet when someone else is talking.	別人在說話時要保持安靜。
Respect other people's things.	尊重他人的物品。
If you make a mess, clean it up.	打翻或弄亂時，請務必清理乾淨。
Share your equipment with others.	與他人分享你的用具。

P2_013

📖 課堂秩序管理

Quiet, please!	請安靜！
Everyone, please be quiet!	大家請安靜！
No talking right now!	現在不要講話！
No talking!	不要說話！
Inside voice, please.	請使用室內音量。
Use your inside voice.	各位請使用室內音量。
Eyes on me!	看著我！
Please look at the screen.	請看螢幕。
Pay attention!	注意；專心！
Eyes on your own paper!	請專心看自己的作業／報告！
Have a seat.	請就座。
Sit down, please!	請坐下！
Raise your hand, please.	請舉手。
Walk, please!	請勿奔跑；請用走的！
Walking feet!	用走的！
Listening ears, please.	請注意聆聽。
Keep your hands to yourself.	把手放好，不要（亂碰）。
Don't touch!	不要碰！

📖 吸引注意力

Can I have your attention?	可以請你們注意一下嗎？
Attention, please.	注意我這裡。
Eyes up here.	看這裡。
Please look at me.	請看我這邊。
Boys and girls, time to quiet down.	同學們，安靜下來。

📖 要求仔細聽、仔細看

This is important.	這很重要。
Please put on your listening ears.	請好好注意聽。
Eyes and ears open, please.	請仔細看、仔細聽。
I need you to listen to this.	我需要你們仔細聽這個。
These instructions are important.	這些指示很重要。

📖 要求看某物或某人

Look at the board.	看黑板。
Look at this example.	看這個例子。
Take a look at page 13.	看第 13 頁。
Eyes on the speaker.	看著講話的人。
Watch me.	注意看我。

📖 請求幫助

I can't get logged into the app.	我無法登入這個應用程式。
I didn't get a copy of the homework.	我沒有拿到作業。
Have you seen my notebook?	你有看到我的筆記本嗎？
Do you have a pencil I can borrow?	你可以借我鉛筆嗎？

📖 離開一下、請假

I'm not feeling well.	我感覺不舒服。
Can I go get a drink of water?	我可以去喝水嗎？

I left my book in my locker.	我把書忘在置物櫃裡了。
I need to leave early for a doctor's appointment.	我需要先離開去看醫生。
I need to use the restroom.	我需要去洗手間。

📖 同學間的衝突

He's copying my work.	他在抄我的作業。
She took my pencil!	她拿了我的鉛筆！
I'm trying to help him, and he won't listen.	我試著幫助他，但他不聽。
He's not helping our group with the project.	他沒有幫忙一起弄這個作業。
She won't stop touching me!	她一直碰我！
He cut in line.	他插隊。
She broke my crayon.	她弄壞了我的蠟筆。
He stole my lunch.	他偷了我的午餐。
She pushed me down!	她把我推倒了！
He won't sit down.	他不肯坐下來。

PART 3

課室
英語句型及用語

Classroom
English
Patterns

UNIT 01 準備上課

📖 就座

Take your seats... 請坐，～

這是提醒學生休息時間結束要開始上課了，或是分配學生座位時可使用的句型，類似的句型有「Please be seated.」。sit down 的字面意思是「坐回你站起來的地方」，而 take your seats 的意思則是「找到自己的座位並坐下」。

Take your seats and we will start the test.　大家請坐，我們要開始考試了。

Take your seats so we can begin.　大家請坐，我們要開始了。

Break time is finished, so **take your seats**.　下課時間結束，大家請坐。

Take your seats and let's start working.　大家請坐，我們開始吧。

Take your seats and get ready to study.　大家請坐，準備來學習吧。

Dialogue

S1 Are you ready for today's test?　你準備好今天的考試了嗎？
S2 No! I forgot to study!　沒有！我忘了念書！
T Take your seats and we will start the test.　大家請坐，我們開始考試。

Dialogue

T Take your seats so we can begin.　大家請就座，我們要開始了。
S What are we going to do today?　我們今天要做什麼呢？
T We are going to practice speaking.　我們要練習口說。
S Good! I love speaking.　太好了！我喜歡口說。

📖 開始上課

Class will begin... 課程將～開始。

這是提醒準備要上課的句型，學會這一句型會很有用。動詞 begin 後面接續各種修飾語，便可以在各情況下宣布準備上課。請注意，在英語中 class 要作為主詞放在句子的開頭。

Class will begin as soon as you sit down.	各位坐下後我們就開始上課。
Class will begin in 15 minutes.	15 分鐘後開始上課。
Class will begin with a spelling test.	課程將從拼字測驗開始。
Class will begin later today.	今天的課程會晚點開始。
Class will begin now.	現在開始上課。

Dialogue

- **T** Please put away your game. 　請把遊戲收起來。
- **S** Why? 　為什麼？
- **T** **Class will begin** in 15 minutes. 　15 分鐘後開始上課。

Dialogue

- **T** Let's welcome our guest speaker. 　我們來歡迎我們的客座講師。
- **S** Aren't we having a test first? 　我們不是要先考試嗎？
- **T** No, **class will begin** later today. 　不，今天的課晚點才開始。

補充 Supplement

📖 暖身

在上正課之前，許多老師會透過暖身運動來讓學生提起精神。以下是一些可以使用的表達。

◎Warm up 暖身

Let's march in place.	我們一起原地踏步吧。
Take a few deep breaths.	做幾次深呼吸。
Follow my lead!	跟著我做！
We're going to do jumping jacks next.	接下來我們要做開合跳。
Take a lap around the gym.	繞體育館跑一圈。

◎Stretching in the classroom 伸展與擺動

Touch your toes.	碰到腳趾。
Shake out your arms and fingers.	抖動手臂和手指。
Reach for the sky!	手伸向天空！
Lean to the side. Now the other side.	斜向這一邊。現在換另一邊。
Make circles with your shoulders.	用肩膀畫圈。

點名

點名時，也可以用英文來進行。以下是一些可以搭配使用的表達。

◎Take a roll call 點名

It's time to take attendance.	現在是點名時間。
Say here when I say your name.	當我念到你的名字時，請答「有」。
Please answer when I call your name.	叫到你的名字時，請回答。
Please respond with here or present.	請答「有」或「在」。
Is Michael here?	Michael 在嗎？

◎Student absent 學生缺席

Luke? He must be absent today.	Luke 人呢？他今天應該沒來。
I haven't seen Sara yet.	我還沒看到 Sara。
Jessica must be sick today.	Jessica 今天肯定是生病了。
Have you seen Beth?	你有看到 Beth 嗎？
Has anyone seen Jane?	有人看到 Jane 嗎？

📖 請拿出課本或文具

Everyone take out... 每個人都拿出～

當你要在課堂上要求學生拿出書本或是拿出必要的物品，或是交作業時，可以使用此句型。everyone 的語意是「每個人、大家」，take out 的語意是「拿出來、掏出來」。另外請注意，everyone 在這裡和 everybody 語意相同，所以要寫作一個單字。但若想強調個人，例如「任何一位～」等時，則是寫作 every one 兩個單字。

Everyone take out your notebooks.	每個人都拿出筆記本。
Everyone take out a blank sheet of paper.	每個人都拿出一張白紙。
Everyone take out your textbooks.	每個人都拿出課本。
Everyone take out your dictionaries.	每個人都拿出字典。
Everyone take out a pen.	每個人都拿出一支筆。

Dialogue

T **Everyone take out** a blank sheet of paper.	每個人都拿出一張白紙。
S Oh no! Not a quiz!	哦不！拜託不要是小考！
T Yes, it's time for a quiz.	是的，現在是小考時間。
S I forgot to do the reading assignment!	我忘了做閱讀作業！

Dialogue

T Everyone take out your textbooks.	每個人都拿出課本。
S What page?	哪一頁？
T Page 57.	第 57 頁。
S Oh good! A new chapter!	哦，太好了！新的一課！

請把東西準備好

Please have your... 請準備好～／請拿出～

這是請學生準備好上課所需物品、作業或簡報時可使用的句型。have 後面接續受詞跟受詞補語時，語意為「讓／使做～」，此時的 have 是使役動詞。

Please have your essay finished by the end of the day.	請在今天結束前完成你們的作文。
Please have your pencil and paper ready.	請準備好你們的鉛筆和紙。
Please have your homework out for collection.	我要收你們的作業，請拿出來。
Please have your answer ready when I call on you.	叫到你們的名字時，請準備好你們的答案。
Please have your books out when the bell rings.	打鐘時，請把書拿出來。

Dialogue

T **Please have your** homework out for collection.	我要收你們的作業，請拿出來。
S Oh no! I forgot mine!	哦不！我忘了帶來了！
T That's okay. You can bring it tomorrow.	沒關係，明天帶來吧。
S Thank you, ma'am.	謝謝老師。

Dialogue

T **Please have your** essay finished by the end of the day.	請在今天結束前完成你的作文。
S I'll never finish in time.	我想我永遠無法在期限內寫完作文。
T Why not?	為什麼不行呢？
S I write too slowly.	我寫字速度太慢了。

📖 翻頁&確認頁碼

Open your books... 把書翻開～

「把書翻開」是老師幾乎每堂課上都會用到的表達之一，可簡單地用「Open your books.」表達，若 your books 後面接續頁數，其語意為「翻到第～頁」。可跟 Turn to page...（翻到第～頁）這個句型互換使用。

Open your books and read the passage.	把書翻開，閱讀這段課文。
Open your books to page 22.	把書翻到第 22 頁。
Open your books and try to find the answer.	把書翻開，試著找出答案。
Open your books to page 98 and look at the chart.	把書翻到第 98 頁，並看一下圖表。
Open your books and check your answers when you are finished.	完成後，把書翻開對答案。

Dialogue

🅣 Let's work on our reading.	我們來閱讀吧。
🅢 What are we going to read?	我們要讀什麼呢？
🅣 **Open your books** and read the passage.	把書翻開，閱讀這段課文。

Dialogue

🅣 **Open your books** to page 22.	翻開你們的書到第 22 頁。
🅢 I'm sorry, what page?	抱歉，翻到第幾頁？
🅣 Page 22.	第 22 頁。
🅢 Oh no! Another vocabulary exercise!	哦不！又是一個單字練習題！

Turn to page... 翻到第～頁

只要知道動詞 turn，就能輕鬆說出跟頁碼相關的表達。有些老師會說 Turn to the page，但這是錯誤的表達。不需要加冠詞，只要在 page 後面加上頁碼數字就行了。類似的句型有 Open your books...（把書翻開…）。

Turn to page 17.	翻到第 17 頁。
Turn to page 5 for the glossary*.	翻到第 5 頁去查術語表。
Turn to page 20 for the answers.	翻到第 20 頁去對答案。
Turn to page 80 for a definition.	翻到第 80 頁去查定義。
Turn to page 32 for more information.	翻到第 32 頁來瞭解更多資訊。

* Turn to page 後面接「for +名詞」或 to 不定詞時，表示該頁上有必須看的內容。

Dialogue

T Where did we stop yesterday?	我們昨天到哪了？
S Chapter 1, page 17.	第 1 章，第 17 頁。
T **Turn to page** 17.	翻到第 17 頁。
S Yes, sir.	好的，老師。

Dialogue

S What does "inconsistent" mean?	「inconsistent」是什麼意思？
T **Turn to page** 80 for a definition.	翻到第 80 頁去查看定義。
S It says, "lacking agreement."	上面寫著「缺乏共識」。
T I guess that's one definition.	我想這是這單字的其中一個定義。

📖 教室管理

I want you guys to... 希望大家～／麻煩大家～

要在課堂上向學生提出要求或指示時，很適合使用這個句型。guy 在字典上的解釋為「男生、男子」，但在口語中，guys 如 people 一樣指的是任何人，既可用於男性，亦可用於女性。無論是兩個人或是全班學生，都可以用 you guys 來指稱眼前看到的所有學生們。

I want you guys to be quiet.	麻煩大家安靜。
I want you guys to pay attention.	希望大家集中注意力。
I want you guys to turn to page 6.	麻煩大家翻到第 6 頁。
I want you guys to listen.	請大家仔細聽。
I want you guys to study.	希望你們好好學習。

Dialogue

- **T** Everyone, quiet down! — 大家安靜！
- **S1** Why? What's going on? — 為什麼？怎麼了嗎？
- **T** **I want you guys to** pay attention. — 我希望你們集中注意力。
- **S2** Oh, the film's about to start. — 哦，看來電影就要開始了。

Dialogue

- **T** I'm separating you two gossips. — 我要你們這兩個愛講話的人分開。
- **S1** What for? — 為什麼？
- **T** **I want you guys to** study. — 我希望你們好好學習。

Everyone, calm down... 大家都冷靜下來～

這是老師管控吵鬧學生的必備句型。calm down 的語意是讓緊張或激動的狀態「平靜或冷靜下來」，所以「Everyone, calm down...」表示「大家都冷靜下來」的意思。除此之外，calm down 後面可以 and 連接其它動詞，例如 calm down and focus、calm down and continue working... 等。

Everyone, calm down now.	大家都冷靜下來。
Everyone, calm down. The excitement is over.	大家都冷靜下來，平復一下激動的情緒。
Everyone, calm down and continue working.	大家都冷靜下來，繼續做好自己手邊的工作。
Everyone, calm down, so we can start.	大家都冷靜下來，這樣我們才可以開始。
Everyone, calm down and focus.	大家都冷靜下來，集中注意力。

Dialogue

- **T** **Everyone, calm down**. The excitement is over.　大家都冷靜下來，平復一下激動情緒。
- **S** Was there really a fire in the building?　大樓裡真的發生火災了嗎？
- **T** No, it was a false alarm.　不，只是虛驚一場。
- **S** Good.　太好了。

Dialogue

- **S** This museum is fantastic!　這間博物館太棒了！
- **T** All right, **everyone, calm down** and focus.　好了，大家都冷靜下來，集中注意力。
- **S** There's so much to see here.　這裡有很多東西可以看。
- **T** Yes, but we're here specifically for the Egyptian exhibit.　對啊，但我們來這裡是為了看埃及的展覽。

Please quiet down... 請安靜～

quiet down 的語意是「降低聲量」，是用來讓周圍的人安靜下來的表達用語。當您想讓課堂上吵鬧的孩子們安靜一下，或是當您需要安靜地觀看或學習某些內容時，都很適合使用這個表達句型。類似的表達句型有「Let me have your attention, please.」跟「Keep silent, please.」等。

Please quiet down because it's time to take the test.	請安靜，準備要考試了。
Please quiet down or you won't hear the correct answer.	請安靜，否則你將聽不到正確答案。
It's getting too loud in here, so **please quiet down**.	太吵了，請安靜一點。
Break time is over, so **please quiet down**.	下課時間結束了，請安靜。
Please quiet down, everyone.	請大家安靜。

Dialogue

S1 Did you study last night?	你昨晚唸書了嗎？
S2 No, I watched TV. Why?	沒有，我看了電視。怎麼了嗎？
S1 You forgot something important!	你忘了一件重要的事！
T **Please quiet down** because it's time to take the test.	請安靜，準備要考試了。

Dialogue

S1 Do you want to play football after school?	放學後要去踢足球嗎？
S2 Sure, that sounds great.	好呀，聽起來很有趣。
S1 Should we ask Billy, too?	我們要問一下 Billy 嗎？
T Brandon, Luke! **Please quiet down** or you won't hear the correct answer.	Brandon、Luke！請你們安靜，否則會聽不到正確答案。

Please stop... 請停止～／請別～

這是當您想阻止對方的行為時可以使用的表達句型。stop 後面通常會搭配動詞-ing。stop 用於祈使句時語氣非常強烈，可能會讓聽者感到畏縮，所以除非情況非常緊急，否則通常會在句首或句尾加上 please。

Please stop complaining.	請別抱怨了。
Please stop using your dictionary so often.	請別這麼常查字典了。
Please stop what you are doing.	請停下你手邊的事。
Please stop talking so loudly.	請別大聲喧嘩。
Please stop and think before you answer.	回答問題之前請先想想。

Dialogue

S1 This exercise is boring.	這個練習題很無聊。
S2 I agree. Let's do something fun.	我也覺得，我們做一些有趣的事情吧。
T **Please stop** complaining. It's time to study.	別抱怨了，現在是念書時間。
S1 Yes, sir.	好的，老師。

Dialogue

T **Please stop** talking so loudly.	別大聲喧嘩。
S Why?	為什麼？
T Because it's time to work on your reading.	因為該是你們閱讀的時候了。
S Oh, I'm sorry.	哦，對不起。

It's time to... 是時候～／該來～／～的時間到了

想讓學生們知道是時候做某件事時，可以使用 It's time to... 句型。例如，你可以用這個句型來表達是時候進行小考、檢查作業或複習今天學到的內容。除此之外，還可以用「for + 名詞」來替代 time 後面接續的「to 不定詞」，例如 It's time for bed.（該睡覺了）、It's time for lunch.（該吃午飯了）等。

It's time to take a quiz.	小考的時間到了。
It's time to review our work.	是時候複習功課了。
It's time to check your homework.	檢查作業的時間到了。
It's time to announce your final test scores.	是時候公佈期末考成績了。
It's time to go over the essay.	是時候複習文章了。

Dialogue

T Close your books, everyone.	大家把課本收起來。
S Why?	為什麼？
T **It's time to** take a quiz.	小考的時間到了。
S Oh no!	哦不！

Dialogue

T Get out your red pens, please.	請拿出你們的紅筆。
S What's going on?	為什麼？
T **It's time to** check your homework.	檢查作業的時間到了。
S Should we circle our mistakes with the red pen?	我們要用紅筆圈出寫錯的地方嗎？

Raise your hand if... 如果～，請舉手

我們通常會要求學生舉手來向老師尋求幫助或表達需求，在這種情況下就可以使用這個表達句型。raise 的語意是「舉起」，if 後面要接舉手的原因。類似的表達句型為「Put your hand up...」。

* 當老師在課堂上點名，叫到學生的名字時，學生應該要怎麼回答呢？很多人會回答「Yes.」或「Yes, here I am.」，但其實只要簡單地說「Here.」就行了。除此之外，當您被點名起來回答問題時，也只要說「Yes.」或「Yes, sir (ma'am).」就行了。

Raise your hand if you need help.	若需要幫助請舉手。
Raise your hand if you have any questions.	若有問題請舉手。
Raise your hand if you've finished the test.	如果你們寫完考卷，請舉手。
Raise your hand if you need to use the bathroom.	如果你想上廁所，請舉手。
Raise your hand if this is unclear.	如果這個不清楚，請舉手。

Dialogue

T The test will take 45 minutes.	考試時間是 45 分鐘。
S What if we finish early?	如果我們提前完成呢？
T **Raise your hand if** you've finished the test.	如果你們寫完考卷，請舉手。
S Okay.	好的。

Dialogue

T You're sure you understand my instructions?	你們都懂我的說明嗎？
S We understand.	我們都懂了。
T **Raise your hand if** this is unclear.	如果這個不清楚，請舉手。
S No, it's very clear.	不用，我們確實都理解了。

UNIT 02　提醒、要求與關心

📖 提醒要做與不要做的事

Please avoid... 請避免～／請不要～

P3_013

這是傳達跟校園生活有關的課堂規定時可使用的表達用語。除此之外，想特別強調某一特定學習內容時也可使用這個表達句型。本句型中的 avoid 是表示「遠離」可能有危險或令人不愉快的事物，avoid 後面要接動名詞。

Please avoid making mistakes.	請避免犯錯。
Please avoid using your dictionary.	請避免使用字典。
Please avoid repeating the same word.	請避免重複使用相同的單字。
Please avoid speaking in languages other than English.	請避免說英語以外的語言。
Please avoid writing down what you want to say.	請不要寫下你想說的話。

Dialogue

T **Please avoid** using your dictionary.	請避免使用字典。
S What should we do if we don't know a word?	如果遇到我們不懂的字怎麼辦？
T Use the context to guess the meaning.	試著透過上下文來猜測其意。
S Okay. I'll try.	好的，我試試看。

Dialogue

T **Please avoid** repeating the same word.	請避免重複使用相同的單字。
S How can I do that?	那我該怎麼做呢？
T Use pronouns or synonyms.	可以使用代名詞或同義詞。
S Oh, I see!	哦，我明白了！

67

Try not to... 儘量不要～

Try to 的語意是「試著～」，所以「You should try to...」或「Let's try to...」意味著「你應該要做～」跟「一起做～」，用作勸告或建議。反之，想表達「儘量不要做～」時，要在 to 前面加上 not，即透過 **Try not to** 來闡述其意，這是可用來傳達注意事項或警告的表達句型，其語意相當於「Stop...」、「Don't...」這類的否定命令，但語氣較為柔和。

Try not to forget your homework.	儘量不要忘了你的作業。
Try not to use your dictionary.	儘量不要使用字典。
Try not to be late.	儘量不要遲到。
Try not to rely on your notes.	儘量不要依賴你的筆記。
Try not to confuse these two words.	儘量不要搞混這兩個單字。

Dialogue

T Now it's time to give a presentation.	現在是發表的時間。
S I think I'm ready.	我準備好了。
T **Try not to** rely on your notes.	儘量不要依賴你的筆記。
S I hope I can remember everything.	我希望我能記住一切。

Dialogue

T **Try not to** confuse these two words.	儘量不要搞混這兩個單字。
S Which ones?	哪兩個？
T "Quite" and "Quiet."	「Quite」和「Quiet」。
S Oh, these are very similar.	哦，這兩個字真的很像。

Would everyone return...? 請大家回到～／交回～／歸還～　P3_015

這是用來告訴別人將物品放回原位的表達句型。此外，當您想要回借出去的蠟筆或色鉛筆等物品時，這也是一個很好的表達句型。這句型中使用的 return 在作為不及物動詞時，其語意是「回～、返回～」，但作為及物動詞時，其語意是「還、歸還」，小心不要混淆。

Would everyone return to the English classroom?	請大家回到英語教室。
Would everyone return these pens after class?	請大家下課後歸還這些筆。
Would everyone return their English dictionaries?	請歸還你們的英文字典。
Would everyone return these notebook computers?	請大家歸還筆記型電腦。
Would everyone return the test papers?	請大家交卷。

Dialogue

- 🅣 Use the red pens to correct your homework.　用紅筆批改作業。
- 🅢 I hope I don't have too much red on my homework.　希望我的作業上不會有太多紅字。
- 🅣 **Would everyone return** these pens after class?　請大家下課後歸還這些筆。
- 🅢 Sure. No problem.　當然，不用擔心。

Dialogue

- 🅢 I didn't know we were having a test today.　我不知道我們今天有考試。
- 🅣 I told you guys last week.　我上週就告訴你們了。
- 🅢 Come on, Mr. Jones.　有嗎？Jones 老師。
- 🅣 **Would everyone return** the test papers?　請大家交卷。

Don't neglect... 別疏於～／別忽視～

相當於「Be sure to ～」句型，這是另一個可用來叮嚀學生某件事的表達句型。有很多事情是學生不應該忽視的，例如做筆記、寫日記、預習、複習等，可以使用這個句型來提醒他們這些事情的重要性。荒廢學業的英文說法是「neglect one's studies」或「ignore one's schoolwork」。另外還要注意一件事，ignore 是及物動詞，因此後面必須加上一個名詞作為其受詞。

Don't neglect to take notes.	別忽視作筆記這件事。
Don't neglect to attend class on time.	別忽視準時上課這件事。
Don't neglect your journal.	別忽視寫日記這件事。
Don't neglect your homework.	別忽視你們的作業。
Don't neglect your responsibility.	別疏於自己的職責。

Dialogue

S It's difficult to finish all my homework.	要完成所有作業是一件難事。
T Where are you falling behind?	你目前卡在哪裡？
S I can't seem to make a daily journal entry*.	我似乎無法天天寫日記。
T **Don't neglect** your journal.	別忽視寫日記這件事。

* entry 的語意為「記錄」，所以「make a daily journal entry」的語意是「天天寫日記」。

Dialogue

T That's all for today.	今天就到此為止。
S Great! Let's go relax!	太好了！休息時間到了！
T **Don't neglect** your homework.	別忽視你們的作業。
S Don't worry. We won't.	別擔心，我們不會的。

Don't forget... 別忘了～

這是可以用來提醒學生下節課需要準備什麼的表達用語。請記住一點，想表達「忘記要去做某件事」時，forget 後面要接 to 不定詞，想表達「不記得做過了某件事」時，forget 後面則是要接動名詞。

Don't forget to do your homework.	別忘了寫作業。
Don't forget that we have a test tomorrow.	別忘了明天有考試。
Don't forget to read chapter 5.	別忘了要念第 5 課。
Don't forget about the school festival.	別忘了校慶。
Don't forget to write your name on your paper.	別忘了在作業上寫下自己的名字。

Dialogue

- **T** What are you going to do this evening? 　今天晚上要做什麼？
- **S** I'm going to play soccer with my friends. 　我要和朋友們去踢足球。
- **T** **Don't forget** to do your homework. 　別忘了寫作業。
- **S** I won't. 　我不會忘記的。

Dialogue

- **T** It's time to give me your writing assignment. 　是時候交作文作業了。
- **S** Here is mine. 　這是我的。
- **T** **Don't forget** to write your name on your paper. 　別忘了在作業上寫上自己的名字。
- **S** Oh! How silly of me! 　啊！對哦！我真蠢！

Don't lose your... 別弄丟你的～

這是適合用來叮嚀對方不要忘記帶下堂課所需物品或作業的表達用語。lose 是表示「弄丟、失去」物品的動詞，不僅能用來描述弄丟物品或金錢這種有形的東西，也能跟 forget 一樣用來表達「失去～的記憶」之意。

Don't lose your homework.	別弄丟你的作業。
Don't lose your backpack.	別弄丟你的書包。
Don't lose it.	別弄丟它。
Don't lose your notebook.	別弄丟你的筆記本。
Don't lose your pencil box.	別弄丟你的鉛筆盒。

Dialogue

T Everyone line up by the door. It's time to go.	大家都到門口排隊，該走了。
S1 Hey, your backpack is open.	嘿，你的書包開了。
S2 Thanks. I'd better close it.	謝謝提醒，我馬上關上。
S1 **Don't lose your** homework!	別弄丟你的作業。

Dialogue

T Here is your homework.	這是你的作業。
S I'll put it in my folder.	我會把它放到我的資料夾裡。
T Good. **Don't lose** it.	好的，別弄丟它。
S Don't worry. I won't.	別擔心，我不會的。

📖 時間上的叮嚀

You have... minutes...
你們有～分鐘時間～／距離～還有～分鐘時間

學校生活必須按照上課時間、下課時間、考試時間等時間表進行，因此經常需要提前告訴學生他們還剩下多少時間。尤其是考試時間結束前常聽到「還

剩下 10 分鐘」之類的話，這個表達句型在這種情況下很有用，其字面意思為「你們有～分鐘做～」。

You have 5 **minutes*** to finish your quiz.	你們還有 5 分鐘時間來完成測驗。
You have several **minutes** to complete the essay.	你們還有幾分鐘時間寫完作文。
You have a few **minutes** until recess.	距離下課只剩下幾分鐘時間。
You have 10 **minutes** to take questions.	你們有 10 分鐘時間來回答問題。
You have 5 **minutes** to memorize this paragraph.	你們有 5 分鐘時間來背這一段。

* 時間單位較長時，此句型中的 minutes 能以 hours、days、months、years 等替代。此外，可利用 to 不定詞來具體描述還有多少時間做某事。

Dialogue

T Class, **you have** 5 **minutes** to finish your quiz.	同學們，你們還有 5 分鐘的時間來完成測驗。
S But I'm only halfway through!	但是我才完成一半！
T Then you will need to work fast.	那你們就快點做吧。
S I'll never finish.	我想我絕對寫不完。

Dialogue

T Each student will give a brief presentation.	每個學生都要做一個簡短的報告。
S Will there be time afterwards for questions?	稍後會有時間問問題嗎？
T **You have** 10 **minutes** to take questions.	你們有 10 分鐘時間來回答問題。
S That sounds good.	太好了。

📖 請注意這裡

Turn your attention to... 注意聽～／注意看～／專心～

這是想將一個人的注意力或焦點從其它地方「轉向某處」時可使用的表達句型。動詞 turn 的基本語意是「改變方向」，當你要某人專心一點時，就能使用這個句型，非常適合用在正在大聲喧嘩或開玩笑的學生。類似的表達句型有「Pay attention to...」跟「Give one's attention to...」，想要求對方全神貫注時，可以在 attention 前面加上 full，以 full attention 來表達其意。

Turn your attention to the blackboard.	注意看黑板。
Turn your attention to our speaker.	專心聽演講者。
Turn your attention to the screen.	注意看螢幕。
Turn your attention to your homework.	專心做作業。
Turn your attention to the question.	專心看這個問題。

Dialogue

🇹 Bill, please stop talking to Walt.	Bill，別再跟 Walt 聊天了。
🇸 I was only borrowing a pen.	我只是借了一支筆。
🇹 **Turn your attention to** our speaker.	專心聽演講者。
🇸 Oh, all right.	好，我知道了。

Dialogue

🇹 **Turn your attention to** the question.	專心看這個問題。
🇸 Which one?	哪一題？
🇹 The one on page 45.	第 45 頁的那一題。
🇸 Oh, I see.	好，我知道了。

Please give your attention to... 請注意～／請專心～

雖然也可簡單地用「Please! Attention!」或「Attention, please!」來表達，但「Please give your attention to...」中使用了介系詞 to，可指出應該要將注意力放在何處，類似的表達句型有「Please pay attention to...」。前一課提到的 Turn your attention to... 句型指的是要對方將注意力從其它事物轉移（turn）到（to）另一目標，兩者略有不同。

Please give your attention to the lesson.	請專心聽課。
Please give your attention to Carl's presentation.	請注意聽卡爾的演講。
Please give your attention to section 3.	請注意看第 3 節。
Please give your attention to this picture.	請注意看這張圖片。
Please give your attention to the test.	請專心考試。

Dialogue

- Ⓣ Put your book away*, Lisa. ── Lisa，把妳的書收起來。
- Ⓢ But I'm getting to the good part! ── 但我快看到最精彩的部分了！
- Ⓣ **Please give your attention to** Carl's speech. ── 請注意聽 Carl 的演講。
- Ⓢ Aw, all right. ── 好啦，知道了。

* Put away 的意思是「收起來」，也就是在不使用時將東西放回原處，有些人可能會把它跟 put aside 搞混，但 put aside 的意思是「留出」「存放」物品或金錢以供日後使用。

Dialogue

- Ⓣ You should study all of the material. ── 你們必須看完資料的所有內容。
- Ⓢ Is there anything we should focus on? ── 有什麼需要特別注意之處嗎？
- Ⓣ **Please give your attention to** section 3. ── 請注意看第 3 節。
- Ⓢ Thanks for the hint. ── 感謝您的提示。

Listen up, everyone, ... 各位,請認真聽~

想表達「聽好!」時,可以用 Listen!,但若能加上 up 改用「Listen up!」的話,可增添傾聽之意。**Listen up, everyone** 之後會出現「介系詞+名詞片語」,句中的介系詞可用 for 或 to。舉例來說,「Listen up for the phone.」的語意是「仔細聽是否有人打電話過來」。

Listen up, everyone, to today's speaker.	各位,請認真聽今天演講者的發言。
Listen up, everyone, for announcements.	各位,請認真聽廣播。
Listen up, everyone, to my report.	各位,請認真聽我的報告。
Listen up, everyone, to the principal.	各位,請認真聽校長講話。
Listen up, everyone, for instructions.	各位,請認真聽指示。

Dialogue

🅣 **Listen up, everyone**, to today's speaker.	各位,請認真聽今天演講者的發言。
🅢 Who is he?	他是誰呢?
🅣 This is Bob Wilson, our head teacher!	他是你們的導師,鮑伯威爾遜!
🅢 Cool!	哇!

Dialogue

🅢 What's the principal doing here?	校長來這裡做什麼?
🅣1 He has some bad news.	他要說一些壞消息。
🅢 What? What is it?	什麼?是什麼壞消息?
🅣2 **Listen up, everyone**, to the principal.	各位,請認真聽校長講話。

要求

Everyone, please... 請各位～

在美國，經常會聽到父母或老師對孩子說 Say, please.，這句話的字面意思就是「請說」。當你需要以較為正式的命令句來向學生們下指令時，請加上 please，這麼一來孩子們就會自然而然地學會更多禮貌用語。除此之外，在前面加上 everyone 的話，可更清楚地表明這項指令是針對所有學生的。

Everyone, please listen.	請各位注意聽。
Everyone, please make a list.	請各位列出清單。
Everyone, please close your books.	請大家闔上書本。
Everyone, please use your red pens.	請各位都使用紅筆。
Everyone, please wait right here.	請各位在這裡等著。

Dialogue

T It's time for the test.	考試時間到了。
S Already?	已經到了嗎？
T **Everyone, please** close your books.	請大家闔上書本。
S All right, here we go!	好的，開始吧！

Dialogue

T Does everybody have a ticket?	大家都有票嗎？
S Yes, we do!	是的，當然有！
T **Everyone, please** wait right here.	請各位在這裡等著。
S All right.	好的。

Could you all please...？請大家都～

與其說「安靜點！」，「請大家都保持安靜」聽起來會較為友善。「**Could you all please...?**」是當老師想友善地向學生提出指令或要求時使用的表達句型。句子結構較為複雜，但語意與 Please 相同。You all 中的 you 跟 all 是同位語。

Could you all please take out your books?	請大家把書拿出來。
Could you all please sit down?	請大家都坐下。
Could you all please get ready to take the test?	請大家都準備好進行考試。
Could you all please turn to page 5?	請大家都翻到第 5 頁。
Could you all please turn in your homework?	請大家交作業。

Dialogue

T **Could you all please** take out your books? — 請大家把書拿出來。
S Oh, no! I forgot mine. — 哦，不！我忘了帶書。
T You can share with Johnny. — 你可以和 Johnny 一起看。
S Yes, ma'am. — 好的，老師。

Dialogue

T **Could you all please** get ready to take the test? — 請大家準備好進行考試。
S1 Test? What test? — 考試？什麼考試？
S2 Did you forget? — 你忘了嗎？
S1 I guess I did! — 我想是的！

Everyone needs to... 每個人都要～

當老師向所有學生下達指令時,可用「Everyone needs to...」這個句型。在出作業時使用這個表達句型的話,此表達帶有一種「沒有例外,全部都要做」之意味。

Everyone needs to take out a piece of paper.	每個人都要拿出一張紙。
Everyone needs to memorize this sentence.	每個人都要記住這句話。
Everyone needs to bring a pencil.	每個人都要帶一支鉛筆。
Everyone needs to turn in the homework.	每個人都要交作業。
Everyone needs to be prepared for a quiz tomorrow.	每個人都要為明天的測驗做好準備。

Dialogue

T **Everyone needs to** take out a piece of paper.	每個人都要拿出一張紙。
S I don't have one. I forgot my notebook.	我沒有紙,我忘了帶筆記本。
T Ask your friend if you can borrow one.	看看能不能向朋友借一張。
S Yes, ma'am.	好的,老師。

Dialogue

T **Everyone needs to** turn in the homework.	每個人都要交作業。
S1 Oh no! I left mine at home!	哦不!我把作業留在家裡了!
S2 Maybe Mr. Smith will let you turn it in tomorrow.	也許 Smith 老師會讓你明天再交作業。
S1 I hope so.	但願如此。

Keep working... 繼續～

「keep+原形動詞+-ing」的語意是「繼續做某件事」，所以「keep working」表示「繼續工作」。當您需要在學生做練習題時暫時離開教室一下，就可以用這個表達句型，要他們不要搗蛋，繼續做練習題。

Keep working until the bell rings.	請繼續（寫），直到鈴聲響起。
Keep working while I help Sally.	在我幫助 Sally 的同時，大家繼續（寫題目）。
Keep working until I tell you to stop.	在我告訴你停止之前，請繼續（寫）。
Keep working while I prepare the next exercise.	在我準備下一個練習題的同時，請繼續（寫）。
Keep working and don't be distracted.	請繼續（寫），不要分心。

Dialogue

S How much longer do we have to write?	我們還要寫多久？
T **Keep working** until the bell rings.	請繼續寫，直到鈴聲響起。
S Oh no! That's another hour!	哦不！那還有一個小時！
T That's not too long.	這不算太長。

Dialogue

T Is anyone having problems with this exercise?	這個練習題有誰遇到問題的嗎？
S I'm a little confused*.	我有點困惑。
T Okay. **Keep working** while I help Sally.	好的，在我幫助 Sally 的同時，大家繼續作題。
S Thank you.	謝謝。

* 「I'm a little confused.」的語意是「我有點困惑」，相似表達句型有「I'm a little lost.」、「This is a little over my head.」、「You've lost me.」等。

The last thing I want you to do is...
我希望你們做的最後一件事～

要提醒學生最後要做的某件事時，可以使用這個表達句型。此外，您也可以用此句型來總結當天課程內容。is 後面接續可作為其補語的名詞或 to 不定詞。

The last thing I want you to do is to make a list of words to study.	我希望你們做的最後一件事是整理要學習的單字。
The last thing I want you to do is to solve the exercise on page 59.	我希望你們做的最後一件事是完成第 59 頁的練習題。
The last thing I want you to do is to make a plan for tomorrow's presentation.	我希望你們做的最後一件事是規劃明天的報告。
The last thing I want you to do is to choose a topic for your essay.	我希望你們做的最後一件事是選出作文主題。

Dialogue

- **T** **The last thing I want you to do is** to solve the exercise on page 59.
- **S** Do we have enough time?
- **T** Yes. It's a pretty short exercise.
- **S** Okay.

我希望你們做的最後一件事是完成第 59 頁的練習題。
我們有足夠的時間嗎？
有，這只是一個簡短的練習題。
知道了。

Dialogue

- **T** **The last thing I want you to do is** to choose a topic for your essay.
- **S** I'm having trouble deciding.
- **T** You should write about something that interests you.
- **S** That's the problem. I'm interested in everything!

我希望你們做的最後一件事是選出作文主題。
難以抉擇。
寫你感興趣的事情。
這就是問題所在，我對一切都感興趣！

I need you to... 我要你們～

「**I need you to** +原形動詞」這種句型是英語母語人士常用的表達方式。need 不僅可用來表示「需要～」，還用來表示非常重要而必須去做的一件事。因此，當老師想要求學生做某些事時，只要使用「I need you (guys) to...」這個句型就行了。類似的表達句型有「I want you guys to...」。

I need you to be on time.	我要大家都能準時到達。
I need you to stop talking.	我要你們別再說話了。
I need you to watch me carefully.	我要你們注意我這邊。
I need you to speak English with confidence.	我要你們能自信地說英語。
I need you to actively involve yourself in other activities.	需要大家更積極參與其它活動。

Dialogue

- **T** Jeremy and Ben, **I need you to** stop talking. — Jeremy 和 Ben，我要你們別再說話了。
- **S** We're talking about our homework. — 我們正在談論作業。
- **T** I realize that, but I need your attention right now. — 我知道，但我希望你們現在能專心一點。
- **S** Okay, Mrs. Anderson. — 知道了，Anderson 老師。

Dialogue

- **T** We're starting at 8:00 tomorrow. — 我們明天 8:00 開始。
- **S** Okay, Mrs. Anderson. Don't worry. — 知道了，Anderson 老師，不用擔心。
- **T** **I need you guys to** be on time. — 我要大家都能準時到達。
- **S** All right. We will be there for sure. — 好的，一定會準時的。

關心與協助

The head teacher wants to see you... 班導師～要見你

在台灣的學校，我們常會提到班導，英文是 head teacher。但有別於台灣，在英語系國家當要用英語稱呼老師時，不會用「Teacher！」，而是用如「Mr. Johnson」、「Mrs. Peterson」直接稱呼其名字。

The head teacher wants to see you in his office.	班導師想在老師辦公室見你。
The head teacher wants to see you about your score.	班導師想跟你談談你的成績。
The head teacher wants to see you in 10 minutes.	班導師 10 分鐘後要見到你。
The head teacher wants to see you right away.	班導師現在就要見你。
The head teacher wants to see you after class.	班導師下課後要見你。

Dialogue

- **T** Jess, can you stay after school?　　Jess，下課後可以留下來嗎？
- **S** Sure, why?　　好啊，怎麼了嗎？
- **T** **The head teacher wants to see you about your score.**　　班導師想跟你談談你的成績。
- **S** Uh oh.　　哎呀。

Dialogue

- **T** Clara, please report to the office.　　Clara，請到辦公室報到。
- **S** Is something wrong?　　怎麼了嗎？
- **T** **The head teacher wants to see you right away.**　　班導師現在就要見你。
- **S** Okay.　　知道了。

Can I help you...? 我能幫你～嗎？

想詢問學生是否需要幫助時可以使用這個表達句型。在各種課堂情況下，當學生似乎不知所措無法獨力完成課業時，您可以透過這個句型來提供幫助。當學生想要幫助老師時，也可以使用這個句型。

Can I help you* solve the problem?	我能幫你解決問題嗎？
Can I help you find the answer?	我能幫你找到答案嗎？
Can I help you clean the board?	我能幫你擦黑板嗎？
Can I help you put the books away?	我能幫你把書本收好嗎？
Can I help you with it?	我能幫你嗎？

* help 是及物動詞，在需要幫助的部分是名詞的情況下，會搭配介系詞 with 組成「Can I help you with +名詞」。也可改用動詞在此表達形式中：「Can I help you + (to)原形動詞」。

Dialogue

- **T** That's all for today.　　今天就到此為止吧。
- **S** **Can I help you** clean the board?　　我能幫你擦黑板嗎？
- **T** That's very helpful of you.　　你真是我的小幫手。
- **S** It's no problem at all.　　不客氣。

Dialogue

- **T** Let's begin the exercise.　　我們開始做練習題吧。
- **S** I don't understand the first question.　　我不理解第一題。
- **T** **Can I help you** with it?　　我能幫你嗎？
- **S** Yes, please.　　好的，請幫我。

Would you care for...? 你想要~嗎？

care for 的語意是「喜歡~、想要~」，所以「Would you care for...?」的意思是「你想要~嗎？」。當您想詢問學生們是否需要或想要特定物品時，可以使用這個表達句型。類似的表達句型有「Would you like...?」。

Would you care for a few more minutes to think?　你要幾分鐘時間思考嗎？

Would you care for a snack?　你想要吃點零食嗎？

Would you care for a suggestion?　你想要我提個建議嗎？

Would you care for a hint?　你需要提示嗎？

Would you care for some help?　你需要幫忙嗎？

Dialogue

- T Can you answer the question?　你能回答這個問題嗎？
- S Hmm...　唔…
- T **Would you care for** a few more minutes to think?　你要幾分鐘時間思考嗎？
- S Yes, please.　是的，拜託了。

Dialogue

- S Hmm. I'm not sure what the past tense of "go" is.　唔…我不確定「go」的過去式是什麼。
- T **Would you care for*** a hint?　你需要提示嗎？
- S Yes, please.　需要，拜託了。
- T It rhymes with "rent."　它與「rent」押韻。

*「Would you care for...?」也有「您想吃~嗎？」之意。舉例來說，「Would you care for coffee?」的語意是「您想喝杯咖啡嗎？」，「Would you care for something to drink?」的語意是「您想喝點什麼嗎？」。

You will need... 你們需要～

need 是用來提及非常重要或必要的事物，所以當一個句子中包含 need 時，儘管語意會根據語境而略有不同，但都是用來提及具強制性的要求。在課堂上講解一項活動或方法時，可以用這個句型來提及要準備的物品或必須要做的事情。

You will need 45 minutes for the test.	你們需要 45 分鐘來考試。
You will need a pair of scissors.	你們需要一把剪刀。
You will need a partner.	你們需要一個搭檔。
You will need more time.	你們需要更多的時間。
You will need to review your notes.	你們需要複習筆記。

Dialogue

S How do we make a paper chain?	我們要怎麼製作紙鏈呢？
T **You will need** a pair of scissors.	你們需要一把剪刀。
S I've got them right here.	剪刀在我這裡。
T Now, go get some colored paper.	現在去拿一些色紙吧。

Dialogue

T This game requires four hands.	這個遊戲需要用到四隻手。
S Four hands?	四隻手嗎？
T Yes. **You will need** a partner.	是的，你們需要一個搭檔。
S Ah, I get it.	哦，我明白了。

When in doubt, ... 如有疑問／不確定的話，～

這句型中省略了 When 跟 in doubt 之間的主詞跟動詞，此句型中的 when 也能用 if 替代，改成 if in doubt。此句型中的 in doubt 的語意是「不確定、有疑問」。很多學生都會因為羞於承認自己不懂而不敢主動發問，此時可試著說「When in doubt, please feel free to ask.（如有問題，請隨時發問）」，讓學生可以更自在地提出問題。

When in doubt, check your notes.	不確定的話，就查看筆記。
When in doubt, ask.	如有疑問，請發問。
When in doubt, use words you know very well.	不確定的話，就使用你熟悉的詞彙。
When in doubt, think about the grammar of the sentence.	如有疑問，請想想該句子的文法。
When in doubt, try to remember yesterday's lesson.	不確定的話，請試著回想昨天的課程。

Dialogue

- 🇹 It's time for your presentation. — 現在輪到你發表了。
- 🇸 What if I get lost when I'm speaking? — 如果我講到一半忘詞了怎麼辦？
- 🇹 **When in doubt,** check your notes. — 不確定的話，就查看筆記。
- 🇸 That's good advice. — 好主意。

Dialogue

- 🇹 Are you having any problems? — 有什麼問題嗎？
- 🇸 Yes. I'm not sure if I'm saying the sentence clearly. — 有，我不確定我是否準確地說出了這個句子。
- 🇹 **When in doubt,** use words you know very well. — 不確定的話，就使用你熟悉的詞彙。
- 🇸 I'll try. — 好的。

Feel free to... 請隨時～／請自在～

帶有「不要猶豫做～」的語意，是可以用來鼓勵學生積極參與課堂的表達句型。**Feel free to** 一般是用於祈使句，to 後面要接原形動詞。

Feel free to ask a question at any time.	有問題隨時發問。
If you need some help, **feel free to** talk to me.	如果你需要幫助，請隨時跟我說。
Feel free to stay after class if you need extra help.	如果你需要更多協助，下課後可留下來。
Feel free to use your dictionary for this part of the exercise.	練習題的這部分可以隨意使用字典。
If you forget the pattern, **feel free to** look at your notes.	如果你忘記這個句型，請隨時查看筆記。

Dialogue

T Practice the new vocabulary with your partner.	請跟你的搭檔一起練習新單字。
S What should we do if we get confused?	有不清楚之處時該怎麼辦？
T **Feel free to** ask a question at any time.	有問題可隨時發問。
S Thanks, Mr. Smith.	謝謝 Smith 老師。

Dialogue

S I don't understand this grammar exercise.	我不懂這個文法習題。
T Have you read the instructions?	你看過解釋了嗎？
S Yes, but it still isn't clear.	看了，但是還是無法完全理解。
T **Feel free to** stay after class if you need extra help.	如果需要更多幫助，下課後可以留下來。

Take a moment to... 花點時間～

想告訴某人可以花點時間去做某件事時,可以使用這個表達句型。take time 的語意是「花時間」,若將 time 改成 a moment 時,語意即成了「花點時間去做某件事」。

Take a moment to collect your things.	花點時間收拾一下你的東西。
Take a moment to catch your breath.	花點時間喘口氣。
Take a moment to yourself.	給自己一點時間。
Take a moment to thank our speaker.	讓我們花點時間感謝講者。
Take a moment to relax.	花點時間放鬆一下。

Dialogue

S I get so nervous during oral exams.	我在口試時感到非常緊張。
T You need to find a way to relax.	你需要找到放鬆的方法。
S That's hard to do with all these people around.	周圍有這麼多人,很難放鬆。
T **Take a moment to** yourself.	給自己一點時間。

Dialogue

S I'm so nervous about my speech.	我對我的演講感到非常緊張。
T **Take a moment to** relax.	花點時間放鬆一下。
S I'm not sure I can.	我不確定能不能做到。
T Just take some deep breaths.	試著深呼吸。

Take your time... 慢慢來～／花點時間～

當您希望您的學生不要敷衍了事,而是花時間細心地去做某件事時,請使用這個表達句型。如果您只是說「Take your time!」,語意是「慢慢來,沒有必要著急」。time 後面接「in+動名詞」,但有時會省略 in。

Take your time and try not to make any mistakes.	慢慢來,盡量不要犯錯。

Take your time completing the questionnaire.	慢慢填寫問卷,不用著急。
Take your time when writing sentence.	寫句子時慢慢寫。
Take your time in choosing a partner.	花點時間選擇搭檔。
Take your time in group discussion.	花點時間進行小組討論。

Dialogue

S I'm really worried about this test.	我真的很擔心這次考試。
T **Take your time** and try not to make any mistakes.	慢慢來,盡量不要答錯。
S What if I don't have enough time?	如果作題時間不夠呢?
T Don't worry. You've got plenty of time.	別擔心,時間很充裕。

Dialogue

S I can't write this sentence correctly.	我無法正確地寫出這句子。
T **Take your time** when writing sentence.	寫句子時要慢慢來。
S Yes, sir. Is this right?	好的,老師,這有寫對嗎?
T Excellent! You did it!	太棒了!你做到了!

P3_037

Does anyone need...? 有人需要~嗎?

這是在上課期間進行課堂活動,想跟學生們確認是否需要什麼東西時可使用的表達句型。及物動詞 need 後面可接需求物或 to 不定詞。當學生需要什麼時會說「我有需要」,即「Here!」。

Does anyone need more time?	有人需要更多時間嗎?
Does anyone need more tape?	有人需要更多膠帶嗎?
Does anyone need further explanation?	有人需要進一步說明嗎?
Does anyone need a hand?	有人需要幫忙嗎?

Does anyone need to use the bathroom?　　有人需要去上廁所嗎？

Dialogue

- S How much time do we have left to finish the test?　　距離考試結束還有多久時間？
- T You have 15 minutes.　　還剩 15 分鐘。
- S I don't think I can finish in 15 minutes.　　我想我無法在 15 分鐘內完成試卷。
- T **Does anyone need** more time?　　有人需要更多時間嗎？

Dialogue

- T As I told you, this assignment will be difficult.　　正如我告訴過你們的，這份作業會很難。
- S I'll say it is. We are all struggling with it.　　確實如此，我們全都痛苦掙扎。
- T **Does anyone need** a hand?　　有人需要幫忙嗎？
- S I think we could all use your help.　　我想我們全都需要您的幫助。

📖 確認狀況與進度

Is that what...? 這是～的嗎？

P3_038

這是可用來確認學生的意圖的表達句型。what 在這個句型中是作為關係代名詞，包含了先行詞，用來表示「做的～事」，並引導名詞片語。

Is that what you meant?	你是這個意思嗎？
Is that what you wanted?	這是您要的嗎？
Is that what you need?	這是您需要的嗎？
Is that what you had in mind?	這是你想要的嗎？
Is that what we were supposed to do?	這是我們該做的嗎？

Dialogue

- **S** Here is the sentence we wrote, Mr. Smith.　Smith 老師，這是我們寫的句子。
- **T** Let me see it.　讓我看看。
- **S** **Is that what** you wanted?　這是您要的嗎？
- **T** Yes. This looks correct.　是的，看起來是對的。

Dialogue

- **T** You didn't study and you failed the test.　你沒有唸書，結果考試不及格。
- **S** I'm sorry.　抱歉。
- **T** **Is that what** you had in mind?　這是你想要的嗎？
- **S** No, sir.　不是的，老師。

Are you done with...?　～完了嗎？

done 的語意為「結束、完成」，相當於 finished。因此，Are you done with...?所表達的語意會隨著 with 後面的內容不同而異，例如「～結束了嗎？」、「～都完成了嗎？」或「～都用完了嗎？」等。當 Are you done with 後面接續物品時，語意是詢問該物品是否已用好了，若後面接續考試、作業、筆記、書等時，其語意則是詢問與該名詞相關的動作是否已完成。

Are you done with that pencil?	鉛筆用完了嗎？
Are you done with your essay?	作文寫好了嗎？
Are you done with your homework?	作業寫完了嗎？
Are you done with your project?	作業完成了嗎？
Are you done with that book?	這本書讀完了嗎？

Dialogue

T **Are you done with** your essay?	作文寫好了嗎？
S Almost.	差不多了。
T You'd better hurry. You only have 5 more minutes.	你最好快點，你只剩下 5 分鐘了。
S I will.	我會的。

Dialogue

T **Are you done with** your homework?	作業寫完了嗎？
S Yes, sir.	是的，老師。
T All right. Please submit it.	好的，請交上來。
S Here you are.	給您。

How many of you...? 你們之中有多少人～？

大家都熟悉「How many...?」這個句型吧？在這裡加上 of you，變成「How many of you...?」的話，語意是「你們之中有多少人～」。將這個句型稍微再變化一下，用 us 替代 you，改成「How many of us...?」的話，語意為「我們之中有多少人～」，而「How many of them...?」則表示「他們之中有多少人」。

How many of you need more time?	你們之中有多少人需要更多時間？
How many of you completed the assignment?	你們之中有多少人完成作業了？
How many of you haven't given a presentation?	你們之中有多少人還沒報告？
How many of you haven't got a test paper yet?	你們之中有多少人還沒拿到考卷？

Dialogue

T Don't forget. Your essays are due on Friday.	別忘了，星期五前要繳交你們的作文。
S What? I can't possibly be done by then.	什麼？到那時我不太可能完成。
T **How many of you** need more time?	你們之中有多少人需要更多時間？
S We all do!	我們都需要！

Dialogue

T **How many of you** completed the assignment?	你們有多少人完成作業了？
S I did, Ms. Peterson.	我做完了，Peterson 老師。
T Did you find it difficult?	你會覺得很難嗎？
S Not particularly.	沒有特別困難的地方。

I'm still waiting for... 我還在等～

這個表達句型可用於向學生提出問題後等待學生的答案，或出作業後等待提交的情況下，「wait for +名詞」的語意是「等待～」，「wait for +名詞+ to 不定詞」則表示「等待某事發生」。

I'm still waiting for your answer.	我還在等你的答案。
I'm still waiting for you to give me your homework.	我還在等你交作業。
I'm still waiting for your response.	我還在等你的回答。
I'm still waiting for you to finish.	我還在等你完成。

Dialogue

T What's the answer to number 7?	第 7 題的答案是什麼呢？
S Let me think.	讓我想想。
T Well?	嗯？
S Hmm.	唔…
T **I'm still waiting for** your answer.	我還在等你的答案。

Dialogue

S Goodbye, Mr. Smith.	Smith 老師再見。
T **I'm still waiting for** you to give me your homework.	我還在等你交作業。
S Oh! I forgot. Here it is.	哦！我忘了。這是我的作業。
T Thank you. Goodbye!	謝謝，再見！

Which one of you...? 你們之中哪一位～？

疑問詞 which 表示「哪一位（人）或哪一個（東西）」，所以「Which one of you」的語意是「你們之中的哪一位」，這句也可以改成「Which one of you guys」或「which of you」。當您想問一群學生之中的某一位時，就可以使用這個表達句型。

Which one of you* wrote this?	這是你們之中哪一位寫的？
Which one of you has the dictionary?	你們之中哪一位有字典？
Which one of you did the work?	這是你們之中哪一位做的？
Which one of you needs my help?	你們之中哪一位需要我的幫忙？
Which one of you knows the answer?	你們之中哪一位知道正確答案？

* which 也可以用在事物上，which one of these cars 表示「這些車中的某一輛」。

Dialogue

T Which one of you wrote this?	這是你們哪一位寫的？
S Why do you ask?	為什麼這麼問？
T It's quite good.	寫得太好了。
S Oh. In that case, I wrote it!	哦。那樣的話，那是我寫的！

Dialogue

T Have you looked at the question?	你們仔細看過題目了嗎？
S Yes, we have.	是的，我們有。
T Which one of you knows the answer?	你們之中哪一位知道正確答案？
S I do!	我知道！

Are there any...? 有～嗎？

這是透過改變「There are...」句型的語序形成的疑問句句型。在「Are there...?」中加上 any，就變成詢問未指定人事物存在與否的句型。類似的表達句型是「Do you have any...?」。想詢問「有什們問題嗎？」時，可以用「Are there any questions?」。「Do you have any questions?」也是不錯的表達方式。

Are there any volunteers?	有志願者嗎？
Are there any good ideas?	有什麼好的想法嗎？
Are there any absentees?	有同學缺席嗎？
Are there any test papers left?	還有考卷嗎？
Are there any questions?	還有什麼問題嗎？

Dialogue

T Okay. Let's take the roll*. **Are there any** absentees?	好的，來點名吧！有同學缺席嗎？
S I don't think Johnny's here today.	Johnny 今天沒來上課。
T Is he sick?	他生病了嗎？
S I'm not sure.	我不確定。

* roll 是意思是「點名冊」或「名單」，所以 take the roll 表示「點名」，與其類似的表達用語還有 call the roll 跟 call the names。

Dialogue

T We will leave at 8:00 for the museum.	我們 8:00 要出發去博物館。
S I'm so excited!	真令人興奮！
T **Are there any** questions?	你們還有什麼問題嗎？
S Yes, should we bring a lunch?	有，需要帶午餐嗎？

強調

What I'm trying to say is that... 我想說的是～

字面上的意思是「我想說的是～」，當您因為對方不理解自己說的話而需要重複一遍，或是當你想透過附加說明來強調自己說過的話時，都可以使用這個表達句型。除此之外，還可以在冗長的解釋之後，以「我想說的是～」這句話來吸引聽眾注意您的結論。

What I'm trying to say is that you need to study harder.	我想說的是，你需要更努力學習。
What I'm trying to say is that your last test score was a little low.	我想說的是，你上次的考試成績有點差。
What I'm trying to say is that this is going to be on the test.	我想說的是，這可能會出現在考試中。
What I'm trying to say is that you have to be in class on time.	我想說的是，上課千萬別遲到。

Dialogue

- T: Maybe you should study a little more in the future.
- S: What do you mean?
- T: **What I'm trying to say is that** you need to study harder.
- S: I understand. I'll try to work harder.

也許你未來應該要更專注於學習才行。
您的意思是什麼呢？
我想說的是，你需要更努力學習。
我知道了。我會更加努力的。

Dialogue

- T: I hope you are all paying more attention to this exercise.
- S: What?
- T: **What I'm trying to say is that** this is going to be on the test.
- S: Oh, I see! We'd better take notes!

我希望大家都能更專注於這道練習題。
什麼？
我想說的是，這題會出現在考試中。
哦，我明白了！我們最好做個筆記！

In the meantime, ... 在此期間，～／與此同時，～

當老師正在做某件事，例如發考卷、去一趟辦公室或在黑板上寫將要學習的內容之際，若想讓學生們在同一時間去做其它事時，就可以使用這個表達句型。meantime 指的是「一件事結束與下一件事開始之間的短暫時間」，與 meanwhile 語意相近。

In the meantime, review your notes.	在此期間，請複習你們的筆記。
In the meantime, don't chat with your partner.	在此期間，請不要與你的夥伴聊天。
In the meantime, sit still.	在此期間，請安靜地坐著。
In the meantime, review your summary.	與此同時，請看一下摘要。
In the meantime, close your eyes.	在此期間，請閉上眼睛。

Dialogue

🅣 We will begin our presentations in 3 hours.	報告將於三小時後開始。
🅢 What should we do until then?	在那之前我們要做什麼？
🅣 **In the meantime,** review your notes.	在此期間，請複習你們的筆記。
🅢 I've been doing that all morning!	我整個上午都在複習！

Dialogue

🅣 Your presentation is next, Bob.	Bob，下一位就輪到你報告了。
🅢 I'm so nervous*, I don't know what to do with myself.	我很緊張，不知道如何是好。
🅣 **In the meantime,** sit still.	在此期間，請安靜地坐著。
🅢 It's hard to sit still when I'm trembling!	我緊張的時候很難安靜地坐著。

* 大家應該都已經很熟悉表達擔心和緊張的句型「I'm so nervous.」了。表達緊張，像 nervous 這樣的類似單字還有 tense、keyed up、worked up，這些都是比較不熟悉的表達用語，請牢記在心。

Can someone carry...? 有人能幫我搬一下～嗎？

您可能還記得，在問句中使用 some 表示期待得到肯定的答案。當您需要有人自願幫忙搬課堂用品或教室桌椅時，可以使用這個表達句型。carry 的語意是「移動、運輸」某物，而且後面必須接續受詞。也可運用之前學到的 **I need a volunteer to...** 句型，以「I need a voluntary to carry...」來表達也行。

Can someone carry my books?	有人可以幫我搬一下我的書嗎？
Can someone carry these chairs?	有人可以幫我搬一下這些椅子嗎？
Can someone carry some boxes for me?	有人可以幫我搬一些箱子嗎？
Can someone carry this stuff for me?	有人可以幫我搬一下這個東西嗎？
Can someone carry my assignment?	有人可以幫我拿一下作業嗎？

Dialogue

T How did you break your arm?	你是怎麼弄傷了手臂？
S I fell off my bicycle.	我從腳踏車上摔了下來。
T Do you need any help?	需要幫忙嗎？
S That would be great. **Can someone carry** my books?	那就太好了，有人可以幫我搬一下我的書嗎？

Dialogue

T You sure bring a lot of food to our study group.	你為我們的讀書會帶來了很多食物。
S I get hungry when I study.	我唸書時總是肚子餓。
T Do you need help carrying anything?	需要幫你搬什麼東西嗎？
S **Can someone carry** my assignment?	有人可以幫我拿一下作業嗎？

Is that okay with...? ～可以嗎？／～同意嗎？

這是可以用來確認某個決定或計畫不會對他人造成傷害的表達句型，介系詞 with 後面接續人物名詞。也可以使用 fine 來代替句中的 okay。

Is that okay with Sally?	這個 Sally 可以嗎？
Is that okay with the teacher?	老師會同意嗎？
Is that okay with the principal?	校長會同意嗎？
Is that okay with your mother?	你媽媽會同意嗎？
Is that okay with you?	你覺得可以嗎？

Dialogue

T What's wrong, Johnny?	Johnny，怎麼了？
S1 I don't understand the exercise. Can I work with Sally?	這個練習題我不太懂，能跟 Sally 一起解題嗎？
T **Is that okay with** you, Sally?	Sally，妳可以嗎？
S2 It's no problem. I can help.	沒問題，我可以幫忙。

Dialogue

T Let's begin our writing.	我們開始寫作吧。
S I want to use my dictionary. **Is that okay with** you?	我想查字典，您覺得可以嗎？
T I'm sorry, but dictionaries are not allowed for this exercise.	抱歉，這個練習題不允許使用字典。
S This is going to be difficult.	那寫起來就困難了。

It's been ... since ... 自從～已經～了

當事情進展不順利，或想訓斥因為進度緩慢而無法按時交作業的學生，又或者是想解釋某件事情的進度時，都可以用到這個表達句型。It's 是 It has 的縮寫，since 子句中的動詞必須是過去式。

It's been a week **since** I gave you the assignment.	自從我出作業給你到現在已經一週了。
It's been a long time **since** we studied that.	自從我們上次學習這個，已經過一段時間了。
It's been an hour **since** he started working.	自從他開始工作到現在已經一個小時了。
It's been 5 minutes **since** I asked you the question.	自從我問你問題已經過 5 分鐘了。
It's been hard to study **since** I lost my dictionary.	自我弄丟了字典以來，學習起來就困難重重。

Dialogue

T Brian, where's your project?	Brian，你的作業在哪裡？
S I'm not finished with it yet.	我還沒完成
T **It's been** a week **since** I gave you the assignment.	自從我出作業給你到現在已經一週了。
S I'll try to finish it tonight.	我今晚會完成的。

Dialogue

T Why have you been doing so poorly this week?	這個星期為什麼你們的學習態度這麼差？
S **It's been** hard to study **since** I lost my dictionary.	自從我弄丟了字典之後，學習起來就困難重重。
T Maybe you should buy a new one.	也許你應該買一本新的。
S I guess you're right.	我想您說得對。

The only thing that … is … 唯一的～是～

當學生們詢問是否有其它或更簡單的方法來做某事時,可以用這個句型來表達:「這是唯一的方法」。The only thing 的語意是「唯一的事」,that 後面緊跟著用來說明 thing 的關係代名詞子句,is 後面則接上解釋具體方法的名詞。

The only thing that will help you speak well **is** practice.	有助於讓你把話說好的唯一方法就是多練習。
The only thing that you must use on this test **is** the past tense.	這次考試中,你唯一必須使用的是過去式。
The only thing that might be useful **is** your dictionary.	你唯一能用的就是字典。
The only thing that we have time to review **is** chapter 6.	我們唯一有時間能複習的是第 6 章。

Dialogue

S What can I do to improve?	我該怎麼做才能改善?
T **The only thing that** will help you speak well **is** practice.	有助於讓你把話說好的唯一方法就是多練習。
S What's the best way to practice?	最好的練習方法是什麼?
T Come to class every day.	每天都來上課。

Dialogue

S I have a lot of questions.	我有很多問題想問。
T **The only thing that** we have time to review **is** chapter 6.	我們唯一有時間能複習的是第 6 章。
S Good. That's the most difficult part.	沒問題,那是最難的一課。
T What are your questions?	你的問題是什麼呢?

103

This is the last... 這是最後一次～

last 的語意是「最後的」，所以當您想在課堂上對動來動去的孩子們說：「這是最後一題了，加油」時，就可以使用這個表達句型。除此之外，也可利用這個句型來警告孩子們，例如「不要再這樣做了，這是最後一次警告」的英語表達就是「This is the last warning. Don't do it again.」。

This is the last test of the year.	這是今年的最後一次考試。
This is the last opportunity to ask questions before the test.	這是考試前最後一次提問的機會。
This is the last day of class.	這是最後一天上課。
This is the last chance.	這是最後一次機會。
This is the last warning.	這是最後一次警告。

Dialogue

🅣 **This is the last** test of the year.	這是今年的最後一次考試。
🅢1 That's wonderful!	太棒了！
🅢2 Don't get too excited. It's going to be difficult.	別太興奮，考試應該會很難。
🅢1 You're right.	你說得對。

Dialogue

🅣 **This is the last** day of class.	今天是最後一天上課。
🅢 Now it's time for summer vacation*!	放暑假了！
🅣 Don't forget everything you have learned.	不要忘記你所學的。
🅢 Don't worry. We won't.	別擔心。我們不會。

* 當我們提到「假期」或「放假」時，經常會使用 vacation 這個單字。另一方面，break 可表示春假這種短暫的「假期」。此外，holiday 指的是依國家、民族所制定的國定假日跟紀念日，而「休假」或「請假」則大多用 day off。

Without a doubt, ... 毫無疑問，～

這是用於描述明顯且確定之事物的表達句型，老師在課堂上講解時常會用到這個句型。因為是副詞片語，所以可以放在句中或句末。也可以省略冠詞，直接說 without doubt。類似的表達句型包括「needless to say」、「out of doubt」、「undoubtedly」等，請一併學習並熟記。

Without a doubt, you need to raise your grade.	毫無疑問，各位需要提高成績。
Without a doubt, this is the best paper I've read.	毫無疑問，這是我讀過的最好的文章。
Without a doubt, you will pass.	毫無疑問，你會通過的。
Without a doubt, I know the result.	毫無疑問，我知道結果。
Without a doubt, I will pass the test.	毫無疑問，我會通過考試。

Dialogue

- 🅣 Daniel, I'm very impressed with your essay.
  Daniel，你的文章給我留下了深刻的印象。
- 🅢 Thank you, Mr. Wilcox.
  謝謝 Wilcox 老師。
- 🅣 **Without a doubt,** this is the best paper I've read.
  這毫無疑問是我讀過的最好的文章。
- 🅢 Wow! I'm flattered.
  哇！受寵若驚！

Dialogue

- 🅢 If I don't pass the test, Dad will kill me.
  如果我沒通過考試，爸爸就會殺了我。
- 🅣 **Without a doubt,** you will pass.
  毫無疑問，你會通過的。
- 🅢 How can you be so sure?
  您怎麼能這麼肯定？
- 🅣 I know you did your best for the test.
  我知道你在這次考試已經盡了全力。

徵求自願者

I need a volunteer to... 我需要一名自願者來～

當您在課堂上需要學生提供幫忙，無論大事或小事時，這是一個很有用的表達句型。volunteer 這個單字有兩個語意，一個是無報酬做某事的「志工」，一個是沒人指使之下自願挺身而出做某事的「自願者」，在這句型中解釋成「自願者」應該會更為適當。

I need a volunteer to pass out these papers.	我需要一名自願者來發這些資料。
I need a volunteer to read aloud.	我需為一位願意大聲朗讀的人。
I need a volunteer to move these desks out of the classroom.	我需要一個自願者來將這些桌子搬出教室。
I need a volunteer to help me.	我需要一名自願者來幫助我。
I need a volunteer to set up the overhead projector.	我需要一名自願者來架設投影機。

Dialogue

T **I need a volunteer to** pass out these papers.　　我需要一名自願者來發這些資料。
S I'll do it, Mrs. Carlson.　　Carlson 老師，我可以幫忙。
T Make sure everyone gets a green sheet and a yellow sheet.　　請確認你們每個人都拿到了綠色和黃色的紙。
S No problem.　　沒問題。

Dialogue

T **I need a volunteer to** read aloud.　　我需為一位願意大聲朗讀的人。
S I'm too shy to read.　　我太害羞了，無法大聲朗讀。
T Don't worry. You'll do fine!　　別擔心。你會做得很好的！
S All right. I'll try.　　好，我盡力。

Can someone...? 有誰能～嗎？

當您不想一個一個叫人起來「你來試試看」,而是想透過「有人能～嗎?」來鼓勵學生自願參與時,就可以使用這個表達句型。這個句型主要用於預期對方會積極回應,而不是在不確定的情況下。如果學生想引起老師的注意,就會舉手說:「我!」。

Can someone* carry these chairs?	有誰可以搬走這些椅子嗎?
Can someone hand me that pen?	有誰能把那支筆遞給我嗎?
Can someone answer the question, please?	有誰能回答這個問題嗎?
Can someone come to the board and solve the problem?	有誰能走到黑板這邊解這道題嗎?
Can someone tell me where Mali is?	誰能告訴我馬利在哪裡嗎?

* 一般來說,any 用於疑問句和否定句,some 用於肯定句,那麼為什麼 someone 是用於疑問句呢?當在疑問句中使用 some 時,這表示您期盼得到肯定的答覆。

Dialogue

T Let's rearrange the classroom so we can watch this English movie.	我們需要重新整理一下教室來**觀賞**這部英語電影。
S Okay. That sounds great!	好啃,聽起來不錯!
T **Can someone** carry these chairs?	有人可以**搬走**這些椅子嗎?
S I can do it.	我可以。

Dialogue

T **Can someone** tell me where Mali is?	誰能告訴我馬利在哪裡嗎?
S1 Is it in South America?	是在南美洲嗎?
T Sorry. Wrong continent.	我很遺憾,但並非在此大陸。
S2 I know! Mali is in Africa!	我知道!馬利在非洲!
T That's right!	沒錯!

Who's going to...? 誰將～呢？／誰要～呢？

「be going to...」解釋為「將要～」，表示不久的將來會發生某件事，所以「Who's going to...?」的語意是「誰要～呢？」。除此之外，這句型也能用來表達主詞的意圖或意願，解釋成「誰想試著～呢？」。

Who's going to be first?	誰會是第一名呢？
Who's going to win the prize?	誰將贏得那個獎品呢？
Who's going to read the sentence?	誰要來讀這一句呢？
Who's going to go on the trip?	誰要去旅行呢？
Who's going to erase the board?	誰要來擦黑板呢？

Dialogue

T The winner will get a new backpack!	優勝者將獲得一個新背包！
S **Who's going to** win the prize?	誰將贏得那個獎品呢？
T Whoever gets the highest score.	得分最高者。
S I hope I win!	真希望是我！

Dialogue

T We're finished for the day.	今天就到這裡。
S Hurray! Time to play!	哦耶！玩的時間到了！
T **Who's going to** erase the board?	誰來擦黑板呢？
S I will!	我來擦！
T Thank you, Bobby.	謝謝 Bobby。

說明原因

That's because... 那是因為～

在回答學生的問題與困惑時,「That's because...」正是可以用來明確指出問題之原因的表達句型。「That's why...」因為跟此句型相似而容易被人搞混,但其語意是「所以～」。請注意 because 後面接續「原因」,但 why 後面接續「結果」。

That's because the verb is in the wrong place.	那是因為動詞放錯位置了。
That's because we have a test tomorrow.	那是因為我們明天要考試。
That's because you left early.	那是因為你早退了。
That's because you're speaking too quickly.	那是因為你說話速度太快了。
That's because you didn't join us for a discussion.	那是因為你沒有參與討論。

Dialogue

S: We are reviewing a lot today.	我們今天複習了超多內容。
T: **That's because** we have a test tomorrow.	那是因為我們明天要考試。
S: Oh! I forgot!	啊!我忘了!
T: Then you'd better pay more attention to the class.	那你上課最好要更專心一點。

Dialogue

T: What's wrong?	怎麼了?
S: I'm making a lot of mistakes.	我犯了太多錯誤。
T: **That's because** you're speaking too quickly.	那是因為你說話速度太快了。
S: I'll try to slow down.	我會儘量放慢語速。

📖 表達動機

I just wanted to... 我只是想～

此句型主要是用來聲稱自己沒有任何特殊意圖，來解釋自己的想法或感受。這裡的 just 的語意是「只是」之意。to 後面接續「know/see/ ask/tell + if 子句」，表達「我想知道～」、「我想看看～」等意思。

I just wanted to ask a quick question.	我只是想問一個簡單的問題。
I just wanted to know if you were ready.	我只是想知道你們是否準備好了。
I just wanted to ask you the time.	我只是想問現在幾點了。
I just wanted to tell you about the homework.	我只是想告訴你們關於作業的事。
I just wanted to see if you understood.	我只是想知道你是否懂了。

Dialogue

🇹 Yes, Billy? Do you have a question?	是的，Billy？你有什麼問題嗎？
🇸 **I just wanted to** ask you the time.	我只是想問現在幾點了。
🇹 It's 3 o'clock.	現在 3 點了。
🇸 It's almost time to go home!	快到回家的時間了！

Dialogue

🇹 What's the answer to number 2?	第 2 題的答案是什麼？
🇸 It's A. I'm not finished with the exercise yet.	是 A，但我還沒做完所有的習題。
🇹 That's okay. **I just wanted to** see if you understood.	沒關係，我只是想知道你是否懂了。
🇸 Oh, I see.	好的。

I just wanted to let you guys... 我只是想讓你們～

you guys 的語意是「你們、各位、大家」，是英文母語人士隨意稱呼聚在一起的某群人（無關性別）時經常使用的一個詞。在這個表達句型中，「let + 受詞 + 原形動詞」的語意是「讓～」，用原形動詞表達您想允許對方去做的事。

I just wanted to let you guys know that I'll be absent tomorrow.	我只是想讓你們知道我明天不能來。
I just wanted to let you guys practice for a few minutes.	我只是想讓你們練習一會兒。
I just wanted to let you guys take a break.	我只是想讓你們休息一下。
I just wanted to let you guys have a few minutes before the test.	我只是想讓你們在考前有一點準備的時間
I just wanted to let you guys try it first.	我只是想先給你們試試看。

Dialogue

T **I just wanted to let you guys** know that I'll be absent tomorrow.	我只是想讓你們知道我明天不能來學校。
S Who will teach us?	誰會來教我們？
T There will be a substitute teacher.	會有一位代課老師。
S I hope she's nice!	希望她是一位好人！

Dialogue

S What are we going to do next?	我們接下來做什麼？
T **I just wanted to let you guys** have a few minutes before the test.	我只是想讓你們在考試前有一點準備的時間。
S Test? What test?	考前？什麼考試？
T Did you forget?	你忘了嗎？

UNIT 03 課程與教材

📖 確認上課主題

Let's review... 我們複習一下～

根據上下文，review 可用來表達「檢視，檢查」之意，尤其在美式英語中，會用 review 來表達「複習（學科）」。而在英式英語中，用來表達「校正、修正」的 revise 也會用來表達「複習」。本課提到的「Let's review + 名詞」是用來指示學生們複習某事的表達句型，別忘了 review 後面要接續名詞作為受詞。

Let's review yesterday's lesson.	我們複習一下昨天的課程。
Let's review chapters 5 through 8.	我們複習一下第 5 章到第 8 章。
Let's review the passive voice.	我們複習一下被動語態。
Let's review chapter 2.	我們來複習一下第二章。
Let's review the new vocabularies we learned yesterday.	我們來複習一下昨天學的新單字。

Dialogue

Ⓢ What are we going to do first? 我們要先做什麼呢？
Ⓣ **Let's review** yesterday's lesson. 讓我們回顧一下昨天的課程。
Ⓢ Okay. I remember it was about verbs. 好的，我記得是跟動詞有關。
Ⓣ That's right. It was about the past tense. 沒錯，是關於過去式。

Dialogue

Ⓣ **Let's review** chapters 5 through 8. 讓我們複習一下第 5 章到第 8 章。
Ⓢ I've already forgotten a lot. 很多內容都忘光了。
Ⓣ Don't worry. You'll remember easily. 別擔心，很容易就會回想起來的。
Ⓢ I hope so. 希望如此。

Let's go over... 我們來（仔細）看看～

在一堂課開始之際，想讓學生回顧上一堂課所學的內容，又或想在課堂中重新提及先前教過的內容來幫助學生理解其內容時，可以使用本課的句型。go over 表示「仔細查看」，語意與 review 相似，但 go over 的意思是仔細查看重要部分，review 的意思則是複習課程全部內容以加深記憶或總結事實。

Let's go over the new vocabulary.	我們來看看新單字。
Let's go over chapter 3.	我們來看看第 3 章。
Let's go over your essay together.	我們一起來看看你的作文。
Let's go over your homework.	我們來看看你的作業。
Let's go over the words you don't know.	我們看看你不認識的單字。

Dialogue

🅣 **Let's go over** chapter 3. Any questions?	讓我們來看看第 3 章，有什麼問題嗎？
🅢 Yes. I don't understand the sentence on page 23.	有，我看不懂第 23 頁的句子。
🅣 Which sentence?	是哪一句呢？
🅢 The one at the bottom.	最下面那一句。

Dialogue

🅢 I'm having a lot of problems with my writing.	我在寫作方面遇到很多問題。
🅣 **Let's go over** your essay together.	我們一起看看你的作文。
🅢 Okay. I think that will help a lot.	好的，我認為這會很有幫助。
🅣 The first paragraph looks pretty good to me.	第一段看起來很不錯。

Our English lesson today will cover...
今天的英文課，我們要來學～

這是可在課程開始時使用的表達句型，用來提前告知當天課程將學習到的內容。動詞 cover 的語意是「包含（某範圍）」跟「涉及（某主題）」，後面接續課堂上要講述的內容即可。在某些情況下，若課程主要是以討論方式進行的話，可以用 discuss 或 talk about 來取代本句型的 cover。

Our English lesson today will cover* the past tense.	今天的英文課，我們要來學過去式。
Our English lesson today will cover action verbs.	今天的英文課，我們要來學動作動詞。
Our English lesson today will cover animal names.	今天的英文課，我們要來學動物的名稱。
Our English lesson today will cover the alphabet.	今天的英文課，我們要來學字母。

* 在 Our English lesson today will cover...這個句型中，cover 的中文語意是「涵蓋、涉及」，所以也可用 concern 和 be about 來取代。

Dialogue

T **Our English lesson today will cover animal names.**	今天的英文課，我們要來學動物的名稱。
S You mean names like, "Spot" or "Fuzzy?"	您指的是「Spot」或「Fuzzy」之類的名字嗎？
T No. Names like "Dog," "Cat," and "Bird."	不是這些，而是像狗、貓和鳥這樣的名稱。
S Oh, okay.	哦，好的。

Dialogue

T **Our English lesson today will cover the alphabet.**	今天的英文課，我們要來學字母。
S Will we have to memorize the alphabet?	我們必須背字母嗎？
T Yes, it will be on the big test.	當然，大考會考字母。

This morning, we will... 今天早上我們要～

這是在開始介紹課程進度或在早自習提醒學生當天課程表時，可用的表達句型。可根據情況不同使用其它片語來取代本句型中的 This morning。改用 during the vacation 時，其語意為「在這個假期期間～」，想表達「在這個學期中～」，就要改用 In this session。若想表達「在未來一年期間～」時，改用「throughout the year」就行了。

This morning, we will learn many new words.	今天早上我們要學習許多新單字。
This morning, we will study chapter 14.	今天早上我們要上第 14 章。
This morning, we will learn about Switzerland.	今天早上我們要認識瑞士。
This morning, we will practice some new skills.	今天早上我們要練習一些新技能。
This morning, we will write a story.	今天早上我們要來寫一篇故事。

Dialogue

- **T** **This morning, we will** study chapter 14. — 我們今天早上要上第 14 章。
- **S** I can't believe we've gotten this far in the book. — 不敢相信我們已經到這一課了。
- **T** Yes. Soon we will be finished! — 是的，我們很快就會讀完這本書了。
- **S** I can't wait! — 等不及了！

Dialogue

- **T** **This morning, we will** write a story. — 我們今天早上要來寫一篇故事。
- **S** That sounds hard. — 聽起來很難。
- **T** Don't worry. It can be quite fun. — 別擔心，這應該會很有趣。
- **S** I hope so! — 但願如此！

Let's begin by... 我們先～／我們先從～開始

這是用來陳述第一個課程的活動時的表達句型。類似的表達句型有「Let's start with...」。begin by 的語意為「從做～開始」，此時的 by 指的是手段或方法，當 by 後面接續動詞 -ing 形式，則表達「透過／藉由～」。相反地，當課程結束，想表達「以做～來結尾」時，則要用「end by + 動詞 -ing 形式」。

Let's begin by practicing pronunciation.	我們先從練習發音開始吧。
Let's begin by reviewing yesterday's grammar.	我們先回顧昨天學過的文法。
Let's begin by telling our partners about our weekends.	我們先和搭檔談談自己的週末。
Let's begin by taking a short quiz.	我們先來做個小測驗。
Let's begin by learning some new words.	我們先開始學一些新單字。

Dialogue

T **Let's begin by** practicing pronunciation.	我們從練習發音開始吧。
S Pronunciation is hard work.	發音真的好難。
T It's good exercise for your mouth.	這可是一種很好的口腔運動鍛鍊。
S That's one way to think about it.	從某種層面上來說是這樣吧！

Dialogue

T **Let's begin by** reviewing yesterday's grammar.	我們先回顧昨天學過的文法。
S Good. It's really difficult.	好，真的很難。
T Do you have any specific questions?	你們還有什麼特別想問的嗎？
S I don't understand any of it.	我一個也搞不懂。

Are we going to talk about...? 我們要來談談～嗎？

當您在跟學生們進行協商，或者試著想跟學生們對某個學習主題展開對話時，可以使用這個表達句型。雖然是疑問句，但更像是提出一個「我們來談談～」的建議，而不是期待對方的回答。類似的表達句型有「Let's talk about...」跟「Why don't we talk about...?」。

Are we going to talk about grammar?	我們要來談談文法嗎？
Are we going to talk about the test?	我們要來談談考試嗎？
Are we going to talk about your essay?	我們要來談談你的作文嗎？
Are we going to talk about the details of the story?	我們要來討論一下這個故事的細節嗎？
Are we going to talk about something interesting?	我們要來談談有趣的事嗎？

Dialogue

T **Are we going to talk about** the test?	我們要來談談考試嗎？
S1 Yes.	好的。
S2 How long will we have to take it?	我們考試時間多長？
T 30 minutes.	30 分鐘。

Dialogue

S **Are we going to talk about** something interesting?	我們要來談談有趣的事嗎？
T Okay. We are going to talk about grammar!	好啊，我們來談談文法。
S That's not interesting.	文法也不有趣呀。
T Sometimes it is.	偶爾也很有趣。

Let's look at ... 我們來看看～

這是跟學生討論問題時可用的句型。這裡的 look 與其解釋成「看到」，用「思考、檢查」會更容易理解。類似的表達句型有「讓我們想一想～」語意的「Let's think about...」，而「Let's think about this another way.」的語意則為「讓我們換個方式思考一下」。

Let's look at this another way.	我們換個角度來看看這個問題。
Let's look at your homework.	我們來看看你的作業。
Let's look at your essay.	我們來看看你的作文。
Let's look at this more carefully.	我們再仔細地看看這個。
Let's look at this right after we finish this chapter.	這一章結束後，我們再來看看這個。

Dialogue

T **Let's look at** your homework.	我們來看看你的作業。
S How did I do?	我寫得如何？
T I think you're confused. There are many mistakes.	我想你沒有搞懂，有很多錯誤。
S Can you explain it to me?	您能跟我說明一下嗎？

Dialogue

S I think I'm confused about the writing assignment.	我覺得好像搞不太清楚要怎麼寫作文作業。
T **Let's look at** your essay.	我們來看看你的作文。
S What do you think?	您覺得怎麼樣？
T It looks fine. I think you understand.	看起來不錯，我想你都理解。

說明主題特色

Our guest today is... 今天的嘉賓是～

這是當學校有特別講座時，想介紹講者時可使用的表達句型。美國的學校會舉辦一個名為職涯探索日（career day*）的講座，邀請來自各業界之嘉賓蒞臨演講，讓學生有機會聽到各領域的人對各種職業的看法，並思考他們的才能和未來。

*「運動會」稱作 field day；拍畢業照的「拍照的日子」則稱作 Picture Day。除此之外，back-to school Day 則相當於我們的「返校日」。

Our guest today is very interesting.	今天的嘉賓很有趣。
Our guest today is a famous politician.	今天的嘉賓是一位著名的政治家。
Our guest today is a very successful businessperson.	今天的嘉賓是一位非常成功的商人。
Our guest today is going to speak about America.	今天的嘉賓要來談論美國。

Dialogue

- T: **Our guest today is** very interesting. 今天的嘉賓很有趣。
- S: Who is it? 是誰？
- T: She's an astronaut who has traveled to outer space! 她是到外太空旅行過的太空人！
- S: Wow! That's great! 哇！太棒了！

Dialogue

- T: **Our guest today is** a very successful businessperson. 今天的嘉賓是一位非常成功的商人。
- S: What kind of business? 從事什麼行業呢？
- T: She owns a software company. 她經營著一間軟體公司。
- S: That sounds like an interesting job. 聽起來是一項很有趣的工作。

This book is... 這本書～

在學校裡免不了會談論到書，像是課本、參考書、童書、漫畫書等等。談論到書籍時，請試著使用句型 This book is...。這是在學期初介紹教科書，或想向學生推薦一本書時可用的表達句型。可以在 is 後面接續各式各樣的補語來描述該本書的特徵或內容。

This book is very interesting.	這本書很有趣。
This book is quite difficult.	這本書相當難。
This book is full of useful words.	這本書有很多有用的單詞。
This book is for students to use.	這本書適合學生。
This book is too long and boring.	這本書過於冗長且無聊。

Dialogue

S Can you recommend something good to read?	您能推薦值得一讀的好書嗎？
T **This book is** very interesting.	這本書很有趣。
S What is it about?	那是什麼樣的書呢？
T It's about a dinosaur.	是關於恐龍的書。

Dialogue

T This homework may take a long time.	這個作業可能需要花費很多時間。
S Why? It looks short.	為什麼？看起來很短。
T Yes, but **this book is** quite difficult.	確實如此，但這本書相當難。
S Oh, I see.	啊，原來如此。

📖 提示接下來的主題

After lunch, we will... 午餐後,我們將～

這是想介紹下午課程時可使用的表達句型。After lunch 的語意雖然是「午餐後」,在校園內使用此句型主要用來表達「下午的課表」。除此之外,想表達「放學;下課」時,可用 after school。

After lunch, we will take a short quiz.	午餐後,我們將進行一個小考。
After lunch, we will watch a movie about whales.	午餐後,我們將觀看一部有關鯨魚的電影。
After lunch, we will memorize the new information.	午餐後,我們將背熟新的資訊。
After lunch, we will prepare our presentations.	午餐後,我們將準備演講。
After lunch, we will take a field trip.	午餐後,我們將去戶外教學。

Dialogue

🅣 **After lunch, we will** take a short quiz.	午餐後,我們將進行一個小考。
🅢 Oh no! I can't remember anything!	哦不!我什麼都忘光了!
🅣 Relax. It's not too difficult.	放輕鬆,測驗不會太難。
🅢 I'm still nervous!	我還是很緊張!

Dialogue

🅣 **After lunch, we will** take a field trip.	午餐後,我們將去戶外教學。
🅢 Where are we going?	我們要去哪裡?
🅣 To the zoo.	去動物園。
🅢 That sounds great!	聽起來很棒!

解說

Let me tell you about... 我來告訴各位～／我來跟各位說～

您可以用這個表達句型在學期初向學生介紹自己，或在課堂上向學生解釋課程內容。當您想向別人講一個故事時，對方可能已經聽過這個故事或不想聽這個故事，所以最好用較有禮貌的表達用語「**Let me tell you about...**」來帶出談話的主題。

Let me tell you about the history of the United States.	我來跟各位說明美國歷史。
Let me tell you about your homework.	我來跟各位說明你們的功課。
Let me tell you about how English verbs work.	我來跟各位說明英文動詞的作用。
Let me tell you about next week's test.	我來跟各位說明下週的考試內容。
Let me tell you about the project.	我來跟各位說明這個專題。

Dialogue

T **Let me tell you about** next week's test.	我來跟各位說明下週的考試內容。
S What's going to be on it?	考試範圍在哪裡？
T Chapters 1 to 15.	從第 1 課到第 15 課。
S Wow! That's a lot!	哇！好多喔！

Dialogue

T **Let me tell you about** the project.	我來跟各位說明這個專題。
S What are we going to do?	我們要做什麼呢？
T We're going to write and perform a play.	我們將寫一個劇本並進行表演。
S That sounds like fun!	聽起來很有趣！

Let me explain... 我來解釋一下～

這是一個經常出現在課堂上進行說明（包含遊戲規則）之前的重要表達句型，其語意是「我要跟你們講解一下，請仔細聽好」，所以在解釋之前，很適合用這句話來吸引孩子們的注意力。類似的表達句型為「Let me tell you...」。

Let me explain the homework.	我來解釋一下作業。
Let me explain how to do this exercise.	我來解釋一下這個練習題該怎麼做。
Let me explain what I want you to do.	我來解釋一下我要你們做什麼。
Let me explain today's lesson.	我來解釋一下今天的課程。
Let me explain how this assignment should be done.	我來解釋一下該如何做這個作業。

Dialogue

T **Let me explain** how to do this exercise.	我來解釋一下這個練習題該怎麼做。
S It looks difficult.	看起來很難。
T Don't worry. It's easy.	別擔心，很簡單的。
S Okay. What should we do?	好的。我們應該怎麼做呢？

Dialogue

S The homework looks difficult.	作業看起來很難。
T **Let me explain** how this assignment should be done.	我來講解一下該如何做這個作業。
S What do we do first?	我們首先應該要做什麼呢？
T Find the words in your dictionary.	從你的字典裡找出這些單字。

That's the way... ～就是～／～正是～

way 後面接續子句時，語意為「以那個方式做」或「就應該這樣做」。當學生的表現是老師想要的結果時，老師可以使用這個句型表達「沒錯，就是這樣」來給予正面回饋。舉例來說，「**That's the way** I like it.」的語意是「這就是我喜歡的方式」，「**That's the way** it should be.」則表示「沒錯，就應該是這樣」。

That's the way you have to do it.	這正是你們要做的事。
That's the way they say it in America.	美國人就是這麼說的。
That's the way I like it.	這就是我喜歡的方式。
That's the way it works.	這就是它的運作方式。
That's the way the teacher showed us.	老師就是這麼教我們的。

Dialogue

S It's difficult to write all the answers to these questions.	寫出這些問題的所有答案並不容易。
T **That's the way** you have to do it.	這正是你們要做的事。
S I know that, but I don't have to like it.	我知道，但這並不表示我必須喜歡這件事。
T Stop complaining!	別再抱怨了！

Dialogue

T Any questions?	你們還有什麼問題嗎？
S I understand "lift" but I don't understand "elevator."	我理解「lift」，但我不懂「elevator」。
T **That's the way** they say it in America.	美國人就是這麼說的。
S How strange!	這很奇怪！

請學生仔細聽（看）

Watch closely... 注意看～／仔細觀察～

是跟「Look carefully...」類似的表達句型，look 跟 watch 都具有「注意看」之意。這是要求仔細觀察並跟著做（或解題）時可用的表達句型，經常出現在練習題的題目說明中。

Watch closely and you'll see what my tongue does.	仔細觀察我的舌頭是如何移動的。
Watch closely and you'll see the shape of my mouth.	如果你仔細觀察，就能看到我嘴巴的形狀。
Watch closely because this is hard to see.	這個很難看出來，所以要仔細觀察。
Watch closely so you don't get lost.	仔細看的話就不會感到迷失。
Watch closely for the way my teeth touch my lips.	仔細觀察我的牙齒接觸嘴唇的方式。

Dialogue

- 🅣 Try saying the word, "thorough."
- 🅢 That's difficult to say.
- 🅣 **Watch closely** and you'll see what my tongue does. "Thorough."
- 🅢 I see! It touches your upper teeth.

試著唸這個單字「thorough」。
太難唸了啦。
仔細觀察我的舌頭是如何移動的，「thorough」。
我明白了！舌頭要碰到上牙齦。

Dialogue

- 🅣 Let's watch this film with subtitles.
- 🅢 It's hard to follow.
- 🅣 **Watch closely** so you don't get lost.
- 🅢 I'll have to learn to read faster.

大家透過字幕來看這部電影吧。
搭配字幕去看有點吃力。
仔細看的話就不會感到迷失。
我要學著看快點。

125

Listen carefully... 注意聽～

listen 的語意是「聽」，carefully 的語意是「仔細地、謹慎地」，所以當您想告訴對方這是重要內容而需要專心聆聽時，很適合使用這個表達句型。尤其在聽力課經常會用到這個句型。想利用這個句型來表達「仔細看～」時，可以說：「Look (at) ～carefully.」。

Listen carefully and fill in the blanks.	注意聽並填空。
If you don't **listen carefully** or you won't know what to do.	如果你不注意聽，就會不知道該做什麼。
Listen carefully or you will get confused.	如果你不注意聽，可能會一頭霧水。
Listen carefully to the story.	認真聽故事。
Listen carefully and then try to answer the questions.	認真聽講並試著答題。

Dialogue

🆃 Now it's time to practice listening.	現在是練習聽力的時候了。
🆂1 Oh, this is going to be easy.	哦，應該很容易吧。
🆂2 Yeah, I can understand everything!	對啊，全都能聽懂！
🆃 If you don't **listen carefully** or you won't know what to do.	如果你不仔細聽，就會不知道該做什麼。

Dialogue

🆂 How do we do this exercise?	這個練習題該怎麼做呢？
🆃 **Listen carefully** and then try to answer the questions.	認真聽講並試著答題。
🆂 Should we write the answers?	我們必須要將答案寫下來嗎？
🆃 No, just discuss them with your partner.	不用，只要跟你的搭檔討論答案。

確認是否跟上進度

Can everyone see...? 大家都能看到～嗎？／大家都懂～嗎？

在使用黑板或投影機等視覺輔助設備時，可使用這個表達句型來確認學生是否都有看到畫面。除此之外，也可用「Is there anyone who can't see...?（有人看不到～嗎？）」。see 除了「看見」之外，還有「知道、明白」之意，所以可用「Can everyone see...?」來詢問「每個人都明白～嗎？」。

Can everyone see the blackboard?	大家都能看到黑板嗎？
Can everyone see the screen?	大家都能看到螢幕嗎？
Can everyone see this graph?	大家都能看到這張圖表嗎？
Can everyone see this picture?	大家都能看到這張照片吧？
Can everyone see how this works?	大家都懂這是如何運作的嗎？

Dialogue

T **Can everyone see** this graph?	大家都能看到這張圖表嗎？
S I can't see it, Mrs. Wilber.	Wilber 老師，我看不到。
T Move closer. It shows the distribution of your grades.	再靠近一點，這張圖顯示了大家的成績分布。
S I'm not so sure I want to see that.	我不太確定我真的想看到它。

Dialogue

T **Can everyone see** this picture?	大家都能看到這張照片吧？
S I think it's a cucumber.	看起來像一條黃瓜。
T No, you were close. It's a "zucchini."	不是，但很接近了，這是「櫛瓜」。
S What's a zucchini?	櫛瓜是什麼？

確認是否有問題

Any questions...? 有什麼疑問嗎？

這是用來確認學生是否有疑問時可用的表達句型，也可簡單地用「Any question...?」來詢問，也可用完整的句型來詢問，例如「Are there any questions?」或「Do you have any questions?」。

Any questions before we finish?	在我們結束之前還有什麼問題嗎？
Any questions about the assignment?	關於作業有什麼問題嗎？
Any questions about what will be on the test?	對考試內容有疑問嗎？
Any questions before you take the test?	在考試前還有什麼想問的嗎？
Any questions about the article?	對這篇文章還有什麼疑問嗎？

Dialogue

T **Any questions** about the homework?	關於作業還有什麼問題嗎？
S How long should our essays be?	我們的作文應該要寫多長呢？
T One page is long enough.	一頁就夠了。
S Oh good. That's not too long.	哦，太好了，那就不會太長。

Dialogue

T **Any questions** before you take the test?	在考試前還有什麼想問的嗎？
S Can we use our dictionaries?	我們可以使用字典嗎？
T Of course not!	當然不行！
S This is going to be hard!	這場考試會很難！

Do you see...? 你理解～嗎？／你有看到～嗎？

當您想確認學生們對於作業內容的理解程度，或確認是否已理解時，就可以使用這個表達句型。「**Do you see...?**」既有「你看到～嗎？」的意思，也可解釋為「你理解～嗎？」，來確認對方是否已經理解。

Do you see how easy it is?	你知道這有多簡單嗎？
Do you see the verb in this sentence?	你有找到這句子中的動詞嗎？
Do you see any words you don't know?	你有看到不認識的單字嗎？？
Do you see where the comma should go?	你知道逗號該放在哪裡嗎？
Do you see the answer to the question?	你知道這個問題的答案嗎？

Dialogue

🇹 Have you finished reading the story?	讀完這個故事了嗎？
🇸 Yes. I'm finished.	嗯，我都讀完了。
🇹 **Do you see** any words you don't know?	你有看到不認識的單字嗎？？
🇸 No. I understand them all.	沒有，都認識。

Dialogue

🇹 There is a problem with this sentence.	這句話有問題。
🇸 What's wrong with it?	哪裡錯了？
🇹 **Do you see** where the comma should go?	你知道逗號該放在哪裡嗎？
🇸 Oh, now I see. It should go right there.	啊，我明白了，應該放在那裡。

📖 回到上一步

Could we go back to...? 我們回到～好嗎？

go back 的語意是「回去」，所以當課堂上的對話偏離主題，想表達「我們回到課堂／課本」，或是當你在找某一個頁面時，都可以使用這個表達用語。順便一提，go over 的語意是「仔細查看」，所以當有人說 Could we go over～? 時，其語意是「我們好好地來看一下～好嗎？」。

Could we go back to question number 5?	我們回到第 5 題好嗎？
Could we go back to chapter 17?	我們回到第 17 章好嗎？

Could we go back to the last exercise?	我們回到上一個練習題好嗎？
Could we go back to what we studied yesterday?	我們回到昨天上的內容好嗎？
Could we go back to number 7?	我們回到第 7 題好嗎？

> Dialogue

🅣 **Could we go back to** question number 5?	我們回到第 5 題好嗎？
🅢 Why?	為什麼？
🅣 I don't think you guys understand it.	因為你們似乎還沒理解這一題。
🅢 Actually, that's true.	事實上，確實如此。

> Dialogue

🅣 Our next exercise is on page 103.	下一個練習題在第 103 頁。
🅢 **Could we go back to** the last exercise?	我們回到上一個練習題好嗎？
🅣 Okay. What's your question?	好啊，有什麼問題嗎？
🅢 I don't understand number 13.	第 13 題我不太理解。

📖 進行下一步

Let's move on to... 我們接著進行～／我們開始進行～

當您結束某項活動並想要繼續下一項活動時，這會是一個很好用的表達句型。尤其在上台報告時，經常會用到這個句型。此外，當您想要請下一位簡報者發表、轉換至新的主題、進到下一章或投影片，甚至是改變對話主題時，也都可以使用這個句型。Let's go to~ 也是此情況下常使用的表達句型。

Let's move on to chapter 7.	我們接著上第 7 課。
Let's move on to a new topic.	我們接著來上新的主題。

Let's move on to the next part of the exercise.	我們來看下一個練習題。
Let's move on to the fun part.	我們接著來上有趣的部分。
Let's move on to your homework.	我們來看看各位的作業。

Dialogue

🅣 **Let's move on to** chapter 7.	我們接著上第 7 課。
🅢 I'm sorry, but I don't understand chapter 6 yet.	抱歉,但我還無法理解第 6 課。
🅣 Okay. **Let's review**.	好的,我們再來複習一遍。
🅢 Thank you, sir.	謝謝老師。

Dialogue

🅢 This exercise is really difficult.	這個練習題真的很難。
🅣 **Let's move on to** the fun part.	我們接著進入有趣的部分吧。
🅢 What's the fun part?	什麼是有趣的部分呢?
🅣 Lunch time!	午餐時間!

📖 按順序說明

First of all, ... 首先,～

這是想依序說明各種活動,或介紹課程內容時可用的表達句型。此外,當您想指出許多事情中最重要的事情,或指出應該擺在最優先順位的事項時,這也是個很好用的表達句型。

First of all, learning a new language should be fun.	首先,學習新語言應該是有趣的。
First of all, let's practice saying the alphabet.	首先,我們來練習唸字母。
First of all, try to remember how to pronounce the new word.	首先,試著記住這個新單字的發音方式。

131

First of all, we need to memorize these new words. 首先，我們要記住這些新單字。

First of all, think about what you want to say. 首先，想想你想說什麼。

Dialogue

Ⓢ English is too difficult. What should we do? 英語太難了，我們該怎麼做呢？

Ⓣ **First of all,** learning a new language should be fun. 首先，學習新語言應該是有趣的。

Ⓢ How can we have fun in English class? 我們要怎麼讓英文課變有趣呢？

Ⓣ Let's try creating a story! 我們來編個故事吧！

Dialogue

Ⓣ Today we are going to read a story. 今天我們來讀一個故事。

Ⓢ That sounds difficult. 聽起來很難。

Ⓣ **First of all,** we need to memorize these new words. 首先，我們要記住這些新單字。

Ⓢ That will make it easier. 這樣會輕鬆一點吧。

P3_079

Next, ... 接下來，～

這是在完成一項活動並打算繼續進行下一項活動時可用的表達句型，尤其在進行簡報時，經常會用到這個句型。Next 後面會接一個句子，來簡要說明將要做什麼事。

Next, we're going to watch a short film. 接下來，我們來看一部短片。

Next, try to guess the answer. 接下來，試著猜猜看答案。

Next, write down your answer. 接下來，寫下你的答案。

Next, I'd like you to open your books. 接下來，請打開你們的書本。

Next, practice with a partner. 接下來，請與搭檔一起練習。

Dialogue

- **T** First, make sure you understand the question. 首先，請確認你是否理解這個問題。
- **S** It looks pretty easy to me. 看起來完全難不倒我。
- **T** Next, try to guess the answer. 接下來，試著猜猜看答案。
- **S** That's a little harder! 有點困難！

Dialogue

- **T** Next, I'd like you to open your books. 接下來，請打開你們的書本。
- **S** What page? 哪一頁？
- **T** Page 34, please. 請翻到第 34 頁。
- **S** Thank you. 謝謝。

📖 詢問學生想法

What do you think about...? 你對～有什麼看法呢？

P3_080

這是想詢問學生意見或鼓勵學生積極參與時可用的表達句型。舉例來說，針對某主題的討論來徵求意見時，可以使用「What do you think about this topic?」來鼓勵學生發表意見、參與討論。

What do you think about this assignment?	你對這份作業有什麼看法呢？
What do you think about the test?	你對這次考試有什麼看法呢？
What do you think about Bob's opinion?	你對 Bob 的意見有何看法呢？
What do you think about this exercise?	你對這個練習題有什麼看法呢？
What do you think about this class?	你覺得這門課怎麼樣？

133

Dialogue

T **What do you think about** Bob's opinion? 　　你對 Bob 的意見有何看法呢？
S I disagree. 　　我不同意。
T What's your opinion? 　　那你有什麼看法呢？
S I think soccer is the best sport. 　　我認為足球是最好的運動。

Dialogue

T **What do you think about** this exercise? 　　你對這個練習題有什麼看法呢？
S It's difficult, but helpful. 　　這題很難，但很有幫助。
T Good. We're going to do another one like it tomorrow. 　　好的，明天我們來做另一道類似的習題。
S Oh no! 　　哦不！

Does anyone have...? 有人（有）～嗎？／誰（有）～嗎？　P3_081

想詢問「誰有～？」時可以使用這個表達句型，動詞 have 後面可接各類名詞。Does anyone 後面不僅可以接 have，還可以接各種動詞，例如「Does anyone know...?（有人知道～嗎？）」、「Does anyone see...?（有人看到～嗎？）」。

Does anyone have a question?　　有人有任何疑問嗎？
Does anyone have experience with dogs?　　有人有養狗的經驗嗎？
Does anyone have something to share?　　有人有什麼可以分享的嗎？
Does anyone have an objection?　　有人反對嗎？
Does anyone have an extra pen?　　誰有多餘的鉛筆嗎？

Dialogue

T The test will cover chapters 3 through 5.　　考試範圍將涵蓋第 3 課至第 5 課。
S I don't feel ready for this exam.　　我覺得自己還沒準備好要考試。
T Let's review then. **Does anyone have** a question?　　那我們來複習一下，有人有任何疑問嗎？
S I have a lot of questions, actually.　　其實我有很多問題想問。

Dialogue

T Let's talk about adverbs. **Does anyone have** an objection?　　我們來談談副詞，有人反對嗎？
S I don't.　　我沒意見。
T All right then! What's an adverb?　　好的！那麼，什麼是副詞呢？
S Please explain it.　　請說明一下。

Can anyone tell me...? 誰能告訴我～？

P3_082

我們都很熟悉「Can you tell me...?」這個句型，但如果將句中的 you 替換成 anyone，改成「**Can anyone tell me**...?」的話，則是指要求任何認識的人回答，是課堂上非常實用的句型。

Can anyone tell me the time?	誰能告訴我現在幾點了？
Can anyone tell me the spelling of "difference"?	誰能告訴我「difference」的拼寫呢？
Can anyone tell me the difference between "on" and "above"?	誰能告訴我 on 和 above 的差別？
Can anyone tell me today's date in English?	誰能用英文告訴我今天的日期？
Can anyone tell me what chapter we are going to study today?	誰能告訴我今天要上第幾課呢？

Dialogue

T **Can anyone tell me** today's date in English?　　誰能用英文告訴我今天的日期？
S March 11th, 2010.　　2010 年 3 月 11 日。
T You're close. It's the other month that starts with "M."　　很接近了，但應該是另一個以「M」開頭的月份。
S Ah, May 11th, 2010.　　啊，是 2010 年 5 月 11 日。

Dialogue

T **Can anyone tell me** what chapter we are going to study today?　　誰能告訴我今天要上第幾課呢？
S I think we were going to review chapter 8.　　我想我們要複習第 8 課。
T Oh yes, that's right.　　噢，沒錯。
S Should we form study groups?　　我們要成立讀書會嗎？

Please explain... 請解釋一下～

explain 的語意是「說明、解釋」，這是想在辯論課等活動中要求學生詳細解釋觀點時可用的表達句型。當學生想請老師在課堂上解釋他們不理解的內容時，也可以使用這個表達句型。在 explain 後面會接作為受詞的名詞或是表示「如何」的副詞 how。若接的是 why 子句，其語意是「做某事的理由」或「為什麼做某事」。

Please explain your answer.	請解釋一下你的答案。
Please explain what you mean.	請解釋一下你的意思。
Please explain why you were late.	請解釋一下你遲到的原因。
Please explain this exercise.	請說明一下這個練習題。
Please explain the rule again.	請再解釋一次規則。

Dialogue

- T: What do you think, Bobby? — Bobby，你覺得怎麼樣？
- S: I think pizza is the best food. — 我覺得披薩是最棒的食物。
- T: **Please explain** your answer. — 請解釋一下你的答案。
- S: Well, it's delicious and it's easy to eat. — 嗯，披薩很美味，而且吃起來很方便。

Dialogue

- T: Do the exercise on page 34. — 試著做第 34 頁的練習題。
- S: **Please explain** this exercise. — 請說明一下這個練習題。
- T: Just fill in the blanks. — 填空即可。
- S: Oh, now I understand. — 哦，我現在明白了。

Which one do you...? 你～哪一個呢？

P3_084

which 是個疑問詞，用於選擇一個或從幾個之中選出一部分的情境。當您想要對方回答單一選項時，可以用「which one」；想要對方回答一個以上的選項時，則要用複數形「which ones」來詢問。除此之外，這句型中的不定代名詞 one 也可以替換成 which person、which book 等特定名詞。

Which one do you want?	你想要哪一個呢？
Which one do you need?	你需要哪一個呢？
Which one do you mean?	你指的是哪一個呢？
Which one do you think is best?	你認為哪一個最好呢？
Which one do you understand better?	你比較瞭解哪一個呢？

Dialogue

- S: I don't understand this question. — 我不明白這個問題。
- T: **Which one do you** mean? — 你指的是哪一題呢？
- S: Number 13. — 第 13 題。
- T: I'll explain it to you. — 我來解釋一下。

Dialogue

- **T** Did you read the three stories? 　　這三個故事都讀了嗎？
- **S** Yes, ma'am. 　　是的，老師。
- **T** **Which one do you** think is best? 　　你認為哪一個最好呢？
- **S** The one about the dragon. 　　關於龍的故事。

📖 學習上的指示與建議

Please follow... 請按照～／請遵循～

follow 除了表示「跟隨」另一個人，還有「遵循／根據某人指示或勸告」之意。當您在閱讀單字或句子時想要求對方準確地閱讀，或想要求對方根據指令來進行遊戲或活動時，就可以使用這個表達句型。

Please follow the instructions.	請按照指示進行。
Please follow the example.	請按照範例進行。
Please follow my lead.	請跟著我做。
Please follow the pattern.	請遵循該模式。
Please follow the form.	請按表格填寫。

Dialogue

- **T** Now begin the exercise. 　　現在開始試著做練習題。
- **S** I don't know what to do. 　　我不知道該怎麼做。
- **T** **Please follow** the instructions. 　　請照指示進行。
- **S** But they're in English! 　　但指示都是用英文寫的！

Dialogue

- **T** Now try to say your own sentence. 　　現在試著用你自己的句子來表達。
- **S** How can I do that? 　　我該怎麼做呢？
- **T** **Please follow** the example. 　　請按照範例進行。
- **S** Oh, that's not too hard. 　　噢，好像沒那麼難。

If you get confused, ... 如果你感到困惑，～

學習英語時會遇到很多令人困惑的事情，例如詞義、拼字和文法。這是一個用來告訴困惑的孩子們該如何解決問題的表達句型。「get + 過去分詞」是一個被動句，語意是「變得～或成為～（某種狀態）」。被動形式通常用「be + 過去分詞」表示，但在口語中常用「get + 過去分詞」來強調動作的含義。除了 get 之外，也可以用 become 或 grow。

If you get confused, just tell me.	如果你感到困惑，請告訴我。
If you get confused, try slowing down.	如果你感到困惑，請慢慢來。
If you get confused, check your book.	如果你感到困惑，請翻書查看。
If you get confused, ask your partner for help.	如果你感到困惑，請向你的夥伴求助。
If you get confused, let me know.	如果你感到困惑，請讓我知道。

Dialogue

T Try using the new grammar in a conversation with your partner.
跟你的搭檔練習對話時，試著使用這個新文法。

S That sounds hard.
聽起來很困難。

T **If you get confused,** ask your partner for help.
如果你感到困惑，請向你的夥伴求助。

S I may have to ask a lot!
我可能會問很多問題！

Dialogue

T Now read this story.
現在請閱讀這個故事。

S I'm not sure I can understand all of these words.
我不確定我能否理解這所有的單字。

T **If you get confused,** let me know.
如果你感到困惑，請讓我知道。

S Thank you, sir.
謝謝老師。

Focus on... 專注於～／注意～／把重點放在～

focus on 的語意是「專注於～、專心於～」。當您想提及活動過程中需格外注意的部分時，或想讓不認真聽課的學生們專心一點時，就可以使用這個表達句型。類似的表達句型是「concentrate on...」，兩個句型中的 on 後面都要接續名詞或動名詞。

Focus on the meaning of the sentences.	把重點放在理解句子含義。
Focus on speaking fluently.	專注於口語流利。
Focus on speaking accurately.	專注於準確說話。
Focus on the pronunciation of the words.	注意單字的發音。
Focus on saying the word correctly.	專心地把這個單字唸好。

Dialogue

T Let's read this passage.	我們一起閱讀這段文字。
S Do you have any advice for understanding it well?	為了更好地理解內容，您有什麼建議嗎？
T Well, **focus on** the meaning of the sentences.	嗯，重點放在理解句子含義。
S I'll try.	我會試試看的。

Dialogue

S I make a mistake every time I say this word.	我每次說這個字時都會出錯。
T **Focus on** saying the word correctly.	專心地把這個單字給唸好。
S What do you mean?	這句話是什麼意思？
T Don't worry about the meaning of the word. Just think about the sound.	只考慮發音，毋須在意單字的意思。

Notice... 請注意～

notice 的語意是「注意、留意」，此表達句型常出現在各練習題的說明文字或文法講解中，用來講解或進行某活動時須注意或留意某內容。notice 是感官動詞，所以受詞補語是原形動詞，若受詞補語是以「to + 原形動詞」形式出現，則為被動語態。that 子句也可以當作受詞，例如「Notice that... 」。

Notice the spelling of these two words.	請注意這兩個單字的拼寫法。
Notice the structure of this sentence.	請注意這個句子的結構。
Notice the tense of this verb.	請注意這個動詞的時態。
Notice the way this word is used.	請注意這個單字的用法。
Notice the pronunciation of this word.	請注意這個單字的發音。

Dialogue

T **Notice** the spelling of these two words.	請注意這兩個單字的拼寫。
S "chicken" and "kitchen."	「chicken」和「kitchen」。
T Sometimes they can be confusing.	有時這兩個單字可能會被搞混。
S That's true.	確實如此。

Dialogue

T **Notice** the structure of this sentence.	請注意這個句子的結構。
S It looks very complicated.	看起來很複雜。
T You will understand it after I explain it.	聽完我的解釋後就會明白了。
S I hope so.	希望如此。

You should all... 你們都應該～

should 是類似 ought to 的建議表達用語，語意為「應該做某事」、「需要做那件事」。此外，must 或 have to 則是用來表示必須完成的義務，不是單單只做某件事比較好，而是不做不行。

You should* all study chapter 7.	你們都應該研讀第 7 課。
You should all keep a diary.	你們都應該寫日記。
You should all take your time.	你們都應該要花點時間來完成。
You should all prepare for the test.	你們都需要準備考試。
You should all follow my instructions.	你們都要遵照我的指示。

* 有別於 should，had better 大多解釋為「做某事會更好」，具有命令的語氣，有一種「如果你不做某事，就會有不好的結果」的意味，請謹慎使用。

Dialogue

- **T** Over the next week, please write about your daily life. 　下週開始請寫一下你們的日常生活。
- **S** How should we do that? 　我們該怎麼做呢？
- **T** **You should all** keep a diary. 　你們都應該寫日記。
- **S** I see. We just write it down. 　好的，我們會寫下來的。

Dialogue

- **T** This assignment is difficult. 　這個作業很難。
- **S** You're not kidding. 　確實如此。
- **T** **You should all** take your time. 　你們都需要花點時間來完成。
- **S** No problem! 　沒問題！

I recommend... 我推薦～／我建議～

這是向學生們推薦好教材或學習方法時可用的表達句型。recommend 為及物動詞，有時以簡單的名詞為受詞，但大多以 that 子句為受詞。此時，that 可以省略，子句中的動詞要用「should+原形動詞」的形式。通常 should 會被省略，只留下原形動詞，使用前請務必熟記句型結構。

I recommend you do a Google search.	我建議你們使用 Google 進行搜尋。
I recommend you form a study group.	我建議你們去成立一個的讀書會。
I recommend you keep a diary in English.	我建議你們用英文寫日記。
I recommend you read this book.	我推薦你們讀這本書。
I recommend you use an English dictionary.	我建議你們使用英文字典。

Dialogue

- **T1** I can't find any information about "English Learning Programs." 　我找不到任何有關「英語學習課程」的資訊。
- **T2** **I recommend** you do a Google search. 　我建議你使用 Google 進行搜尋。
- **T1** What should I search for? 　我該搜尋什麼？
- **T2** Just type in "English Learning Programs." 　試著在 Google 搜尋欄中輸入「英語學習課程」。

Dialogue

- **S** I'm having trouble improving my vocabulary. 　我在增加單字量方面遇到了困難。
- **T** **I recommend** you read this book. 　我推薦你讀這本書。
- **S** Will it help me? 　這對我有幫助嗎？
- **T** Yes. It has a lot of good words in it. 　有，這本書裡有很多好詞彙。

If you have a question, ... 有任何疑問，~

課堂結束時，最少不了的環節就是學生們問問題。無論是在課堂上還是日常生活中，這是英語會話中十分常見的句型。這是用來提醒對方有問題時該怎麼做的表達句型，並在 question 後以祈使句的形式描述具體的行動指示。如果您想請對方毫不猶豫地提問，可以使用「Feel free + to 不定詞」或「Don't hesitate + to 不定詞」。

If you have a question, raise your hand.	有任何疑問，請舉手。
If you have a question, write it down.	有任何疑問，請寫下來。
If you have a question, ask it now.	有任何疑問，請現在就發問。
If you have a question, see me.	有什麼問題都可以來找我。
If you have a question, check your notes.	有任何疑問，請看一下您的筆記。

Dialogue

T Save your questions for the end of the class. 　　有問題的話，請課程結束時再提出來。
S I'll never remember them. 　　那時我就已經忘記問題了。
T **If you have a question,** write it down. 　　如有任何疑問，請寫下來。
S I guess that will work. 　　這樣應該行得通。

Dialogue

T The test begins in two minutes. 　　兩分鐘後開始考試。
S I don't feel ready for it. 　　我覺得自己還沒準備好。
T **If you have a question,** ask it now. 　　如有任何疑問，請現在就發問。
S How long is the test? 　　考試要多長時間？

As you listen, ... 邊聽～邊～／聽的時候，～

這是在聽音檔、看影片等來進行學習時可用的表達句型。類似的表達句型有「While listening...」跟「While you listen...」。當您想表達「邊聽邊在答案紙上標記你的答案」時，可以用「While you listen, mark your answer sheets.」。

As you listen, see if you can understand what the man says.	聽聽看你能不能聽懂這位男生在說什麼。
As you listen, copy what you hear in your notebook.	邊聽邊在筆記本上寫下聽到的內容。
As you listen, pay attention to the woman's pronunciation.	聽的時候，注意這位女生的發音。
As you listen, think about the following questions.	邊聽邊思考下面的問題。

Dialogue

🅣 Now we are going to do a listening exercise.	現在我們來做聽力練習吧。
🅢 What should we do?	我們該做什麼呢？
🅣 **As you listen,** see if you can understand what the man says.	聽聽看你能不能聽懂這位男子在說什麼。
🅢 I hope he doesn't speak too quickly.	但願他不會說得太快。

Dialogue

🅣 This is a dictation exercise.	現在是聽寫練習時間。
🅢 What's a dictation exercise?	什麼是聽寫練習？
🅣 **As you listen,** copy what you hear in your notebook.	一邊聽一邊在筆記本上寫下聽到的內容。
🅢 Oh, I understand.	哦，我明白了。

Take care to... 確保～／注意～

這是用來說明考前注意事項、學校生活的注意事項，以及出作業時的表達句型。「Take care to...」的語意是「注意～」，to 後面要接原形動詞。將 take 改成 give 時語意不變。

Take care to spell the word correctly.	確保單字拼寫正確。
Take care to finish on time.	確保按時完成。
Take care to use the correct verb.	確保使用正確的動詞。
Take care to read the instructions.	請仔細閱讀說明。
Take care to write down every word.	確保寫下每一個字。

Dialogue

T **Take care to** read the instructions.	請仔細閱讀說明。
S They seem pretty easy.	看起來很簡單。
T But if you do the exercise wrong, you'll get a zero*.	但如果你這個練習題做錯了，你就會得到零分。
S All right. I'll read them again.	好的，我會再讀一遍的。

Dialogue

T I'm going to read a story. You should write what I say.	我要唸一段故事，你們把我說的寫下來。
S That doesn't sound too hard.	這聽起來不太難。
T **Take care to** write down every word.	確保寫下每一個字。
S Every word?	每一個字嗎？

＊ 當學生的考試成績很糟時，老師可能會對學生說：「You'll get a zero.」。類似的表達句型為「You'll fail.」跟「You'll flunk」，這裡的 fail 跟 flunk 都表示「不及格」。

UNIT 04 發講義或教具

📖 發東西下去

Everyone, take a... 請各位～／請大家各～

這是發講義或考卷給學生時可用的表達句型。這裡的 everyone 指的是「所有人、大家」，在教室中用來稱呼「學生們」或「孩子們」。在課堂上發的「講義、印刷物」，英文是 handout，而「分發、發放」這個行為的動詞則是 hand out。相反地，想表達「拿；收」時，則使用 take、get、receive 等。

Everyone, take a number.	請大家各拿一個號碼。
Everyone, take a handout.	請大家各拿一份講義。
Everyone, take a test and pass them back.	請各位做個測試，然後傳回來。
Everyone, take a questionnaire.	請各位填寫問卷。
Everyone, take a name tag.	請各位領取自己的名牌。

Dialogue

🅣 **Everyone, take** a number.	請大家各拿一個號碼。
🅢 What's this for?	這是做什麼用的？
🅣 To determine the order of your speech.	決定你們發言的順序。
🅢 I hope I get a high number!	希望能拿到數字較大的號碼！

Dialogue

🅣 **Everyone, take** a handout.	大家各拿一份講義。
🅢 I love crossword puzzles!	我喜歡玩填字遊戲！
🅣 This one features all biology terms.	這次主題跟生物學的術語有關。
🅢 It sounds difficult.	聽起來很難。

I'm handing out... 我要把～發下去

還記得前面提到過的 hand out 吧？這是用來描述「將～發給多人」的表達用語，可替換成 give out 使用。相反地，當學生向老師「提交」作業時，則要使用 hand in。

I'm handing out your assignments.	我要把你們的作業發下去。
I'm handing out the report cards at the end of class.	我要在課程結束時把成績單發下去。
I'm handing out the final projects.	我要把期末作業發下去。
I'm handing out permission slips*.	我要把家長同意書發下去。
I'm handing out the new textbooks.	我要把新的課本發下去。

* 所謂 permission slip，指的是家長或監護人同意學生參加學校校外教學等的同意書。

Dialogue

S What are those folders you're holding, Ms. Park?	Park 老師，你手上拿的是什麼文件？
T **I'm handing out** your assignments.	我要把你們的作業發下去。
S What is it?	什麼樣的作業？
T You will be practicing sentences in the past tense.	你們要練習用過去式造句。

Dialogue

T You'll need your parent's permission to participate.	你們需要得到爸媽的同意才能參加。
S Should we have them call the school?	需要請爸媽打電話給學校嗎？
T No, **I'm handing out** permission slips.	不用，我要發家長同意書。
S Oh, okay.	哦，知道了。

Take one and... 拿一張（個）～

發講義（handout）時，可以先用 Everyone! 來吸引所有人的注意力，然後再說「**Take one and...**」，這句話的意思就是一人拿一個，不要全拿走。在發講義時，經常會說「**Take one and** pass the rest back/backwards.（每個人拿一份，然後將其餘的往後傳）」。一份講義的英文說法是 one copy 或 a copy。

Take one and fill it out.	拿一張填寫。
Take one and pass the rest back.	拿一張，其餘的往後傳。
Take one and write your name on it.	拿一張並在上面寫上你們的名字。
Take one and put it in your folder.	拿一張並放進你們的資料夾內。
Take one and have your parents sign it.	拿一份並請你們的父母簽名。

Dialogue

- **S** What are these cards? 這些卡片是什麼？
- **T** They're for recording your medical information. 它們是用來記錄你的健康資訊的。
- **S** Do we all need to take one? 每個人都要拿一張嗎？
- **T** Yes. **Take one and** fill it out. 是的，拿一張並填寫。

Dialogue

- **T** I have the semester schedule for you. 這是你們學期的課表。
- **S** Are there copies for everyone? 每個人都要拿一張嗎？
- **T** Yes. **Take one and** pass the rest back. 是的，拿一張，其餘的往後傳。
- **S** Wow, it looks like we're going to be busy. 哇，看起來我們會很忙。

📖 多拿一張時

Who has an extra...? 誰有多的～嗎？

上課上到一半時，有時會出現需要跟學生確認是否備妥必要物品的情況。若有學生沒有該必要物品，例如有學生沒帶筆時，就要詢問「誰有多餘的筆？」，此時就能說「Who has an extra pen?」，只要將 an extra 放在受詞位置就行了。

Who has an extra pen?	誰有多的筆嗎？
Who has an extra piece of paper?	誰有多的紙嗎？
Who has an extra notebook?	誰有多的筆記本嗎？
Who has an extra test paper?	誰有多的考卷嗎？
Who has an extra paper clip?	誰有多的迴紋針嗎？

Dialogue

Ⓢ Ms. Wilson, I can't take the quiz.	Wilson 老師，我不能參加小考。
Ⓣ Why not?	為什麼？
Ⓢ I forgot my pen.	我忘了帶筆。
Ⓣ **Who has an extra** pen?	誰有多餘的筆？

Dialogue

Ⓣ Open your notebook and write down these words.	打開你的筆記本，寫下這些單字。
Ⓢ I haven't got a notebook yet.	我沒有筆記本。
Ⓣ You should ask to borrow* one.	你應該要跟別人借一本。
Ⓢ **Who has an extra** notebook?	誰有多餘的筆記本嗎？

* borrow 的語意是跟某人「借（某物）」，lend 的語意則是「借（某物）給」某人。因此，borrow 後面只有一個直接受詞，lend 後面既有直接受詞，也有間接受詞。

UNIT 05 課堂練習、作業與考試

📖 出作業

Tomorrow's assignment is... 明天的功課是～

P3_098

這是出功課時可用的表達句型。assignment 的語意是「任務，功課」，是個難度略高於 homework 的單字，但使用頻率卻跟 homework 一樣高。「今天有作業」的英文說法是「You have homework today.」，「今天沒有作業」的英文說法則是「There's no homework for today.」。

Tomorrow's assignment is to write a paragraph about your family.	明天的功課是寫一段關於家庭的文章。
Tomorrow's assignment is to memorize* 10 new words.	明天的功課是要背十個新單字。
Tomorrow's assignment is to read this article.	明天的功課是閱讀這篇文章。
Tomorrow's assignment is to read a story in the newspaper.	明天的功課是要閱讀報紙文章。

* memorize 的意思是「背誦」，「完成作業」的英文動詞是「complete」，寫練習題的英文則是「do the exercise」。

Dialogue

🇹 We are finished for the day.	今天的課程就到這裡吧。
🇸 What is tomorrow's assignment?	明天的功課是什麼呢？
🇹 **Tomorrow's assignment is** to memorize 10 new words.	明天的功課是要背十個新單字。
🇸 Only 10? That will be easy.	只有十個嗎？那很輕鬆嘛。

151

Dialogue

- **T** Don't forget to bring a newspaper tomorrow.　　明天別忘了帶報紙。
- **S** Why do we need to do that?　　為什麼需要帶？
- **T** **Tomorrow's assignment is** to read a story in the newspaper.　　明天的功課是要閱讀報紙文章。
- **S** Oh, I see.　　哦，我明白了。

做課堂練習

This exercise requires you to... 這題練習題是要你～

P3_099

儘管英文學習的捷徑就是反覆練習，但如果只是不斷地重複卻不知道自己在做什麼，就很難達到期望的學習效果。因此，在解題之前，可能有必要指出題目的要點或說明解題方法，在這種情況下就很適合使用這個表達句型。

This exercise requires you to find the correct words.	這題練習題是要你找出正確的單字。
This exercise requires you to use the proper verb form.	這題練習題是要你使用正確的動詞形態。
This exercise requires you to repeat what I say.	這題練習題是要你重複我所說的話。
This exercise requires you to change these sentences.	這題練習題是要你改寫這些句子。
This exercise requires you to use the grammar we learned yesterday.	這題練習題是要你使用我們昨天學過的文法。

Dialogue

- **S** I don't understand the assignment.　　我不明白這個作業。
- **T** **This exercise requires you to** use the proper verb form.　　這個練習題是要你使用正確的動詞形態。
- **S** How will I know which one to use?　　我怎麼知道該用哪一個形態？
- **T** You can check the chart on page 88.　　你可以查看一下第 88 頁的表格。

Dialogue

T **This exercise requires you to** use the grammar we learned yesterday.　這個練習題是要你使用我們昨天學過的文法。

S But I was absent yesterday.　但是我昨天沒來上學。

T Then you will have to work with a partner.　那你需要和你的搭擋一起做。

S Okay. I'll work with Sarah.　好的，我會和 Sarah 一起解題。

Is this problem…? 這個問題～嗎？

P3_100

這是想談論老師出的作業、討論議程或其它問題時可用的表達句型。當學生在課堂上對您提出的問題感到吃力，因而在回答時支支吾吾，此時您便可以在 problem 後面接續形容詞以詢問學生如何看待這問題。可以用 hard、serious、complex、challenging、demanding 等形容詞來表達問題的難度或狀況。

Is this problem solvable?	這個問題是可以解決的嗎？
Is this problem too difficult?	這個問題是不是太難了？
Is this problem complex?	這個問題複雜嗎？
Is this problem familiar?	這個問題會很眼熟嗎？
Is this problem confusing?	這個問題是不是讓人感到困惑？

Dialogue

S We ran out of poster board for our projects.　我們專題需要的海報板用完了。

T **Is this problem** solvable?　這個問題可以解決嗎？

S I think they have more poster board in the Arts room.　我認為美術室裡可能還有一些海報板。

T Why don't you go ask the art teacher?　為什麼不去問問看美術老師呢？

153

> Dialogue

- **T** It seems some of you struggled with number 7.　看來你們一些人正卡在第 7 題。
- **S** That's for sure!　是的！
- **T** **Is this problem** too difficult?　這個問題是不是太難了？
- **S** I think it's too advanced for us.　我認為這題對我們來說太深了。

📖 寫考卷

Please put your name... 請在～寫上你的名字

P3_101

put 的語意是「寫下來、填入」，後面先接受詞，然後再接表示位置的介系詞跟名詞。舉例來說，「請在這張紙上寫下你的名字」的表達是「Please put your name on this piece of paper.」，這表達句型很適合用來提醒常忘記寫名字的孩子們。put 也可用 write 替代。

Please put your name on your paper.　請在報告上寫上你的名字。
Please put your name on your test.　請在考卷上寫上你的名字。
Please put your name on your essay.　請在作文上寫上你的名字。
Please put your name at the top of the paper.　請在報告上方寫上你的名字。
Please put your name on the list*.　請在名單上寫上你的名字。

*「Please put your name on the list.」中的 put 也可用 write、add 等單字替代。

> Dialogue

- **T** Okay. Time's up.　好了，時間到。
- **S** I just finished.　我才剛寫完。
- **T** **Please put your name** on your test.　請在考卷上寫上你的名字。
- **S** Oh yeah! I almost forgot.　哦，對喔！差點忘了。

Dialogue

- **T** This weekend we will have a special class trip.　這個週末將有一個特別的班遊。
- **S** What should we do if we want to go?　想參加的話,該怎麼做呢?
- **T** **Please put your name** on the list.　請在名單上寫上你的名字。
- **S** I'm definitely going to sign up!　我一定要報名!

No cheating... ～不許作弊

P3_102

考試期間的不當行為「作弊」的英文是「cheating」,在其前面加上 no,組合成「No cheating」則表示「不能作弊」。

No cheating on the test.	考試不許作弊。
No cheating or you will flunk.	不許作弊,被抓到的話會不及格。
No cheating will be tolerated.	絕不容忍任何作弊行為。
No cheating this time.	這次不准作弊。
No cheating is my policy.	我的原則就是不准作弊。

Dialogue

- **T** Remember the "golden rule."　請記住「黃金法則」。
- **S** The "golden rule?"　什麼是「黃金法則」?
- **T** You know. **No cheating** on the test.　大家都知道的,考試不許作弊。
- **S** Don't worry. I will never cheat.　別擔心,我絕不作弊。

Dialogue

- **T** If I catch you cheating, you will fail.　如果我發現你們作弊,你們就會不及格。
- **S** Automatically?　一定不及格嗎?
- **T** **No cheating** will be tolerated.　絕不容忍任何作弊行為。

The test will cover... 考試範圍為～

考試是學校生活不可或缺的一部分，想告知考試範圍時，動詞 cover 是一個很好用的字，其語意是「涵蓋、涉及」某個範圍，或「包含」某個地區或領域。cover 是及物動詞，後面要接一個名詞作為其受詞，此時可以把與考試範圍相對應的名詞放在其受詞的位置。

The test will cover the entire semester.	考試範圍將涵蓋整個學期的所有內容。
The test will cover chapters 3, 4, and 5.	考試範圍為第 3、4、5 課。
The test will cover the 12th century.	考試範圍將涵蓋整 12 世紀。
The test will cover our papers.	考試範圍將涵蓋我們的報告。
The test will cover a lot of material.	考試將涵蓋大量的內容。

Dialogue

S How should we study for the test?	我們該如何準備考試呢？
T **The test will cover** the entire semester.	考試範圍將涵蓋整個學期的所有內容。
S That's a lot of material.	內容太多了。
T Yes, but you should know it by now.	是的，但你們現在也該知道那些內容了。

Dialogue

S1 Are you ready for the exam?	準備好考試了嗎？
S2 No. Do you know which chapters we're covering?	還沒，你知道考試範圍是哪幾課嗎？
S1 **The test will cover** chapters 3, 4, and 5.	考試範圍為第 3、4、5 課。
S2 I guess that's not so bad.	哦，我想那不算太多。

The test is... 測驗～

在測驗開始前告知該測驗的範圍、類型與考試時間等資訊時，時常使用這個表達句型。當 based on 出現在 is 之後時，其語意為「測驗是根據～（內容）」。除了 test 之外，還可以用 essay test、placement test、performance test 等來具體描述這是什麼類型的測驗。

The test is based on what we've studied this semester.	測驗範圍出自於我們本學期所學的內容。
The test is based on chapter 8.	測驗範圍出自於第 8 課。
The test is worth 100 points.	測驗滿分為 100 分。
The test is important part of your grade.	這次測驗對你的成績很重要。
The test is based on the exercises we've done in class.	測驗範圍出自於我們在課堂上做過的練習題。

Dialogue

T **The test is** tomorrow, so don't forget to study.	明天要考試了，別忘了念書。
S What's on the test?	會考些什麼？
T **The test is** based on chapter 8.	考試內容出自於第 8 課。
S That's not too much information.	透露這點資訊並不太夠。

Dialogue

T We'll have a test next week.	下週我們要考試。
S I don't feel like studying.	我不想念書。
T You'd better!	你最好還是好好念點書吧！
S Why?	為什麼？
T **The test is** important part of your grade.	這次考試對你們的成績很重要。

繳交作業或考卷

Pass forward your... 把你們的～往前傳

這是要求對方將考卷、作業、父母同意書或活動使用的物品等往前傳時，可用的表達句型。通常在考試的鐘聲響起時，老師會說「好了，把筆放下，把考卷往前傳」，這句話的英文就是「Put your pencils down and pass forward your test papers.」。反之，pass down 指的是自己拿一份考卷等資料，其餘往後傳給下一個人。

Pass forward your exams.	把你們的試卷往前傳。
Pass forward your assignments.	把你們的作業往前傳。
Pass forward your permission slips.	把你們的家長同意書往前傳。
Pass forward your papers.	把你們的報告往前傳。
Pass forward your lists.	把你們的清單往前傳。

Dialogue

T Time's up. *	時間到了。
S But I haven't finished.	但我還沒寫完。
T Too bad. **Pass forward your** exams.	很遺憾，將你的試卷往前傳。
S Well, I probably flunked that test.	好吧，這次考試我可能要考砸了。

*「Time's up.」的 up 表示「結束的、完結的」，很容易被誤以為是介系詞或副詞，但實際上卻是形容詞，作為連接 be 動詞的補語。

Dialogue

T Have you all made a list in English of vegetables?	大家都用英文列出蔬菜清單了嗎？
S Yes.	是的。
T Then please **pass forward your** lists.	那麼，將你們的清單往前傳。
S Wait! Is a tomato a vegetable?	等等！番茄是蔬菜嗎？

Turn in your... 請交～

turn in 的語意是「提交、交出」，是要求對方交作業或交考卷時可用的表達用語。句中的 turn in 可以 submit 或 hand in 等替代。

Turn in your assignment before you leave.	離開前請交功課。
Turn in your test.	請交卷。
Turn in your essay.	請交作文。
Turn in your homework.	請交作業。
Turn in your exercises and I'll correct them.	請交練習題，我要批改。

Dialogue

T Okay. Time is up. **Turn in your** test.	好的，時間到，請交卷。
S1 How do you think you did?	你認為你做得怎麼樣？
S2 I'm not sure. What about you?	我不確定。你呢？
S1 I didn't finish!	我沒寫完！

Dialogue

T **Turn in your** homework.	請交作業。
S I don't have mine.	我沒帶作業來。
T Why not?	為什麼？
S I left it on the bus.	我把它遺忘在公車上了。

The assignment is due... ～前要交功課

這是告知作業繳交期限的表達句型。due 的語意是「預計的、到期的」，後面要接 to 不定詞或介系詞 for、at、in 等。

The assignment* is due by the end of the week.	週五之前要交功課。
The assignment is due next Monday.	下週一要交功課。
The assignment is due in 3 weeks.	三週後要交功課。
The assignment is due at 3:00.	3 點時要交功課。
The assignment is due right before the final test.	期末考前要交功課。

* 如果問略懂英語的人 assignment 和 homework 之間的差別，他們都會回答 assignment 是「作業」，homework 則是「家庭作業」。但事實上，這兩個單字在字義上並沒有什麼差別。不過，homework 是不可數名詞，所以無論有多少作業，都不能稱為 homeworks，而 assignment 是可數名詞，所以如果有多項作業，就要稱為 assignments。

Dialogue

S When should we turn in our homework?	我們什麼時候要交功課？
T **The assignment is due** by the end of the week.	週五之前要交功課。
S How long should they be?	需要寫多長呢？
T Just 2 pages.	兩頁就夠了。

Dialogue

S1 You'd better get busy.	你最好加快腳步。
S2 Why?	為什麼？
S1 **The assignment is due** at 3:00.	3 點時要交功課。
S2 I thought it was due tomorrow.	我以為是明天。

The highest score was... 最高分是～

考完試後，免不了要提到分數，此時可以用語意為「分數、得分」的單字 score。但因為是分數，所以可用表示分數高低的 high、low 來描述分數。當您想詢問對方「考得如何？」時，可以說「How did you do on your test?」。

The highest score* was Jimmy's.	最高分的是吉米。
The highest score was 98.	最高分是 98 分。
The highest score was only 50.	最高分只有 50 分。
The highest score was pathetic.	最高分糟透了。
The highest score was impressive.	最高分是令人印象深刻地高分。

* 考試成績的英文是 test score，多益成績是 TOEIC score，平均考試成績是 average test score，滿分則是 perfect score。而當您想表達「他 SAT 考了滿分」時，可以用「He got a perfect score on the SAT.」，請記住接在考試前面的介系詞 on。

Dialogue

T1 I heard everyone did poorly on the exam.	我聽說大家這場考試都考得不好。
T2 How poorly?	有多糟？
T1 **The highest score was** only 50.	最高分只有 50 分。
T2 Wow, did anyone pass?	哇，有人通過考試嗎？

Dialogue

S How did we do on our essays, teacher?	老師，我們的作文寫得如何？
T Very well, Janet.	Janet，表現得非常好。
S Who got the highest score?	誰得到了最高分呢？
T I can't tell you, but **the highest score was** impressive.	不能告訴你，但最高分是令人印象深刻地高分。

UNIT 06 進行活動

📖 徵求表現機會

Come up to the front and... 到前面來～

這是要求學生上台做報告或解題時可用的表達句型。有時會省略表示強調意味的 up，直接說「Come to the front.」。此外，句中的 to the front 也可用 out 替代，改說「Please come out and...」。另一方面，懲罰學生時，經常會要求學生去教室後面，這種情況的表達用語是「Go to the back of the classroom.」。

Come up to the front and read what you have just written.	到前面來讀一下你剛剛寫的內容。
Come up to the front and give your presentation.	到前面來報告。
Come up to the front and write your answer on the board.	到前面來把你的答案寫在黑板上。
Come up to the front and perform this dialogue.	到前面來演出這段對話。
Come up to the front and give your speech.	到前面來發表。

Dialogue

🅣 **Come up to the front and** read what you have just written.	到前面來讀一下你剛剛寫的內容。
🅢 But I'm too nervous.	但我真的很緊張。
🅣 Don't be nervous. Everybody is going to do it.	沒什麼好緊張的，每個人都要做這件事。
🅢 In that case, I'm not so worried.	那我就放心了。

Dialogue

- 🇹 **Come up to the front and** give your presentation.　　到前面來作報告。
- 🇸 What presentation*?　　什麼報告？
- 🇹 The one I assigned you yesterday.　　昨天交代給你們的作業。
- 🇸 Oh no! I forgot!　　哦不！我忘了！

* presentation 的意思是「報告」，speech 的意思是對著觀眾「演說」，address 的意思則是對於重要問題進行充分準備後所進行的正式「演講」。

Who would like to...? 誰願意～呢？

老師在課堂上詢問學生有誰願意出來解題時，學生們往往會低頭迴避老師的視線。「Who would like to...?」是用來鼓勵學生參與時可用的表達句型。類似的表達句型還有「Who wants to volunteer?」跟「Who wants to try?」。

Who would like to perform this dialogue?	誰願意演出這段對話呢？
Who would like to read this paragraph?	誰願意讀一下這一段呢？
Who would like to answer this question?	誰願意回答這個問題呢？
Who would like to help me with this example?	誰願意為我解釋一下這個例子呢？
Who would like to write the answer on the board?	誰願意把答案寫在黑板上呢？

Dialogue

- 🇹 **Who would like to** perform this dialogue?　　誰願意演出這段對話呢？
- S1 I would!　　我願意！
- 🇹 Okay, who else?　　好，還有誰也想試試？
- S2 Me, too!　　我也願意！

Dialogue

T **Who would like to** read this paragraph?　誰願意讀一下這一段呢？
S I'll do it. Where should I start?　我來，該從哪裡開始讀呢？
T Start from the beginning.　從頭開始。
S Yes, ma'am. 'Once upon a time...'　好的老師。「好久好久以前...」。

Who wants to recite...? 誰想朗誦～？

P3_111

在課堂上請某學生做某件事時，可使用「Who wants to...?」這個表達句型。recite 這個詞主要用於英語課堂，不常用於一般情況，其語意是「在眾人面前背誦一首詩歌或文學作品的一部分」。通常是用 recite poetry、recite a poem 來表示「吟誦／朗誦詩歌」。

Who wants to recite the first poem?　誰想朗誦第一首詩？
Who wants to recite this poem?　誰想朗誦這首詩？
Who wants to recite their own poetry?　誰想朗誦自己的詩？
Who wants to recite the last part of the poem?　誰想朗誦這首詩的最後一部分？
Who wants to recite the next stanza*?　誰願意朗誦下一段？

* stanza 指的是「（詩的）節」。詩一般稱作 poetry，但也可以用 verse 來表達。韻文指的是具有押韻、頭韻等有押韻（rhyme）的「詩句」，自由詩體的英文是 free verse，輓歌的英文則是 elegy。

Dialogue

T Who wants to recite this poem?　誰想朗誦這首詩？
S It looks too difficult.　這首詩看起來太難了。
T It's not so bad. The words are easy.　沒那麼難，用字很簡單。
S Okay, I'll try.　好吧，我來試試。

Dialogue

T This is a lovely poem.　真是一首好詩。
S He is my favorite poet.　他是我最喜愛的詩人。

- **T** Who wants to recite the next stanza? 誰願意朗誦下一段？
- **S** Allow me. 我來吧。

Who can solve...? 誰能解決～？

P3_112

想讓學生有機會在課堂上解題時，可以使用這個表達句型。動詞 solve 的語意是「解決」，所以通常用 problem 作為受詞，以 solve a problem、solve problems 這樣的方式來表達。除此之外，也可用 riddle、quiz、puzzle、mystery 等作為受詞。

Who can solve this problem?	誰能解這個問題？
Who can solve this puzzle?	誰能解開這個謎題？
Who can solve the mystery?	誰能解開這個謎團？
Who can solve our dilemma?	誰能解決我們的困境？
Who can solve this argument?	誰能解決這場爭論？

Dialogue

- **T** Today's challenge question is on the board. 今天的挑戰題在黑板上。
- **S** Holy cow! It looks tough. 天啊！看起來很難。
- **T** **Who can solve** this problem? 誰能解決這個問題？
- **S** Marcus is probably the only one who can. Marcus 可能是唯一能做到的人。

Dialogue

- **S1** Jenny thinks "ain't" is a real word in the English language. Jenny 認為「ain't」在英語中是一個真實存在的單字。
- **T** Is it? 是嗎？
- **S2** I think "ain't" is a slang word*. 我認為「ain't」是一個俚語。
- **T** **Who can solve** this argument? 誰能解決這個爭論？

* slang 指的是日常對話中常會用到，但不被視為標準英文的「俚語」。除此之外，也會使用 slang 一詞來指稱僅由學生、記者等群體才會使用的特殊術語。

Who knows…? 有誰知道～？

who 是主格疑問詞，所以後面會接「did」或「knows」等動詞。換句話說，像「Who did such a bad thing?（誰做了這麼糟的事情？）」這類句子，who 既是疑問詞，也是主格，所以即使是疑問句，語序也不會顛倒。在課堂上提問時，經常會聽到的「有誰知道～？」，只要用「Who knows＋名詞」來表達就行了。know 是及物動詞，所以後面要有受詞。

Who knows what mammals are?	有誰知道什麼是哺乳類動物？
Who knows the time?	有誰知道現在幾點了？
Who knows the answer?	有誰知道答案嗎？
Who knows why Gilbert is not here today?	有誰知道吉伯特今天為什麼缺席嗎？
Who knows what we are going to cover today?	有誰知道我們今天要學什麼嗎？

Dialogue

T I wonder if we have time to finish this exercise.	想知道我們是否有時間完成這個練習題。
S It looks pretty long.	這題看起來很長。
T **Who knows** the time?	有誰知道現在幾點了？
S It's 2:45.	現在是 2 點 45 分。

Dialogue

T How do you spell "thorough?"	「thorough」怎麼拼？
S Hmm. That's a difficult word.	唔，這是一個很難的單字。
T **Who knows** the answer?	有誰知道答案嗎？
S I do. It's "T-H-O-R-O-U-G-H."	我知道，答案是「T-H-O-R-O-U-G-H」。
T That's right!	答對了！

📖 輪流進行

Let's take turns... 我們輪流～吧。

老師會安排很多活動（activity）來讓學生參與課堂，可能會讓學生們玩遊戲或角色扮演。除此之外，也可能進行小組或配對活動，或讓學生按順序輪流進行。take turns 的語意是「輪流做～」，當您想讓學生公平地輪流練習時，就可以使用這個表達句型。

Let's take turns* reading.	我們輪流讀吧。
Let's take turns saying these words.	我們輪流說這幾個單字吧。
Let's take turns asking questions.	我們輪流提問吧。
Let's take turns practicing this sentence.	我們輪流練習這個句子吧。
Let's take turns writing the answers.	我們輪流寫答案吧。

* take turns 後面省略了 at 或 in，直接接動名詞。

Dialogue

- **T** Let's take turns practicing this sentence. Johnny, you're first. 　我們輪流練習這個句子吧。Johnny 從你開始。
- **S1** "I like pizza." 　「I like pizza」。
- **T** Very good. Now you, Sally. 　很好，接著輪到 Sally。
- **S2** "I like pizza." 　「I like pizza」。

Dialogue

- **T** Let's take turns writing the answers. 　我們輪流寫答案吧。
- **S** Why? 　為什麼？
- **T** That way you all get a chance to write. 　這樣每個人都有機會寫答案。
- **S** Oh, I understand. 　好，我知道了。

Whose turn is it to...? 輪到誰～了？

Whose 是疑問代名詞的所有格，語意為「誰的～」，作為所有格關係代名詞時要解釋成「～的～」。這是想詢問「輪到誰了」時非常好用的表達句型，如果加上 to 不定詞，則具體語意就是「輪到你做～了」。

Whose turn is it to speak?	輪到誰發言了？
Whose turn is it to lead the group?	輪到誰帶領小組了？
Whose turn is it to answer?	輪到誰回答了？
Whose turn is it to bring snacks?	輪到誰帶零食了？
Whose turn is it to read a story?	輪到誰讀故事了？

Dialogue

T Everyone, pull up a chair*.	大家坐近一點。
S Is it time for group discussion?	現在是小組討論時間嗎？
T Yes.	是的。
S **Whose turn is it to** lead the group?	輪到誰當組長了？

Dialogue

T It's time to do some reading.	現在是讀書時間。
S Great!	太好了！
T **Whose turn is it to** read a story?	輪到誰讀故事了？
S It's mine!	我！

* Everyone, pull up a chair. 是英語母語人士才會用的口語表達用語。類似的表達句型有「Have a seat.」、「Sit down.」、「Take a load off.」等，特別是「Take a load off.」是好朋友之間使用的非正式用語，所以使用時要小心。

📖 一起覆誦

Repeat after me... 跟著我唸～／跟我一起唸～

這是老師要學生跟著自己唸時可用的表達句型。這個句型還可搭配 line by line、word by word 這類用詞，或是 at a normal speed、slowly、naturally 等這類描述閱讀速度的用語，用途十分廣泛。

Repeat after me: 'go, went, gone.'	跟我一起唸「go, went, gone」。
Repeat after me line by line.	跟著我逐行唸。
Repeat after me: 'To be or not to be.'	跟我一起唸「To be or not to be」。
Repeat after me slowly.	慢慢地跟我一起唸。
Repeat after me while thinking about the meaning of the paragraph.	跟著我唸，並思考這段話的意思。

Dialogue

- 🅣 Let's practice pronunciation. 　我們來練習發音吧。
- 🅢 What should we say? 　我們應該讀什麼呢？
- 🅣 **Repeat after me** line by line. 　跟著我逐行唸。
- 🅢 That's too difficult! 　太難了吧！

Dialogue

- 🅣 It's time to memorize some verbs. Are you ready? 　該背點動詞了，大家準備好了嗎？
- 🅢 Yes, ma'am. 　是的，老師。
- 🅣 **Repeat after me**: 'go, went, gone.' 　跟我一起唸「go, went, gone.」。
- 🅢 Go, went, gone. 　Go, went, gone。

📖 同學間倆倆做練習

Turn to your partner and...
請向你們的搭檔～／請跟你們的搭檔～

turn to 的語意是將視線或臉「轉向～」。想請學生們跟自己旁邊的搭檔一起做什麼時，可以使用這個表達句型。句型中的 and 後面也接續省略主詞的命令句。同學們練習之後，想要求他們角色互換並再做一次時，可以使用「Change the roles and...」來表達。

Turn to your partner and ask him 5 questions.	請向你們的搭檔問五個問題。
Turn to your partner and talk about your weekend.	請跟你們的搭檔談論你的週末。
Turn to your partner and summarize the passage.	請向你們的搭檔總結這段內容。
Turn to your partner and practice saying this sentence.	請跟你們的搭檔練習這些句子。
Turn to your partner and interview him.	請向你們的搭檔進行採訪。

Dialogue

- 🅣 **Turn to your partner and** ask him 5 questions. 　請向你們的搭檔問五個問題。
- 🅢 What should we ask about? 　應該問些什麼呢？
- 🅣 Anything you want to know. 　你想知道的都可以。
- 🅢 I'm going to ask about soccer. 　我要問跟足球有關的問題。

Dialogue

- 🅣 Do you understand what we have read? 　你理解我們剛才讀的內容嗎？
- 🅢 I think so. 　我想我懂。
- 🅣 Then **turn to your partner and** summarize the passage. 　請向你們的搭檔總結這段內容。
- 🅢 That sounds difficult! 　這也太難了吧！

📖 動筆寫

Write this down... 把它寫下來

write down 是表示「寫下來」的動詞片語，主要是要對方寫下你說的內容，如果想加上 this 或 that 這類的代名詞，就把此代名詞放在 Write 和 down 中間，如 Write this down。要學生寫下提到的作業、準備物品，或想要對方抄寫課堂內容時，就可以使用這個表達句型。

Write this down because it's important.	這很重要，把它寫下來。
Write this down and then practice saying it.	寫下來然後練習說出來。
Write this down or you won't remember it later.	把它寫下來，以免以後忘記。
Write this down so you don't forget.	把它寫下來，這樣你就不會忘記了。
Write this down as I say it.	寫下我說的話。

Dialogue

- 🅣 Are you listening? 　你有在聽嗎？
- 🅢 Yes, sir. 　有，老師。
- 🅣 Write this down because it's important. 　這很重要，把它寫下來。
- 🅢 I'm ready. 　我準備來寫。

Dialogue

- 🅢 What chapter are we supposed to read? 　我們該讀哪一課？
- 🅣 Chapter 16. 　第 16 課。
- 🅢 I can never remember the homework! 　我永遠記不住作業！
- 🅣 Write this down so you don't forget. 　把它寫下來，以免以後忘記。

Write your name... 在～寫上你的名字

考試時最重要的是什麼？沒錯，就是在考卷上寫上自己的名字。即使考得再好，得了滿分，如果沒有在考卷上寫上自己的名字也是無濟於事。想要求對方寫下自己的名字，或想確認對方在考試期間是否寫下自己的名字時，都可以使用這個表達句型。

Write your name at the top of your paper.	在報告的上方寫上你的名字。
Write your name on the cover.	在封面上寫上你的名字。
Don't forget to **write your name** on the test.	別忘了在考卷上寫上你的名字。
Write your name on the list if you want to go on the trip.	如果想參加這場旅行，請在名單上寫上你的名字。
Write your name next to the topic you want to write about.	在你想寫的主題旁邊寫上你的名字。

Dialogue

T Next week there will be a special trip to the zoo!	下週我們將有一個特別的動物園之旅！
S That sounds terrific!	聽起來棒極了！
T **Write your name** on the list if you want to go on the trip.	如果想參加這場旅行，請在名單上寫下你的名字。
S I'll do it right now!	我現在就寫！

Dialogue

T You must choose one of these topics for your essay.	你必須為你的文章從中選定一個主題。
S1 I want to write about history.	我想寫歷史。
S2 I want to write about art.	我想寫一些關於藝術的文章。
T **Write your name** next to the topic you want to write about.	在你想寫的主題旁邊寫下你的名字。

UNIT 07 進行討論

📖 出題與開頭

Let's suppose... 假設～

向學生解釋課程內容時，有時需要假設各種情況來幫助他們理解。舉例來說，當你想對學生們說：「假設失敗的話，～」或「假設做了～的話，～」時，相較於 Let's think...，用 Let's suppose...才是更正確的表達句型。因為 think 只是單純的「思考」，suppose 則表示「基於～來思考」。

Let's suppose we're at war.	假設我們正處於戰爭中。
Let's suppose we lived in ancient Rome.	假設我們生活在古羅馬。
Let's suppose we have a fire.	假設我們發生了火災。
Let's suppose we fail.	假設我們考不及格。
Let's suppose there's life on other planets.	假設其它行星上有生命。

Dialogue

🅣 Is killing another person ever acceptable?	剝奪別人的生命是可以被容忍的嗎？
🅢 No, never.	不，絕對無法容忍。
🅣 **Let's suppose** we're at war.	假設我們正處於戰爭中。
🅢 Even then, it's wrong.	即便如此，這也是錯的。

Dialogue

🅣 I hope you're prepared for next week's test.	我希望你們為下週的考試做好準備。

S **Let's suppose** we fail. What will happen to our grades? 假設我們考不及格,成績會發生什麼變化呢?

T It's better not to find out. 無知便是福。

S That makes me nervous! 您這樣說會讓我們很緊張!

Imagine what it was like... 想像一下~是什麼~

P3_121

當您要學生想像一下如果他們正處於過去的某種情況下會有什麼感受時,便可以使用這個表達句型。很多人會因為這個句型看起來有點難而棄之不用,但這是非常有用的句型。

Imagine what it was like to be a western pioneer. 想像一下西部拓荒者是什麼模樣。

Imagine what it was like to live without electricity. 想像一下沒有電的生活是什麼樣子。

Imagine what it was like for the poor. 想像一下貧困的人是什麼感受。

Imagine what it was like in the Dark Ages. 想像一下黑暗時代是什麼模樣。

Imagine what it was like for Princess Diana. 想像一下戴安娜王妃是什麼樣子。

Dialogue

S The flood destroyed so many homes. 洪水摧毀了許多房屋。

T **Imagine what it was like** for the poor. 想像一下貧困的人是什麼感受。

S Yes, but everyone suffers, rich or poor. 是的,但不管是富人還是窮人,每個人都受到了傷害。

T I suppose that's true. 你說得對。

Dialogue

S I can't believe we only have these slow computers to use. 難以想像我們只有這幾台龜速電腦可用。

🅣 **Imagine what it was like** in the Dark Ages. 　　想像一下黑暗時代是什麼模樣。
🅢 I guess it must have been pretty hard. 　　那肯定很艱難吧。
🅣 You should be thankful! 　　你們應該要懂得感恩！

Let's discuss... 我們來討論～／我們來談談～　　P3_122

這是主題討論課堂上常用的表達句型，針對某個主題交換正反雙方的意見。使用這個表達句型時，需要特別小心 discuss 這個單字。discuss 通常會跟 with 或 about 搭配使用，但 discuss 是及物動詞，所以後面不會接續介系詞。跟 with 或 about 搭配使用時，請記得要用於「have a discussion with someone」或「have a discussion about something」。

Let's discuss this question. 　　我們來討論一下這個問題。
Let's discuss this topic. 　　我們來談談這個話題。
Let's discuss the article. 　　我們來討論這篇文章。
Let's discuss your mistake. 　　我們來談談你犯的錯誤。
Let's discuss the questions on page 23. 　　我們來討論一下第 23 頁的題目。

Dialogue

🅣 Did you read page 89? 　　大家都讀了第 89 頁嗎？
🅢 Yes, ma'am. 　　是的，老師。
🅣 Okay, then **let's discuss** the article. 　　好的，我們來討論一下這篇文章。
🅢 I thought it was very interesting. 　　應該會很有趣吧。

Dialogue

🅢 I don't understand what I did wrong. 　　我不知道我做錯了什麼。
🅣 **Let's discuss** your mistake. 　　我們來談談你犯的錯誤。
🅢 I think that would help. 　　這應該會很有幫助。
🅣 Your first problem was pronunciation. 　　第一個問題是發音。

True or false: ... ～，對還是錯？

這是跟學生玩猜謎遊戲時常用的表達句型，只要在 True or false 後面接續一段敘述，像是「Tomatoes are fruit.」就行了。當學生答對時，請回應「Right.」、「Yes.」或「That's right/it/correct.」。反之，當學生答錯時，請以「Not really.」或「Not exactly.」等作為答覆。

True or false: Cats are mammals.	貓是哺乳類動物，對還是錯？
True or false: Tomatoes are fruit.	番茄是水果，對還是錯？
True or false: Some fish can fly.	有些魚會飛，對還是錯？
True or false: The highest mountain is Mt. Everest.	珠穆朗瑪峰是世界上最高的山峰，對還是錯？
True or false: The earth is flat.	地球是平的，對還是錯？

Dialogue

- **T** Let's take a quiz.
- **S** Okay. What's the first question?
- **T** **True or false:** Tomatoes are fruit.
- **S** Hmm. That's a difficult one.

我們來做個小測驗吧。
好啊，第一題是什麼呢？
番茄是水果，對還是錯呢？
嗯，這題有點難。

Dialogue

- **T** **True or false:** The earth is flat.
- **S** It looks flat.
- **T** True, but remember, it's a planet.
- **S** Oh yeah. The earth is not flat. It's a sphere.

地球是平的，對還是錯呢？
感覺是平的。
是的，但請記住地球是一個行星喔。
啊，對哦，地球不是平的，而是球狀。

📖 集思廣益

Can you think of...? 你們能想到～嗎？

相較於讓老師自己講整堂課，更應該讓學生們自己去尋找答案，哪怕過程稍微緩慢或令人沮喪，也要問學生們「你的答案是什麼？」。當您想要像這樣鼓勵學生參與，並徵求其意見時，就可使用這個表達句型。

Can you think of a good question to ask?	你們能想到什麼要問的好問題嗎？
Can you think of any other ideas?	你們還能想到其它方法嗎？
Can you think of a good way to remember this grammar?	你們能想出記住這個文法的好方法嗎？
Can you think of a new sentence?	你們能想出一個新句子嗎？
Can you think of an answer?	你們能想到答案嗎？

Dialogue

- 🅣 Any questions? **Can you think of** a good question to ask? — 還有什麼問題嗎？你們能想到什麼要問的好問題嗎？
- 🅢1 No. You explained everything very clearly. — 沒有，老師已經非常清楚地解釋了所有內容。
- 🅢2 No, ma'am. We don't have any questions. — 沒有，老師，我們沒有任何問題。

Dialogue

- 🅣 What's a good way to learn new words? — 學會新單字的方法是什麼呢？
- 🅢1 We can write a sentence using them. — 我們可以用它們來造句。
- 🅣 Good. **Can you think of** any other ideas? — 很好，你們還能想到其它方法嗎？
- 🅢2 We can make flash cards*. — 我們可以製作單字卡。

*flash cards 指的是老師在課堂上快速閃現的單字、數字、圖片等學習小卡。除此之外，也能表示用比賽期間為體操選手等運動員評分的「記分卡」。

Try to come up with... 試著想出～

提到「come up with」時，最先想到的語意就是「趕上／追上～」，但在這裡是用來表示「想出～」或「提出～」之意。這是用來鼓勵學生參與課堂的表達句型，當您要別人針對某個主題或事件來發表想法或意見時，就能使用這個句型。

Try to come up with a funny story.	試著想出一個有趣的故事。
Try to come up with a better idea.	試著想出一個更好的主意。
Try to come up with a good answer.	試著想出一個好答案。
Try to come up with a solution to the problem.	試著想出一個解決那個問題的辦法。
Try to come up with a new topic.	試著想出一個新主題。

Dialogue

S What's our homework tonight?	我們今晚的作業是什麼呢？
T **Try to come up with** a funny story.	試著想出一個有趣的故事。
S A funny story? That sounds hard.	一個有趣的故事？聽起來有點難。
T It's not so difficult.	其實沒那麼難。

Dialogue

S I want to write about video games.	我想寫一篇跟電玩有關的文章。
T **Try to come up with** a new topic.	試著想出一個新主題。
S Okay. How about sports?	好吧，運動如何？
T I guess that's a little better.	這可能會更好一些。

針對議題探討

It's important to consider... 考慮～是很重要的。

think 的語意很簡單，就是「思考」。反之，consider 的語意是考慮且仔細衡量某種情況，即為了做出決定而仔細思考（think about something carefully）。consider 是及物動詞，所以後面要接名詞或動名詞作為其受詞，或是「疑問詞＋to 不定詞」等。

It's important to consider all possibilities.	考慮所有可能性是很重要的。
It's important to consider the alternatives.	考慮替代方案很重要。
It's important to consider global climate change.	考慮全球氣候變遷很重要。
It's important to consider how to manage your time during the test.	考試時，考慮如何管理時間很重要。
It's important to consider your choice for the essay topic.	思考寫一篇關於什麼的文章很重要。

Dialogue

- T: Do you think there is life on other planets, Bill?
  Bill，你覺得其它行星上有生命嗎？
- S: No, I don't.
  不，我覺得沒有。
- T: **It's important to consider** all possibilities.
  考慮所有可能性是很重要的。
- S: Maybe.
  也許吧。

Dialogue

- T: Don't you care if the polar ice caps melt?
  你不在乎極地的冰川融化嗎？
- S: No, it's just a frozen wasteland.
  不，那只是一塊無用的冰凍荒地。
- T: **It's important to consider** global climate change.
  考慮全球氣候變遷是很重要的。
- S: You say that, but I don't believe in it.
  即使您這麼說，但我有不同看法。

回應對方觀點

There has never been... 從未有過～／沒有比～更～

P3_127

這是以 There has never been 搭配比較級（如 more）的表達句型，語意為「從未有過／從來沒有～」。been 後面接續一般名詞時，只表示「沒做過～；沒有過～」，比較級搭配 than 的話，則表示「從未有過比～更～的～」，所以要區分兩者差異並牢記在心。

There has never been an argument about this.	關於這個，從未有過爭論。
There has never been a more important president than Lincoln.	美國歷史上從未有過比林肯更重要的總統。
There has never been a better humanitarian than Mother Teresa.	沒有比特蕾莎修女更充滿人道主義的人了。
There has never been a funnier comedian than Rob Schneider.	沒有比勞勃・許奈德更搞笑的搞笑藝人了。
There has never been a perfect score in class.	班上從未有人考過滿分。

Dialogue

- 🅣 Have you heard of Mother Theresa? 你聽過德蕾莎修女嗎？
- 🅢 Yes, she helped the poor, didn't she? 有，她就是幫助窮人的人吧？
- 🅣 **There has never been** a better humanitarian than Mother Teresa. 沒有比特蕾莎修女更充滿人道主義的人了。
- 🅢 I'd like to learn more about her. 我想多了解她一點。

Dialogue

- S1 I just love Rob Schneider. 我真的很喜歡勞勃・許奈德。
- S2 **There has never been** a funnier comedian than Rob Schneider. 沒有比勞勃・許奈德更有趣的搞笑藝人了。
- S1 Well, I don't know if I agree with that. 唔，我不確定是否同意這點。
- S2 Name one person who's funnier. 那你試著說出一個比他更有趣的人的名字。

Your theory is... 你的理論～

除了一般學術意義上的「理論」，theory 也能用來表示個人的「觀點、理論、意見」。當老師想針對學生的簡報或言論做出評論時，這會是一個很好用的表達句型。is 後面可添加資訊以說明該理論的內容。

Your theory is flawed.	你的理論是錯的。
Your theory is similar to mine.	你的理論和我的很相似。
Your theory is the best.	你的理論是最好的。
Your theory is worth trying.	你的理論值得一試。
Your theory is okay if you change it a little.	你的理論只要稍作修改就行了。

Dialogue

- 🅣 I want to talk about your ideas further. 我想聽聽你的想法。
- 🅢 Why? 為什麼？
- 🅣 Because I think **your theory is** the best. 因為我認為你的理論是最好的。
- 🅢 Wow! I had no idea. 哇！我不知道您是這麼想的。

Dialogue

- 🅢 I think if we practice these words every day, we will learn them easily. 我想如果我們每天都練習這些單詞，就能輕鬆地將其熟記在心。
- 🅣 **Your theory is** worth trying. 你的理論值得一試。
- 🅢 I will start today! 從今天開始吧！
- 🅣 Okay. Here's the first word. 好的，這是第一個單字。

Can you be more...? 你能夠更～嗎？

當學生迫不急待想急著想下課或開始某活動時，老師可以說「Can you be more patient?（你能耐心一點嗎？）」。「Can you be more...?」是可以用來指出學生缺點的表達句型。more 後面接續形容詞，內容為您希望學生具備哪些素質。

Can you be more specific?	你能夠更具體一點嗎？
Can you be more clear*?	你能夠解釋得更清楚一點嗎？
Can you be more understanding?	你能夠更善解人意一點嗎？
Can you be more enthusiastic?	你能夠更熱情一些嗎？
Can you be more serious?	你能夠更認真一點嗎？

* 「Can you be more clear?」的語意是「您能說得更清楚一點嗎？」，句中的 clear 可替換成 simple，改成「Can you say that in a simpler way?」或「Can you simplify that?」也可表達其意。

Dialogue

S I need more information about tomorrow's assignment.	我需要更多跟明天作業有關的資訊。
T Can you be more specific?	你能夠更具體一點嗎？
S Yes, which writing exercises should we work on?	好的，我們應該要做哪些寫作練習呢？
T You should complete exercises 1 through 45.	你們必須完成第 1 題到第 45 題。

Dialogue

T Do you understand what to write about?	你們知道要寫些什麼嗎？
S Can you be more clear?	你能夠解釋得更清楚一點嗎？
T Yes. Just write about a member of your family.	好的，就是描寫你們的一位家庭成員。
S Oh, now I understand.	哦，我現在明白了。

This will be difficult... 這很難～

在出困難的作業之前，或是講解難懂的內容之前，想吸引學生注意力並安撫他們時，這是一個很合適的表達句型。difficult 後面緊接著 to 不定詞，其語意為「很難做到～」，若接 if 條件子句等則表示「如果～，會很難～」。

This will be difficult to solve.	這個問題很難解。
This will be difficult for all of us.	這對我們所有人來說都很難。
This will be difficult to explain.	這很難解釋。
This will be difficult to manage.	這很難處理。
This will be difficult if no one helps us.	如果沒有人幫我們，這將會很困難。

Dialogue

T We will have to share our room with the other English class.	我們必須和其它英語班共用這間教室。
S But it's too small for 50 people!	但這個教室太小了，容納不了 50 個人！
T I know. **This will be difficult** for all of us.	我知道，這對我們所有人來說都很困難。
S Let's bring in some more chairs, then.	那我們再搬一些椅子過來吧。

Dialogue

T Your explanation is weak*.	你的解釋有點不夠充分。
S You think so?	您是這麼認為的嗎？
T Yes. **This will be difficult** to explain.	是的，這很難解釋。
S I think I can do it.	我想我能做到。

*「Your explanation is weak.」是當對方的解釋不夠充分且缺乏說服力時可用的表達用語。類似的表達句型有「I don't buy your explanation.」或「I don't follow your reasoning.」等。

That's not my idea of... 我不認為～

這在表達「我不這麼認為」的用語中也算複雜的句型。對於學生們的答案當需要給否定的意見時，或當學生給出的答案與您的想法不同時，比起「你錯了」，用「我不那麼認為…」來回應較能顧及到學生的感受。這正是在這種情況下可用的表達句型。

That's not my idea of a good answer.	我不認為這是個好答案。
That's not my idea of an interesting exercise.	我不認為這是一個有趣的練習。
That's not my idea of a high score.	這不是我心目中的高分。
That's not my idea of a difficult exercise.	我不認為這是一個有挑戰性的練習。
That's not my idea of an easy test.	我不認為這是一個簡單的測驗。

Dialogue

T Now copy the paragraph on page 5.	現在請抄第 5 頁的段落。
S **That's not my idea of** an interesting exercise.	我不認為這是一個有趣的練習。
T If you don't like it, maybe you'd prefer some extra homework.	如果你不喜歡這樣的練習，也許你會比較想要額外作業。
S No, thank you. This is fine!	不用了，謝謝，這個就可以！

Dialogue

T We're going to take a test tomorrow.	我們明天要考試了。
S Is it easy?	考試簡單嗎？
T **That's not my idea of** an easy test.	我不認為這是一個簡單的測驗。
S Oh, God!	啊，我完蛋了！

宣布答案

Grades are announced... 成績將於～公布

這個表達句型可用來告知學生他們最關心的成績將在何時公佈、以何種方式公佈。您可以使用未來式句型「Grades will be displayed...」來表示，也能簡單地用現在式句型「Grades are displayed...」。

Grades* are announced at the next class.	成績將在下一堂課上公布。
Grades are announced two weeks after the semester.	成績將於學期結束後兩週公佈。
Grades are announced when all results are in.	成績將在所有結果出來後公布。
Grades are announced to your parents by phone.	將透過電話向家長公佈成績。

*期末考的分數，英文稱作 final grades；期中考的分數，英文稱作 midterm grades。成績單的英文說法則是 report card 或 transcript。

Dialogue

🅣 Grades will be out in a week.	成績將在一週後出來。
🅢 How will we know what we earned?	我們要怎麼知道自己的分數？
🅣 **Grades are announced** at the next class.	成績將在下一堂課上公布。
🅢 Oh! No!	哦！不！

Dialogue

🅢 When will we get our scores?	我們的成績什麼時候才會公布？
🅣 **Grades are announced** when all results are in.	成績將在所有結果都出來後公布。
🅢 So, we have to wait for the late entries?	所以我們要等那些較晚參加的人嗎？
🅣 Sorry, but yes.	很遺憾，是的。

The correct answer is... 正確答案是～

在美國的益智節目上向來賓進行問答時，會使用的句型就是「The correct answer is...」。當然，老師在課堂上也可以用這個句型來向學生宣布正確答案。順便一提，錯誤選項的英文是 incorrect answer 或 wrong answer。

The correct answer is in your book.	正確答案就在你的書裡。
The correct answer is debatable.	正確答案有爭議性。
The correct answer is George Washington.	正確答案是 George Washington。
The correct answer is Italy.	正確答案是義大利。
The correct answer is what we just heard.	正確答案就是我們剛才聽到的。

Dialogue

T Who was the first president of the United States?	美國的第一位總統是誰？
S1 Was it Abraham Lincoln?	是 Abraham Lincoln 嗎？
S2 Was it Bill Clinton?	是 Bill Clinton 嗎？
T **The correct answer is** George Washington.	正確答案是 George Washington。

Dialogue

T What country's capital city is Rome?	羅馬是哪個國家的首都？
S France.	法國。
T Sorry. **The correct answer is** Italy.	很遺憾，但正確答案是義大利。
S Oh, I knew that!	哦，我就知道！

UNIT 08 基本的回應與互動：鼓勵、讚美、責備與拒絕等

📖 鼓勵

There will be extra points... ～將獲得加分。

「獲得額外分數」的英文說法是 earn extra points，「被給予額外分數」的英文說法則是 be given extra points 或 receive extra points。需要注意的是，extra 讀作 [ˋɛkstrə]。

There will be extra points* for early assignments.	如果提前完成作業，將獲得加分。
There will be extra points given to attendees.	參加者將獲得加分。
There will be extra points if your spelling is correct.	如果拼寫正確，將獲得加分。
There will be extra points for anyone who never misses class.	從未缺席的學生將獲得加分。
There will be extra points given to the best presenter.	表現最優異的學生將獲得加分。

*extra points 指的是原始分數之外額外獲得的分數，與 bonus points 同義。

Dialogue

🅣 Please have your assignments turned in by September 12.	請在 9 月 12 日之前交作業。
🅢 What if we finish early?	如果我們提早完成的話呢？
🅣 **There will be extra points** for early assignments.	如果提前完成作業，將給予加分。
🅢 Awesome! I'm almost done already.	太棒了！我已經快完成了。

Dialogue

T Write a list of words that rhyme with "corn." 　　　試著列出跟「corn」押韻的單字。

S That sounds easy. 　　　聽起來蠻簡單的。

T **There will be extra points** if your spelling is correct. 　　　如果拼寫正確，將給予加分。

S All right! 　　　太好了！

Let's try to... 我們試著～吧。

在課堂上，有時不是老師一個人拼命唱獨角戲就能完成的事情，與其給出諸如「做這個！」、「做那個！」之類的指令，偶爾使用「Let's try to...」這個句型來鼓勵學生也是很重要的。「try + to 不定詞」的語意是「嘗試、努力」做某事。作為參考，「try + 動名詞」的語意是「試驗性地做某事」。

Let's try to finish our homework early. 　　　我們試著早點完成作業吧。

Let's try to answer all of the questions correctly. 　　　我們試著準確回答所有問題吧。

Let's try to write as quickly as we can. 　　　我們試著寫快一點吧。

Let's try to avoid using our dictionaries. 　　　試著不要使用字典吧。

Let's try to speak more clearly. 　　　我們試著把話說得更清楚吧。

Dialogue

T Your homework is page 22. 　　　作業在第 22 頁。

S1 **Let's try to** finish our homework early. 　　　我們儘量早點完成作業吧！

S2 Why? 　　　為什麼？

S1 Then we can play video games. 　　　這樣就能打電動了。

Dialogue

T Let's try to avoid using our dictionaries. 試著儘量不要使用字典吧。
S Why? 為什麼？
T We'll be able to read faster that way. 那樣可以更快速地閱讀。
S Oh, I see. 哦，原來如此。

I'm sure that... 我確信～／我相信～

P3_136

當您想斬釘截鐵地說某件事是無誤的事實，可以使用這個表達用語。that 後面若接續帶有鼓勵性或警告性的字眼，則可能表示要對方牢記在心。用 sure 代替 certain，改成「I'm certain that...」時，兩句型的語意相同。

I'm sure that you will understand eventually.	我相信你最終會理解的。
I'm sure that you will do fine.	我相信你會做得很好。
I'm sure that the test will be easy.	我確信這次考試會很簡單。
I'm sure that we will have enough time.	我確信我們會有足夠的時間。
I'm sure that no one else wants the ticket.	我確認沒有人會要那張票。

Dialogue

S This exercise is impossible. 這個練習題是不可能解開的。
T **I'm sure that** you will understand eventually. 我相信你最終會理解的。
S I don't know about that. 我真的看不太懂。
T Just keep trying and you'll get it. 只要繼續努力，你就會明白的。

Dialogue

T Don't forget about the test tomorrow. 別忘了明天的考試。
S1 **I'm sure that** the test will be easy. 我確信這次考試會很簡單。
S2 You always say that. 你總是這麼說。
S1 And I'm always right! 而我總是對的！

There's no time to... 沒時間～

P3_137

這是日常生活中常會用到的表達句型之一，主要用來督促別人因為沒有時間了而要求停止做某件事，要對方專注於更緊急或重要的事情。「There's no time to lose.」的語意是「沒有時間磨蹭了」，即表示「需要抓緊時間」。類似的表達句型還有「There's no time to waste.」。

There's no time to be nervous.	沒時間緊張了。
There's no time to explain.	沒時間解釋了。
There's no time to complain.	沒時間抱怨了。
There's no time to waste.	沒時間可以浪費了。
There's no time to study now.	現在沒時間學習了。

Dialogue

T It's time to do your presentation. 該是你報告的時候了。
S I'm scared to speak in front of the class. 我害怕在全班同學面前講話。
T **There's no time to** be nervous. 沒時間緊張了。
S I guess you're right. 我想您說得對。

Dialogue

T Let's begin the quiz. 現在開始小考。
S Can I have a few more minutes to study? 我可以再多念幾分鐘嗎？
T **There's no time to** study now. 現在沒時間念書了。
S Oh no! 哦不！

If you try to... 如果你試著～／努力～，就～

這是使用 If 的條件句，是想對學生給予建議時非常好用的表達句型。如前所述，「try＋to 不定詞」表示「嘗試、努力」做某事，「try＋動名詞」則表示「試驗性地做某事」。

If you try to speak slowly, you'll make fewer mistakes.	如果你試著放慢説話速度，就會少犯錯。
If you try to study a little bit every day, you won't have to cram*.	如果你試著每天都學習一點，就不用臨時抱佛腳了。
If you try to be on time, you won't miss anything.	如果你努力準時到達，就不會錯過任何事情。
If you try to understand the main idea, it will be easier.	如果你試著理解其要旨，就會更容易。
If you try to memorize the words, you'll see it isn't too hard.	如果你試著記住這些單字，就會發現這並不難。

Dialogue

S I'm having a hard time preparing for tomorrow's test.	我正在準備明天的考試，真的太辛苦了。
T Why?	為什麼？
S There's so much to study.	因為要學習的東西太多了。
T **If you try to** study a little bit every day, you won't have to cram.	如果你試著每天都學習一點，就不用臨時抱佛腳。

*cram 的語意是「塞進」一個狹窄的空間，是描述「在考試前臨時抱佛腳」時常會用到的單字。cram 也當作名詞，舉例來說，cram school 指的是「升學補習班」。

Dialogue

T Let's do some listening practices.	我們來做一些聽力練習吧。
S It's so hard to understand all the details.	聽懂每個細節真的太難了。
T **If you try to** understand the main idea, it will be easier.	如果你試著理解其要旨，就會更容易。
S Okay. I'll try to do that.	好的，我會試試看。

Don't be afraid of... 不要害怕～

語意為「不要怕～」或「不要害怕～」，這是要求猶豫不決的學生們果敢去做某件事時可用的表達句型。of 後面接續名詞或動名詞。

Don't be afraid of a little hard work.	不要遇到一點困難就畏怯。
Don't be afraid of asking questions.	不要害怕提問。
Don't be afraid of speaking English.	不要害怕說英語。
Don't be afraid of making a mistake.	不要害怕犯錯。
Don't be afraid of me.	不要怕我。

Dialogue

T Now we will all memorize this dialogue.	現在我們都要記住這段對話。
S That sounds difficult.	這聽起來很難。
T **Don't be afraid of** a little hard work.	不要遇到一點困難就畏怯。
S I guess I'm kind of lazy.	我想我有點懶惰。

Dialogue

T If you didn't understand, why didn't you ask a question?	如果你不明白，為什麼不發問呢？
S I was too shy.	我太害羞了。
T **Don't be afraid of** asking questions.	不要害怕提問。
S I won't next time.	下次不會這樣了。

Do your best... 盡力～／盡你所能～

這是老師在鼓勵學生時最常使用的表達句型。在 best 後面接續 to 不定詞的話，語意是「盡全力去做～」。其它類似句型還有「You're the best!（你是最棒的！）」、「You are good at this.（這個你很擅長）」跟「You can do it! I know it.（我就知道你辦的到）」等。

Do your best to remember the new vocabulary. 盡力記住新單字。

Do your best to speak correctly. 你必須盡你所能把話說好。

Do your best to be on time. 盡你所能準時到。

Do your best not to make any mistakes. 盡你所能不要犯任何錯誤。

Do your best to write neatly. 盡你所能寫得工整一點。

Dialogue

- **T** **Do your best** not to make any mistakes. 盡你所能不要犯任何錯誤。
- **S** That's easy to say, but difficult to do. 說起來容易，做起來卻很難。
- **T** We can all try. 我們都可試試看。
- **S** I guess that's true. 我想您說得對。

Dialogue

- **T** Sammy, I can't read your handwriting*. Sammy，我看不懂你的筆跡。
- **S** It's difficult to write quickly and clearly. 要寫得又快又工整是很難的。
- **T** **Do your best** to write neatly. 盡你所能寫得工整一點。
- **S** Okay. I'll try. 好的，我會盡力的。

*handwriting 指的是「手寫」。寫字時，要求把每個字母寫清楚時，會用動詞 print 來表達，草寫體的英文說法是 cursive writing。

Don't give up... 不要放棄～

give up 原本是語意為「放棄～、戒除～」的及物動詞，但也可以用作不及物動詞，如「**Don't give up.**」。在口語中，give up on 表示「放棄～」。這是常用來鼓勵那些因為成效不明顯而沮喪的學生的表達句型。

Don't give up just yet.	不要放棄。
Don't give up on yourself.	不要放棄自己。
Don't give up without trying your best.	不要不努力就放棄。
Don't give up and don't give in*.	不要放棄，也不要屈服。
Don't give up your rights.	不要放棄自己的權利。

*give in 表示「屈服」或「讓步」，跟 yield 語意相同。想陳述「屈服於～」時，可以利用介系詞 to，以「give in to」來表達其意。

Dialogue

S I'm never going to learn English!	我永遠不會學好英語的！
T **Don't give up** just yet.	不要放棄。
S Is there anything you can do to help me?	您有什麼辦法可以幫助我嗎？
T I have some written exercises for you.	我會給你一些練習題。

Dialogue

S To study is too hard for me.	念書對我來說太難了。
T You'll get it eventually.	你最終會做到的。
S I don't think I'll be a very good scientist.	我不認為我會成為一位優秀的科學家。
T **Don't give up** on yourself.	不要放棄自己。

📖 給予建議

It doesn't mean... 這並不表示～

當您在解釋某個情況,並想排除任何潛在的誤會時,就可緊接著用「It doesn't mean...」這個句型來進行補充說明。在此句型後面接上子句,以明確指出「這並不表示～」。

It doesn't mean you'll never understand.	這並不表示你永遠無法理解。
It doesn't mean you'll fail the class.	這並不表示你這門課會被當掉。
It doesn't mean you're not smart.	這並不表示你不聰明。
It doesn't mean you can speak well.	這並不表示你可以講得很好。
It doesn't mean you can't do it.	這並不表示你做不到。

Dialogue

🅢 This exercise is impossible.	這個練習題是不可能解開的。
🅣 Why do you say that?	為什麼這麼說?
🅢 I just can't understand it.	我就是無法理解。
🅣 **It doesn't mean** you'll never understand.	這並不表示你永遠無法理解。

Dialogue

🅣 Here are your test scores.	這是你們的考試成績。
🅢1 Oh no! I've got an F.	哦不!我得到 F。
🅢2 Don't worry. **It doesn't mean** you'll fail the class.	別擔心,這並不表示你這門課會被當掉。
🅢1 I hope not!	但願如此!

You should try to... 你應該試著～／你應該儘量～

這是老師和爸媽都很常使用的表達句型，一般用來表示「你應該要嘗試！」或「嘗試看看！」。助動詞 should 雖然解釋成「應該做～」，但有別於 must 或 have to（用來描述絕對要遵守某規定或原則），should 具有「建議做某事；做某事是對的」之意味。

You should try to speak as clearly as possible.	你應該儘量說得清楚點。
You should try to memorize one word a day.	你應該試著每天背一個單字。
You should try to be more careful.	你應該要更小心一點。
You should try to avoid making mistakes.	你應該儘量不犯錯。
You should try to write more quickly.	你應該儘量寫快一點。

Dialogue

S Do you have any advice about how to learn vocabulary?	您能建議我該如何學習單字嗎？
T **You should try to** memorize one word a day.	你應該試著每天背一個單字。
S That doesn't sound like much work.	聽起來不會很費力。
T No, but over the year, you will learn a lot.	確實不多，但只要過了一年，就能學會許多單字。

Dialogue

T Here is your corrected homework.	這是批改過的作業，你的作業。
S Oh no! I forgot to do number 3.	哦不！我忘了做第三題。
T **You should try to** be more careful.	你應該要更小心一點。
S I will next time.	下次我會小心的。

May I suggest…? 我可以建議／提議～嗎？

這是用來向學生提出建議的表達句型。與其使用祈使句來下令「去做～」，不如用「May I suggest…?（我可以建議～嗎？）」這更溫和的方式，來尊重他們的的選擇。當學生在寫作業或解題時不知從何下手時，可以用這種句型提出建議。

May I suggest that you practice with a partner?	我可以建議你和夥伴一起練習嗎？
May I suggest a different answer?	我可以提出不一樣的答案嗎？
May I suggest that we do it differently?	我可以提議我們換個方式進行嗎？
May I suggest that you write down your ideas?	我可以建議你寫下你的想法嗎？
May I suggest that you study a little harder?	我可以建議你再用功一點嗎？

Dialogue

S I'm having a hard time learning these words.	這些單字真的很難學。
T **May I suggest** that you practice with a partner?	我可以建議你和夥伴一起練習嗎？
S How will that help?	會有什麼幫助呢？
T It will be more fun.	讓學習變得更有趣。

Dialogue

T The presentation is tomorrow. Are you ready?	明天要報告了，你都準備好了嗎？
S I'm having a hard time preparing tomorrow's speech.	我為了明天的報告準備得很辛苦。
T **May I suggest** that you write down your ideas?	我可以建議你寫下你的想法嗎？
S That sounds like a good idea.	這聽起來是個好主意。

The best way to ~ is... ～最好的方法是～

學生們總是會問老師說有沒有學好英語的捷徑，此時就該回答：「There is no royal road, but the best way to learn English is to study hard.（這世上沒有捷徑，學習英語最好的方法是努力學習）」。The best way 後面接續 to 不定詞的話，則意味著「做～是最好的方法」。

The best way to learn English **is** to speak a lot.	學習英語最好的方法就是開口多講。
The best way to remember words **is** to say them many times.	記住單字最好的方法就是多説幾遍。
The best way to get a good grade **is** to study hard.	取得好成績的最好方法就是努力學習。
The best way to understand **is** to listen carefully.	要理解的最好方法就是仔細聆聽。

Dialogue

S1 I study a lot, but my English doesn't get better.	我很認真念書，但英語並沒有進步。
S2 Me too. What should we do?	我也是，我們該怎麼辦？
T **The best way to** learn English **is** to speak a lot.	學習英語最好的方法就是開口多講。
S2 Okay.	好的。

Dialogue

T "Fast" means "quick."	「Fast」的意思是「quick」。
S I can never remember new words.	我永遠記不住新單字。
T **The best way to** remember words **is** to say them many times.	記住單字最好的方法就是多說幾遍。
S Okay. Fast, fast, fast, fast...	好的。Fast, fast, fast, fast…

Let's put a little more effort into... 我們再加把勁～吧

在學習過程中，經常會因為成績提升不如預期而感到沮喪。當您想要鼓勵感到失望的孩子時，就可以利用這個表達句型來告訴他們不要放棄，鼓勵他們繼續努力。「put an effort into...」的語意是「為～做出努力」，這裡的 effort 前可接續各種形容詞來修飾。若加上 a little more（多一點～），語意帶有「再努力一點」；若加上 a lot of（很多～），語意則為「多努力」。

Let's put a little more effort into learning this grammar.	我們再加把勁學習這個文法吧。
Let's put a little more effort into writing this essay.	我們再花點功夫寫這篇文章吧。
Let's put a little more effort into finishing this exercise.	我們再加把勁完成這個練習題。
Let's put a little more effort into passing this test.	我們再加把勁通過這次測驗吧。

Dialogue

S We should play a game now!	我們現在應該要玩個遊戲了！
T **Let's put a little more effort into** learning this grammar.	我們再加把勁學習這個文法吧。
S But I'm tired of grammar!	但是我對文法感到厭倦！
T Don't worry. We're almost finished.	別擔心，就快結束了。

Dialogue

S It's almost time to go home.	差不多該回家了。
T Yes, but **let's put a little more effort into** finishing this exercise.	是的，不過我們再加把勁完成這個練習題。
S Okay, I'll do number 8.	好吧，我來做第 8 題。
T That's a good attitude!	這種態度很好！

It would be wise to.... 最好～

老師或家長最常給孩子們的警告性規勸就是「最好～」。從字面意思來看時，其語意是「做～是明智的」，蘊含「如果你不希望以後後悔的話」之意。句中的 wise 可替換成 better，是一個用途多廣的句型。

It would be wise to study for the test.	最好去為這考試念書。
It would be wise to be on time tomorrow.	明天最好準時到。
It would be wise to memorize this vocabulary.	最好記住這個單字。
It would be wise to turn in your homework on time.	最好按時交作業。
It would be wise to review* chapter 6 tonight.	今晚最好複習一下第 6 課。

*複習的英文是 review。那預習呢？可以很簡單地用 preview，但也可以利用動詞 prepare，以「prepare tomorrow's lesson」或「check out new material」來表達。

Dialogue

S I'm sorry I was late again.	很抱歉我又遲到了。
T **It would be wise to** be on time tomorrow.	明天最好準時到。
S I understand. I'll be here on time.	知道了，我會準時到的。
T I hope so.	希望如此。

Dialogue

T **It would be wise to** review chapter 6 tonight.	今晚最好複習一下第 6 課。
S Why?	為什麼？
T Because I might give you a quiz tomorrow.	因為我明天可能會給你們安排個小考。
S Thanks for the hint!	謝謝提點！

You should have... 你早應該要～

「You should have + p.p.」意味著「應該要做某事，結果卻沒做」，當對方原本應該要做某事或採取某行動，卻什麼事都沒做時，就能用此句型來斥責或表示遺憾。例如對方遲到了，我們通常會跟對方說應該要提前打電話；或者如果有考試，我們就會說應該要認真念書。換句話說，這是用來對已發生的事情表達遺憾的句型。相反地，當對方做了不該做的舉動時，請使用「You should have not + p.p.」。

You should have studied harder.	你早應該要更用功念書。
You should have done your homework.	你早應該要做作業。
You should have paid more attention.	你早應該要再專心一點。
You should have gone to bed earlier.	你早應該要早點睡。
You should have eaten breakfast.	你早應該要吃早餐。

Dialogue

- S: I got a terrible grade! 我分數考得很差！
- T: **You should have** studied harder. 你應該要更用功念書。
- S: I did my best! 我已經盡力了！
- T: I think you can do better. 我認為你還可以做得更好。

Dialogue

- T: Okay, let's start the exercise. 好的，我們開始做練習題。
- S: I don't understand what to do. 我不知道該做什麼。
- T: **You should have** paid more attention. 你應該要再專心一點。
- S: I'm sorry. 對不起。

Would you just...? 你能不能～呢？

P3_149

Would you 是請求幫忙的禮貌用語，所以當有人說「**Would you just**...?」，通常是一種比較柔和的命令用語，意思是「你能不能這樣做？」，這裡的 just 意味著「稍微」。不過在語氣上要注意一下，可能會因為語調而聽起來有點不耐煩或不高興，所以使用時要考慮到這一點。

Would you just try harder?	你能不能再努力一點呢？
Would you just try it one more time?	你能不能再試一次呢？
Would you just stop complaining so much?	你能不能不要這麼常抱怨呢？
Would you just give me a second?	你能不能等我一下呢？
Would you just explain it one more time?	你能不能再解釋一遍呢？

Dialogue

T Tonight you need to read all of chapter 5.	今晚你們需要讀完第 5 課全部內容。
S All of it? That's so much!	全部嗎？太多了！
T **Would you just** stop complaining so much?	你能不能不要這麼常抱怨呢？
S Yes, sir. I'm sorry.	好的，老師，對不起。

Dialogue

T Does everyone understand the assignment?	作業大家都清楚了吧？
S **Would you just** explain it one more time?	您能不能再解釋一遍呢？
T No problem. You need to write down 5 words you don't understand.	好的，請大家寫下 5 個不懂的單字。
S Oh! That's easy.	哦！這很容易。

Why don't we...? 我們何不～呢？

這是用來向對方建議「我們一起～吧」的表達句型，是跟「Let's...」類似的句型。而當有人說「Why don't you...?」時，其語意是「你何不～？」，旨在鼓勵對方採取某種行動。

Why don't we try saying it together?	我們何不一起唸出來呢？
Why don't we do it tomorrow?	我們何不明天弄呢？
Why don't we share my textbook?	我們何不一起看我的課本呢？
Why don't we quit for the day?	我們今天何不就到此為止呢？
Why don't we study together?	我們何不一起學習呢？

Dialogue

T Do you understand this sentence?	你看得懂這句話嗎？
S Yes, but I can't pronounce it correctly.	懂，但我發音不標準。
T **Why don't we** try saying it together?	我們何不一起唸出來呢？
S That's a good idea.	好主意。

Dialogue

S1 I forgot my books today.	今天忘了帶我的課本。
S2 You're going to need your English book.	你會需要用到你的英文課本。
S1 I know. I'm not sure what to do.	我知道，但我不知道該怎麼辦。
S2 **Why don't we** share my textbook?	我們何不一起看我的課本呢？

It's not enough to just... 僅僅～是不夠的／光～是不夠的。 P3_151

當您想表達目前為止所做的還不夠，所以還需要更加努力或多做一點時，就可以使用這個表達句型。not enough 的語意是「不夠、不充分」，所以能利用由虛主詞 it 跟 to 不定詞組成的「It's not enough to +原形動詞」來表達「做～是不夠的」之意。在這裡用 just 來修飾不定詞的話，語意會變為「僅僅做～」，可以讓句子更為自然。

It's not enough to just study at the last minute.	臨陣磨槍是不夠的。
It's not enough to just skim the readings.	僅僅只是略讀是不夠的。
It's not enough to just attend class weekly.	僅僅只是每週上課是不夠的。
It's not enough to just memorize this paragraph.	光記住這一段是不夠的。
It's not enough to just solve the questions.	光解題目是不夠的。

Dialogue

S I was up until 3:00 this morning studying for the test.	我為了這考試念書念到凌晨 3 點。
T That's not a good study plan for English class.	這不是學英語的好方法。
S I'm starting to realize that.	我開始意識到這一點了。
T **It's not enough to just** study at the last minute.	臨陣磨槍是不夠的。

Dialogue

S Why did I get such a low score?	為什麼我的分數這麼低？
T **It's not enough to just** attend class weekly.	僅僅只是每週上課是不夠的。
S What else do I need to do?	我還需要做什麼？

🅣 You need to participate in discussions and do your homework. 要參與討論跟做作業。

📖 引導

Wouldn't you like...? 難道你不想～嗎？

P3_152

語意跟「Would you like...?」相差不大，但當您想透過「難道你不想～」來確認學生的想法時，就要使用這個表達句型。Would you like 後面接續名詞，若接的是動詞，則要採用 to 不定詞。

Wouldn't you like to raise your grade? 難道你不想提高成績嗎？
Wouldn't you like my advice? 難道你不想聽我的建議嗎？
Wouldn't you like a front row seat? 難道你不想坐前排嗎？
Wouldn't you like to listen to more details? 難道你不想聽聽更多細節嗎？
Wouldn't you like to know your final grades? 難道你不想知道你的期末成績嗎？

Dialogue

🅣 Stay after class, and I'll help you study. 下課後留下來，我幫你複習課業。
🅢 Nah, I want to go to the soccer game. 不要，我想去看足球賽。
🅣 **Wouldn't you like** to raise your grade? 難道你不想提高成績嗎？
🅢 Yes, but this is a game I don't want to miss. 想啊，但我也不想錯過這場足球比賽。

Dialogue

🅢 My essay paper isn't coming together very well. 我的作文寫得不是很順利。
🅣 **Wouldn't you like** my advice? 你想要聽我的建議嗎？
🅢 Actually, that would be great. 如果可以的話我會很感激。
🅣 Why don't you make an outline first? 為什麼不先列個大綱呢？

There are so many reasons why... ～的理由有很多。

那些喜歡到處找藉口而不念書的學生,每天都會問我好幾次「為什麼我必須這樣做?」,當您想告訴這些孩子「你應該這樣做的原因有很多」時,就可使用這個表達句型。reasons why 的語意是「做～的理由」,此時 why 可以省略,改成 reasons for which 亦可表達相同意思,請一併記住這個句型。

There are so many reasons why you need to learn this grammar.	你應該學習這個文法的理由有很多。
There are so many reasons why you should use your dictionary.	應該要使用字典的理由有很多。
There are so many reasons why you need to do homework.	你應該寫作業的理由有很多。
There are so many reasons why we should discuss this topic.	我們應該討論這個話題的理由有很多。

Dialogue

- **T** **There are so many reasons why** you need to do homework.
- **S** Like what?
- **T** Well, if you study every day, you'll improve your grades more quickly.
- **S** I guess that's true.

你需要寫作業的原因有很多。
比如說?
唔,如果你每天學習,你的成績就能進步得更快。
我想你說得對。

Dialogue

- **T** **There are so many reasons why** we should discuss this topic.
- **S** But it's so boring.
- **T** Maybe. But it's going to be on the test next week.
- **S** Oh! Then let's discuss it.

我們應該討論這個話題的原因有很多。
但是這個話題太無聊了。
也許吧,但它會出現在下週的測驗中。
哦!如果是這樣,那我們來討論一下吧。

Why do you always ...? 為什麼你總是～？

班上難免會有學生不斷犯同樣的錯，講過兩次三次卻還是犯一樣的錯，或是想出各種藉口來替自己辯解，此時為了瞭解學生的想法，便可以使用這個表達句型。這個問句帶有「你為什麼老是這樣？」之意，若將這句型用在只犯過一兩次錯的學生身上，可能會對他們造成傷害，所以要謹慎使用。

Why do you always gossip in class?	為什麼你總是在班上講閒話？
Why do you always forget your books?	為什麼你總是忘記帶課本？
Why do you always say it's too difficult for you?	為什麼你總是說這對你來說太難了？
Why do you always say that word wrong?	為什麼你總是說錯這個字？

Dialogue

S This is so hard!	這太難了！
T **Why do you always** say it's too difficult for you?	為什麼你總是說這對你來說太難了？
S Because it is!	因為確實如此呀！
T I think you just need to try harder.	我認為你需要更加努力。

Dialogue

S **Why do you always** talk so loud when I'm explaining this grammar?	為什麼我在講解這文法時，你總是大聲講話呢？
T I'm sorry, I just get a little excited when thinking of something to share.	抱歉，我只是有點興奮，因為想到一些想分享的事情。
S Could you wait until I finish?	能等我說完再講嗎？
T Sure. I didn't mean to be rude.	好的。我不是故意失禮的。

If I were you, I'd... 如果我是你，我會～

這是在各種情況下都適合用來積極提供建議的表達句型。「If I were you, I'd...」這個句型陳述了與當前事實相反的假設，若 if 子句使用過去式，當 be 動詞是 were 的話，主要子句中就會跟著使用如 would、should、could…等過去式助動詞。

If I were you, I'd study harder.	如果我是你，我會更努力學習。
If I were you, I'd do the homework first.	如果我是你，我會先寫作業。
If I were you, I'd get ready for the test.	如果我是你，我就會準備考試。
If I were you, I'd memorize those words.	如果我是你，我就會記得這些單字。
If I were you, I'd ask the teacher.	如果我是你，我會問老師。

Dialogue

🅣 You did very poorly on the test.	你這次考試考得很差。
🅢 What should I do to improve?	該怎麼做才能改進呢？
🅣 **If I were you, I'd** study harder.	如果我是你，我就會更努力學習。
🅢 Could you be more specific?	能說得更具體一點嗎？

Dialogue

S1 Are you ready to do the assignment?	你準備好做作業了嗎？
S2 I don't understand the grammar.	我不懂這個文法。
S1 **If I were you, I'd** ask the teacher.	如果我是你，我會問老師。
S2 That's a good idea.	這是個好主意。

📖 讚美

I like your... 我喜歡你的～

從字面上來看指的是「我喜歡你的～」，是用來稱讚別人的句型。舉例來說，當學生自我介紹說「My name is Kim Yuna.」時，便可以回答「I like it.」來表示她的名字很好聽。也可用來稱讚別人的服裝、物品，可用「I like your bag.」來稱讚對方的包包，藉此拉近跟學生們之間的距離。

I like your answer.	我喜歡你的回答。
I like your enthusiasm.	我喜歡你的那種熱情。
I like your attitude.	我喜歡你的態度。
I like your idea.	我喜歡你的點子。
I like your way of thinking.	我喜歡你的思考方式。

Dialogue

T Let's learn some new words.	我們來學一些新單字吧。
S Hurray! I love learning new words!	萬歲！我喜歡學習新單字！
T **I like your** attitude.	我喜歡你的態度。
S Thank you.	謝謝。

Dialogue

T Try to think of a topic for your presentation.	試著為簡報想出一個主題。
S1 Let's talk about soccer.	我們來談談足球吧。
S2 **I like your** idea.	我喜歡你的想法。
S1 Thanks!	謝謝！

This is the best... 這是～最～的～

這是用來稱讚別人的表達句型。如果學生從老師那邊獲得到這樣的讚美，大概會覺得自己是全世界最棒的吧？This is the best 後面接續的 I've ever 意味著「直到現在、目前為止」。舉例來說，「You are the best student I've ever taught.」這句話意味著「你是我教過的最好的學生」。

This is the best grade I've ever made!	這是我有史以來取得的最佳成績。
This is the best exercise we've ever done!	這是我們做過最好的練習題。
This is the best essay you've ever written!	這是你寫過最好的作文。
This is the best class I've ever taught!	這是我有史以來教過最好的班級。
This is the best time I've ever had!	這是我有史以來度過最美好的時光。

Dialogue

T **This is the best** essay you've ever written!	這是你寫過最好的作文。
S Thank you.	謝謝。
T Why is it so good?	你怎麼寫得這麼好？
S I spent a long time on it.	我花了很多時間寫的。

Dialogue

T Now we're going to play another game.	現在我們要玩另一個遊戲。
S **This is the best** time I've ever had!	這是我有史以來度過最美好的時光。
T I told you that English could be fun!	我說過英語也可以很有趣的！
S And you were right!	您說得對！

Good work... ～做得很好。

這是用來大力稱讚別人的作品、作業等的表達句型。Good job! 是類似的表達。除此之外，也請記住「Very good!」、「That's very good!」、「Well done!」、「Marvelous!」、「You did a great job!」等相關的表達。亦可以用 excellent 來代替句中的 good。

Good work on the homework.	作業寫得非常好。
Good work is always rewarded.	努力工作總會有回報。
Good work of this kind is rare.	難得看到有人做得這麼好。
Good work, everyone!	大家都做得很好！
Good work on your exam.	你考得非常好。

Dialogue

🅣 **Good work**, everyone!	大家都做得很好！
🅢 Thanks, it was fun performing our play.	謝謝，演出我們的這齣劇真是太有趣了。
🅣 You should all be very proud. It was good.	你們大家都該感到自豪，表現的很棒。
🅢 I think the audience liked it, too.	觀眾們似乎也很喜歡。

Dialogue

🅣 James, I want to tell you something.	James，我想跟你說一件事。
🅢 What is it, Mr. Hamilton?	Hamilton 老師，是什麼事？
🅣 **Good work** on your exam.	你考得非常好。
🅢 Does that mean I passed?	你的意思是我通過了嗎？

It's very ~ of you to ... 你～真是太～了。

這是可用來談論對方行為或向對方表示謝意的表達句型。very 後面可接續各種形容詞來靈活運用，最常使用的形容詞是 nice、kind、wise 等。除此之外，別忘了 to 後面要接原形動詞（即 to 不定詞），to 不定詞是這個句子真正的主詞。

It's very kind **of you to** give me extra help.	你願意給我額外的幫助真是太好了。
It's very wise **of you to** do your homework now.	你能現在就寫作業真是太明智了。
It's very sweet **of you to** write me this card.	你寫這張卡片給我真是太貼心了。
It's very smart **of you to** write down all the new words.	你能把所有新單字都寫下來真是太聰明了。
It's very nice **of you to** help me carry these books.	你幫我提這些書真是太好了。

Dialogue

🅣 Do you understand the homework?	你理解作業內容嗎？
🅢 No. I'm still a little confused.	不太理解，我還是有點困惑。
🅣 Why don't you stay after class and I'll explain it again?	不如你下課後留下來，我再跟你解釋一遍？
🅢 **It's very** kind **of you to** give me extra help.	你願意給我額外的幫助真是太好了。

Dialogue

🅣 Why are you still here? Class is over.	你怎麼還在這裡？已經下課了。
🅢 I'm going to finish this assignment.	我要完成這個作業。
🅣 **It's very** wise **of you to** do your homework now.	你能現在就寫作業真是太明智了。
🅢 I want to have fun later!	我一會兒想去玩！

Congratulations on your... 恭喜你～

當您想對認真學習的學生表示讚揚時，只要在此句型的 your 後面加上你要讚揚的事就行了。要特別注意的是，「congratulation」在拼寫時一定要加上 -s，即寫成 congratulations 才行。也可改用 Congratulations 的動詞表示，即「Congratulate +人+ on +要恭喜之事」，語意為「恭喜某人某件事」。

Congratulations on your prize.	恭喜你得獎了。
Congratulations on your scholarship.	恭喜你獲得獎學金。
Congratulations on your score.	恭喜你取得你的理想成績。
Congratulations on your perfect score.	恭喜你考取完美成績。
Congratulations on passing the test.	恭喜你通過考試。

Dialogue

- **T** I heard you won the poetry contest. 　聽說你贏得了詩歌朗誦比賽。
- **S** Yes, as a matter of fact, I did. 　是的，我確實做到了。
- **T** **Congratulations on your** prize. 　恭喜你得獎了。
- **S** Thank you! 　謝謝！

Dialogue

- **T** Sunny, you had the top score on today's test. 　Sunny，你今天考試得最高分。
- **S** You're kidding! What was it? 　真的嗎？幾分？
- **T** 99. **Congratulations on your** score. 　99 分，恭喜你取得你的理想成績。
- **S** I can't believe it! 　我簡直不敢相信！

📖 拒絕

I'm sorry I can't... 抱歉,我無法～

教導學生時,很多時候他們會提出各式各樣的要求或幫助,在這種情況下想拒絕對方時,很適合用這個表達句型,類似的表達句型有「I'm afraid I can't...」。除此之外,也請同時記住「I'm sorry＋to 不定詞」這用法。

I'm sorry I can't be more specific.	抱歉,我無法說得更具體了。
I'm sorry I can't give you any more hints.	抱歉,我無法給您更多提示。
I'm sorry I can't push back* the test.	抱歉,我無法延後考試。
I'm sorry I can't explain it more clearly.	抱歉,我無法解釋地更詳細。
I'm sorry I can't do better.	抱歉,我沒能做得更好。

*push back 從字面上來看指的是「往後推」,但在這裡指的是將日期往後延的「延期、推遲」。

Dialogue

T Tomorrow's test will cover chapter 7.	明天的考試範圍將涵蓋第 7 課。
S Which part of chapter 7?	第 7 課的哪一部分呢?
T **I'm sorry I can't** be more specific.	抱歉,我無法說得更具體了。
S I guess we'll have to study all of it.	我想我們必須讀第 7 課的所有內容。

Dialogue

T You said it wrong again.	你又說錯了。
S **I'm sorry I can't** do better.	抱歉,我沒能做得更好。
T You'll get it if you practice a little more.	只要再多練習一點就行了。
S I hope so.	但願如此。

I'm sorry to say that... 很遺憾，～

這是向學生傳達壞消息時可以使用的表達句型。反過來說，當您要傳達的是好消息時，請用 happy、glad 或 pleased 來代替 sorry。舉例來說，如果您說「I'm happy to say that...」，則表示「我很高興地說～」。

I'm sorry to say that no one passed the test.	很遺憾，沒有人通過測驗。
I'm sorry to say that you will have to try again.	很遺憾，你必須再試一次。
I'm sorry to say that you will have to stay after class.	很遺憾，你下課後得留下來。
I'm sorry to say that the homework will be a little difficult.	很遺憾，作業會有點難度。
I'm sorry to say that we have many more words to learn.	很遺憾，我們還有很多單字要學。

Dialogue

T **I'm sorry to say that** no one passed the test.	很遺憾，沒有人通過測驗。
S Maybe it was too hard.	也許是因為考試太難了。
T Maybe you didn't study enough.	也可能是因為大家沒有好好唸書。
S I guess that's possible.	或許是吧。

Dialogue

S That's it. I memorized all of the words from chapter 2.	就這樣，我熟記了第 2 課所有的單字。
T **I'm sorry to say that** we have many more words to learn.	很遺憾，我們還有很多單字要學。
S Learning English is going to take a long time.	學習英語真的很費時。
T That's true.	確實如此。

📖 結論

No wonder... 難怪～

這是「It is no wonder that」的省略說法，省略了句中的 It is 跟 that。No wonder 指的是所發生的情況或事件是自然的、不足為奇的，可以用來向學生指出這是由於他們自身的過錯而造成的因果關係。相反地，當您說「It is a wonder that...」，則意味著「～是一件奇怪的事情」。

No wonder you didn't get a high score.	難怪你沒有得到高分。
No wonder you can't understand the lesson.	難怪你聽不懂那門課。
No wonder you can't concentrate.	難怪你無法集中注意力。
No wonder you're flunking.	難怪你會不及格。
No wonder he doesn't understand you.	難怪他聽不懂你在說什麼。

Dialogue

T You did a terrible job on the test.	你這次考試考得很糟。
S I didn't study for it.	我沒有念書。
T **No wonder** you didn't get a high score.	難怪你沒有得到高分。
S I'll do better next time.	下次我會努力的。

Dialogue

T Have you met the new foreign student?	你見過新來的外國學生嗎？
S I tried to speak English to him, but he doesn't understand me.	我試著用英語和他交談，但他不懂我說的話。
T **No wonder** he doesn't understand you. He's from Germany!	難怪他聽不懂你在說什麼，他來自德國！
S Oh! I feel so silly!	哦！我覺得自己好蠢！

The worst part is... 最糟糕的是～

在一一列出對方這段期間犯過了哪些錯誤之後,接著指出在這些錯誤中哪個部分是最糟糕的,在這種情況下可以使用的句型就是「The worst part is...」。請記住這個句型中的「The worst part is」是一個主詞,所以要從 is 處斷開,稍微停頓一下再繼續說下去。

The worst part is we have a test tomorrow, too.	最糟糕的是我們明天還要考試。
The worst part is you didn't even try.	最糟糕的是你根本沒有嘗試過。
The worst part is you didn't do your homework, too.	最糟糕的是你也沒寫作業。
The worst part is we still have to do this exercise.	最糟糕的是我們還得做這練習題。

Dialogue

T Your essays have many mistakes. You need to write them again.	你的作文錯誤百出,必須再寫一次。
S1 Oh no! This is terrible.	哦不!我有大麻煩了。
S2 I know.	我知道。
S1 **The worst part is** we have a test tomorrow, too!	最糟糕的是我們明天還要考試。

Dialogue

T Andy, you're late again. I'm going to take 5 points off of your grade.	Andy,你又遲到了,我要扣你 5 分。
S I'm sorry, sir.	對不起,老師。
T **The worst part is** you didn't do your homework, too.	最糟糕的是你也沒寫作業。
S I'm sorry.	對不起。

📖 責備

There's no excuse for...
沒有任何理由～／～是沒有任何藉口的。

當您想嚴厲斥責某人的錯誤時，可以使用這個表達句型。可以在 for 後面接續名詞或動名詞來指出不能容忍哪一種行為或事件。如果想表達「沒有理由不做～」，請在 -ing 之前加上 not。

There's no excuse for this behavior.	對於這種行為是沒有任何藉口的。
There's no excuse for not being prepared.	沒有理由不做好準備。
There's no excuse for not handing in your homework on time.	沒有理由不按時交作業。
There's no excuse for such low scores.	如此低的分數是沒有任何藉口的。

Dialogue

T: It's time to turn in your homework.	交作業的時間到了。
S: I don't have mine.	我沒有帶作業。
T: Why not?	為什麼沒有呢？
S: I left it at the library*!	我把它遺忘在圖書館了！
T: **There's no excuse for** not handing in your homework on time.	沒有理由不按時交作業。

Dialogue

T: You all did very poorly on your tests.	你們這次考試都考得很差。
S: It was too hard!	太難了！
T: **There's no excuse for** such low scores.	如此低的分數是沒有任何藉口的。
S: I guess we'll have to study harder next time.	下次我們都得更努力學習。

*一起來認識一些跟 library（圖書館）有關的表達用語吧！在圖書館借書（check out）時使用的圖書館借書證稱作 library card，借閱的圖書逾期時則使用「overdue」一詞。除此之外，可透過電腦使用的電子圖書清單稱作 OPAC（Online Public Access Catalog）。

I told you guys to... 我告訴過你們～了。

當您因為有事得稍微離開去一趟辦公室，回來時卻發現學生吵吵鬧鬧、沒有在寫作業時，或者當您要學生整理教室，半小時後回來發現還是老樣子時，又或者當學生找了個藉口，狡辯說不知道作業今天要交，而您想嚴厲斥責對方時，都很適合使用這個表達句型。此句型意味著「我告訴過你們～」，to 的後面要接續您要他們做的事情的原形動詞。

I told you guys to study.	我告訴過你們要好好唸書了。
I told you guys to stop cheating.	我告訴過你們不要作弊了。
I told you guys to be quiet.	我告訴過你們要安靜了。
I told you guys to stop using your dictionaries so much.	我告訴過你們不要老查字典了。
I told you guys to speak English.	我告訴過你們要說英語了。

Dialogue

S This test looks very difficult.	這次考試看起來非常難。
T **I told you guys to** study.	我告訴過你們要好好念書了。
S We did, but maybe not enough.	我們念了，但似乎還是不夠。
T I warned you!	我警告過你了！

Dialogue

T **I told you guys to** be quiet.	我告訴過你們要安靜了。
S We're sorry!	對不起！
T It's okay. Just try to be better.	沒關係，只要再努力一點。
S Yep!	我們會的！

📖 給予評論

I don't like the way... 我不喜歡～的方式。

當您想責罵一個在課堂上態度不佳、言行有誤的學生，或是當您想表達自己的不滿時，很適合使用這個表達句型。這裡的 the way 指的是「做某事的方式」，後面接續以 the way 作為先行詞的關係代名詞 that 子句。

I don't like the way you wrote this sentence.	我不喜歡你這個句子的寫法。
I don't like the way you pronounced that word.	我不喜歡你這個字的發音。
I don't like the way things are going.	我不滿意事情的進展。
I don't like the way you handled this.	我不喜歡你處理這件事的方式。
I don't like the way you gossip.	我不喜歡聽到你說別人的閒話。

Dialogue

- Ⓢ What do you think of my essay? — 你覺得我的文章怎麼樣？
- Ⓣ **I don't like the way** you wrote this sentence. — 我不喜歡你這個句子的寫法。
- Ⓢ What's wrong with it? — 有什麼問題嗎？
- Ⓣ I think you should change this word. — 我覺得這個詞應該改一下。

Dialogue

- Ⓢ We kicked Mark off the team*. — 我們把 Mark 踢出團隊了。
- Ⓣ What? Why? — 什麼？為什麼？
- Ⓢ He was acting like a jerk. — 他一直在耍白癡。
- Ⓣ **I don't like the way** you handled this. — 我不喜歡你處理這件事的方式。

*把 Mark 踢出團隊了的英文表達方式為「We kicked Mark off the team.」，這裡的 kick... off 可替換成 force ... to leave 或 make ... quit。

That's not exactly... 那不完全是～

exactly 是語意為「準確地、正好地、完全」的副詞，所以「That's not exactly...」意味著「不完全是這樣」。exactly 搭配 not 表示部分否定，語意為「不完全是如此」。exactly 在句中可以作為修飾語，也可以在對話中代替 yes，此時的語意是「正是如此」，當有人說「Not exactly!」時，意味著「不一定是那樣的!」。

That's not exactly correct.	這麼說不完全正確。
That's not exactly the right answer.	不完全是正確答案。
That's not exactly what we are going to cover today.	那不完全是我們今天要討論的內容。
That's not exactly my understanding.	那不完全是我所理解的。
That's not exactly the way I'd do it.	那不完全是我的作法。

Dialogue

Ⓢ Christopher Columbus discovered America, right?	哥倫布發現了美洲，對嗎？
Ⓣ **That's not exactly** correct.	這麼說不完全正確。
Ⓢ Who was it, then?	那是誰呢？
Ⓣ Some say it was Amerigo Vespucci.	有人說是 Amerigo Vespucci。

Dialogue

Ⓣ Who can tell me what "patient" means?	誰能告訴我「patient」是什麼意思？
Ⓢ Does it mean "invalid?"	是 invalid 嗎？
Ⓣ Yes, that's one meaning, but **that's not exactly** the right answer.	沒錯，這是其中一個意思，但不完全是正確答案。。
Ⓢ Oh, I know. It also means "uncomplaining."	哦，我知道了。也有 uncomplaining 的意思。

221

Don't underestimate... 不要低估／小看～

estimate 的語意是「測量、評估」，under 則是語意為「低於、不足」等的前綴，所以 underestimate 的語意是「低估」，其反義詞是加上具有 too much 之意的前綴 -over 的 overestimate，語意為「高估」。請一併記住語意為「不要高估」的句型為「Don't overestimate...」。

Don't underestimate the benefits of studying.	不要低估學習的好處。
Don't underestimate your capabilities.	不要低估自己的能力。
Don't underestimate the difficulty of this subject.	不要低估這個科目的難度。
Don't underestimate your teacher.	不要小看你的老師。
Don't underestimate class attendance.	不要低估課堂出勤分數。

Dialogue

S You're my favorite teacher.	你是我最喜歡的老師。
T Why is that?	為什麼呢？
S Because your assignments are so easy.	因為你出的作業很簡單。
T **Don't underestimate** your teacher.	不要小看你的老師。

Dialogue

S Will I pass if I get a high score on the next test?	如果下次考試得高分，我就能通過嗎？
T **Don't underestimate** class attendance.	不要低估課堂出席分數。
S What do you mean?	是什麼意思呢？
T You need to come to class every day.	你必須每天都來上課。

UNIT 09 學生在課堂中的常用句

📖 心情的表達

I can't wait... 我迫不及待要～了。／我等不及要～了。

當殷切地期待某件事時，可以使用的句型正是「**I can't wait...**」。反之，can wait 意味著「可以等待」。**I can't wait** 後面可接續「介系詞+名詞」或「to+原形動詞」。除此之外，也可採用 until 後面接續表達時間的名詞或子句來表達「我不能等到～」。

I can't wait to see my final grade.	我等不及要看我的期末成績了。
I can't wait for the weekend.	我迫不及待週末到來。
I can't wait until we're finished with this exercise.	我迫不及待地想完成這道練習題。
I can't wait to go on the trip.	我等不及要去旅行了。
I can't wait to take the test.	我等不及要參加考試了。

Dialogue

🅣 Now let's do number 17.	現在我們來做第 17 題。
🅢1 **I can't wait** until we're finished with this exercise.	我迫不及待地想完成這道練習題。
🅢2 I know. It's so boring.	我也是，太無聊了。
🅣 You'll never finish by complaining!	光抱怨是無法寫完的！

Dialogue

🅣 Tomorrow's the big exam!	明天有一場非常重要的考試！
🅢1 **I can't wait** to take the test.	我等不及要參加考試了。
🅢2 Are you crazy?	你瘋了嗎？
🅢1 No. I'm just prepared!	沒呀，我已經準備好了！

I'm so glad... 我很高興～

最常聽到的句子就是「**I'm so glad** to meet you.（很高興認識你）」，只要將 meet you 替換成讓你覺得開心之人事物就行了。glad 後面接續 that 子句或 to 不定詞。

I'm so glad you were my teacher.	我很高興您是我的老師。
I'm so glad you made a high score.	我很高興你取得了高分。
I'm so glad I passed.	我很高興我通過了。
I'm so glad we're finished.	我很高興我們完成了。
I'm so glad school is out.	我很高興學校放假了。

Dialogue

T Today is the last day of class.	今天是最後一堂課。
S **I'm so glad** you were my teacher.	我很高興你是我的老師。
T That's very nice of you to say.	謝謝你這麼說。
S You have been very patient and kind.	您非常有耐心又友善。
T Thank you very much.	非常感謝。

Dialogue

S1 That was one tough exam.	這考試真的超難。
S2 I'll say. **I'm so glad** I passed.	我也正想這麼說。很高興我通過了。
S1 Oh, are the grades out already?	哦，成績出來了嗎？
S2 Yes, Mrs. Taylor posted* them today.	嗯，Taylor 老師今天已經公布成績了。

*post 的語意為「公布、發布」或「通知」，是指透過佈告欄來公布成績、公告事項等情況時會使用的單字。想表達「公布在〜」時，請使用介系詞 on。舉例來說，「post a notice on the board」的語意為「在佈告欄發布通知」。

I can't believe... 真不敢相信～

當您聽到令人難以置信的事情時，可以說「真不敢相信」來表達驚訝的心情。這個句型既可以用於不可思議的樂事，也可以用於荒誕的事情。另外要注意的是，當 can 與 see、hear、feel、smell、taste、understand 和 believe 等感官動詞搭配時，can 的語意會弱化，所以 I can't believe 的語意幾乎等同於 I don't believe。

I can't believe how difficult this grammar is.	真不敢相信這個文法會這麼難。
I can't believe you forgot your homework.	真不敢相信你忘了帶作業。
I can't believe what a difficult test this is.	真不敢相信考試會這麼難。
I can't believe I made such a high score.	真不敢相信我得到這麼高的分數。
I can't believe I got an A.	真不敢相信我得到了A。

Dialogue

- S: **I can't believe** how difficult this grammar is. 真不敢相信這個文法會這麼難。
- T: It will get easier if we practice a lot. 多練習幾遍就會變容易的。
- S: I don't think it will ever be easy. 我覺得這永遠不會變容易。
- T: Don't be so negative! 別這麼消極！

Dialogue

- T: Here is your test score. 這是你的考試成績。
- S: **I can't believe** I made such a high score. 真不敢相信我得到這麼高的分數。
- T: You must have studied very hard. 你肯定很用功。
- S: Well, I did my best. 嗯，我盡全力了。

There are so many... ～真的很多。

There are 的語意是「有」，so 的語意為「真的、非常」，用來強調後面的 many。many 後面接名詞，但 many 只修飾可數名詞，所以使用時要注意其後方不能接續如 information 這類的不可數名詞。

There are so many words to memorize!	要背的單詞真的很多！
There are so many grammar rules to learn!	有很多文法規則要學！
There are so many chapters to study.	要念的章節真的很多。
There are so many students in here.	這裡的學生真的很多。
There are so many contestants this year.	今年的參賽者真的很多。

Dialogue

S English is difficult.	英文太難了。
T Why do you say that?	為什麼這麼說？
S **There are so many** grammar rules to learn!	有很多文法規則要學！
T It's not that difficult. It just takes time.	沒那麼難，只是需要一些時間。

Dialogue

T How are the academic contests going?	學術競賽進行得怎麼樣了？
S Very well. A little too well, I think.	很好，我覺得好得有點過頭了。
T What do you mean?	這是什麼意思？
S **There are so many** contestants this year.	今年參賽者實在很多。

📖 表達想法

Don't you think...? 你不覺得～嗎？／你不認為～嗎？

當您假設對方的想法與您相同，並想開口確認時，就可以使用這個表達句型，主要用在期望得到肯定回答並尋求認同的情況下。

Don't you think the homework is difficult?	你不覺得作業很難嗎？
Don't you think it's time to go?	你不覺得是時候該走了嗎？
Don't you think you should get a tutor?	你不覺得你應該找個家教嗎？
Don't you think you should study a little more?	你不覺得你需要再多唸一下書嗎？
Don't you think you'll be able to answer the question?	你不認為你能回答這個問題嗎？

Dialogue

T: Don't forget to finish your homework.	別忘了完成你們的作業。
S1: No problem.	沒問題。
S2: **Don't you think** the homework is difficult?	你不覺得作業很難嗎？
S1: No. It's not so bad.	不會，好像沒那麼難。

Dialogue

S: I'm ready to take a break.	我準備稍微休息一下。
T: **Don't you think** you should study a little more?	你不覺得自己需要再多唸點書嗎？
S: I've been studying for an hour!	我已經唸了一個小時了！
T: Well, learning English takes a lot of work.	噢，學習英語需要付出很多努力。

It's better for me to... 我最好還是～

P3_175

better 的語意是「更好」，因為後面加了 for me，所以語意變成了「我最好還是～」、「～對我來說比較好」。這是當您想表達自己偏好的物品或想法時，可以使用的表達句型。

It's better for me to take notes.	我最好還是作筆記。
It's better for me to sit up front.	我最好還是坐在前面。
It's better for me to focus on pronunciation.	我最好還是專注於發音。
It's better for me to listen twice.	我最好還是聽兩遍。
It's better for me to memorize my speech.	我最好還是記住我的演講稿。

Dialogue

S1 You take a lot of notes in class.	你在課堂上寫了很多筆記。
S2 I don't want to miss anything important.	我不想錯過任何重要的事情。
S1 Why don't you use a tape recorder?	為什麼不使用錄音機呢？
S2 It's better for me to take notes.	我最好還是作筆記。

Dialogue

S1 Kevin, sit back here with me.	Kevin，和我一起坐在後面。
S2 It's better for me to sit up front.	我最好還是坐在前面。
S1 Why is that?	為什麼呢？
S2 I can see the blackboard better.	我可以更清楚地看到黑板。

I didn't mean to... 我不是故意～的。

P3_176

當對方可能會誤解您的時候，可以利用這個句型來表達您真正的意思。「I didn't mean it.」意味「我不是故意的」。相反地，「I mean it.」則意味著「我是認真的」。請別忘了 to 後面要接續原形動詞。

I didn't mean to confuse you.	我不是故意讓你感到混淆的。
I didn't mean to cause a problem.	我不是故意要製造麻煩的。
I didn't mean to take up all of the time.	我不是故意佔用你所有時間的。
I didn't mean to bother you.	我不是故意打擾你的。
I didn't mean to do this.	我不是故意的。

Dialogue

🇹 Robert, you forgot to put your name on your homework.	Robert，你忘了在作業上寫下你的名字。
🇸 **I didn't mean to** cause a problem.	我不是故意要製造麻煩。
🇹 It's okay. I just want to give you credit.	沒關係，我只是想要表揚你。
🇸 It won't happen again.	這種事下次不會再發生的。

Dialogue

S1 What are you going to do this weekend?	這個週末你打算做什麼？
S2 Hush! I'm trying to concentrate.	噓！我正在努力集中注意力。
S1 I'm sorry. **I didn't mean to** bother you.	抱歉，我不是故意打擾你的。
S2 That's okay. This exercise is just a little difficult.	沒關係，這個練習題有點難。

I don't mind... 我不介意～

這個句型跟「I don't care...（我不在乎）」有著細微差別，可用來回覆如「Would you mind if...?」這類問句。**I don't mind** 後面接續的 if 子句是語意為「是否～」的條件子句。mind 後面接動名詞作為受詞，所以接在 mind 後方的動詞一定要採 -ing 形式。

I don't mind if you borrow my dictionary.	我不介意你借用我的字典。
I don't mind staying later.	我不介意待到很晚。
I don't mind volunteering.	我不介意當志工。
I don't mind sitting at the back.	我不介意坐在後面。
I don't mind sharing.	我不介意分享。

Dialogue

S1: Let's do the assignment together. 　　　我們一起做作業吧。
S2: Okay. I can't understand the first word. 　好的，我不懂第一個單字。
S1: **I don't mind** if you borrow my dictionary. 　我不介意你借用我的字典。
S2: Oh, thanks. I left mine at home. 　　　噢，謝謝，我的字典放在家裡。

Dialogue

T: Can some of you stay late tonight? 　今晚你們誰可以待到很晚？
S: **I don't mind** staying later. 　我不介意待到很晚。
T: Great. We need to put away the instruments. 　太好了，我們需要把這些用具收好。
S: I'm happy to help. 　我很樂意幫忙。

That's all I... 這就是我所～的。

當對方不斷催促著你,說著像是「告訴我你所知道的一切」時,你就可用「That's all I heard.(我所聽到的就這些了)」之類的話來打斷對方。請別忘了,That's all 後面要接續子句。

That's all* I took.	這就是我所拿的了。
That's all I said.	這就是我所說的了。
That's all I can do.	這就是我所能做的了。
That's all I want.	這就是我所想要的。
That's all I heard.	這就是我所聽到的。

*「That's all.」跟「That's it.」的語意都是「～就是一切」,但「That's it.」通常用來表示「就是這樣」,所以兩者稍有不同。

Dialogue

S1 Did someone take my pencils?	有人拿走我的鉛筆嗎?
S2 I took one.	我拿了一枝。
S1 But they're all missing.	但我這邊全都不見了。
S2 **That's all** I took.	這是我所拿的了。

Dialogue

S1 Why is Ginny so angry?	Ginny為什麼那麼生氣?
S2 I told her we were leaving early.	我告訴她我們提早離開。
S1 And that's what upset her?	這就是讓她惱火的原因嗎?
S2 **That's all** I said.	我就說了這麼多。

I didn't get... 我沒（獲得）～

當您沒有收到老師發的講義，或是沒有聽懂老師的講解時，都可以使用這個表達句型。用來表達「我沒有收到～」時，句中 get 解釋為「收到、獲得」；而用來表達「我沒聽懂～」時，句中 get 的意思為「理解（understand）、聽懂」。舉例來說，「I didn't get your name.」的語意是「我沒有聽到您的名字。」。

I didn't get a lot of sleep last night.	我昨晚沒有睡很久。
I didn't get a chance to speak.	我沒有機會說話。
I didn't get it right.	我沒有答對。
I didn't get a very high score.	我沒有取得高分。
I didn't get what you said.	我沒聽懂你說的話。

Dialogue

🆃 Why are you making so many mistakes today?	你今天為什麼犯這麼多錯？
🆂 **I didn't get** a lot of sleep last night.	我昨晚沒有睡很久。
🆃 You should try to get more rest.	你應該多休息。
🆂 I will tonight.	我今晚會的。

Dialogue

🆃 How do you feel about your test?	你對你的考試有何感想？
🆂 **I didn't get** a very high score.	我沒有取得高分。
🆃 Why not?	為什麼呢？
🆂 I guess I didn't study enough.	我想是我念得還不夠。

📖 準備要做的事

I'm planning to... 我打算～

這個表達句型的語意為「我打算…」，用來談論尚未付諸實踐但已經想好的計畫。請注意 to 後面要接續原形動詞。

I'm planning to study all night.	我打算熬夜念書。
I'm planning to give you a big homework assignment tomorrow.	我打算明天給大家一份大作業。
I'm planning to go to the library.	我打算去圖書館。
I'm planning to play soccer with my friends.	我打算跟朋友一起踢足球。
I'm planning to write down the sentences.	我打算把這些句子寫下來。

Dialogue

🇹 The test is tomorrow.	明天就要考試了。
🇸1 Oh no! How are we going to pass?	哦不！我們要怎樣才能及格呢？
🇸2 **I'm planning to** study all night.	我打算熬夜念書。
🇸1 I guess I will, too.	我應該也會。

Dialogue

🇹 What are you going to do this evening?	今晚打算做什麼？
🇸 **I'm planning to** play soccer with my friends.	我打算和朋友一起踢足球。
🇹 Well, don't forget to do your homework.	噢，別忘了做作業。
🇸 Oh. Thanks for reminding me.	對喔，謝謝您的提醒。

I was just going to... 我（剛剛）正打算要～

be going to... 的語意是「打算做～」。這是一個加了語意為「剛剛、現在」的 just 的表達句型，當老師詢問「某某事做了嗎」時，學生們最常見的回答是「我正要這麼做」，此時就可以使用這個句型，to 後面接續原形動詞，而 be about to 是類似的表達句型。

I was just going to apologize for my behavior.	我（剛剛）正打算要為我的行為道歉。
I was just going to ask a question.	我（剛剛）正打算要問問題。
I was just going to look up this word.	我（剛剛）正打算要查這個字。
I was just going to take out my pencil.	我（剛剛）正打算要拿出鉛筆。
I was just going to hand it in.	我（剛剛）正打算要把它交出去。

Dialogue

T Christopher, why are you playing with your backpack?	Christopher，為什麼在玩你的背包？
S **I was just going to** take out my pencil.	我剛正打算要拿出鉛筆。
T Well, hurry up and pay attention.	噢，那就趕快拿出來，專心一點。
S I'm sorry, sir.	對不起，老師。

Dialogue

T Mary, where's your homework?	Mary，妳的作業呢？
S **I was just going to** hand it in.	我剛正想要把它交出去。
T Okay. Thank you.	好的，謝謝。
S It sure was hard!	作業真的很難！

建議

We'd better... 我們最好～

We'd better 是「We had better」的縮寫，是給予建議的表達，語意為「這樣做會更好～」。但當 had better 的主詞不是 I 或 We 的情況下，而是 you 時聽起來會像是忠告、命令，有時甚至像是威脅，所以最好不要對長輩或上司使用這個句型。

We'd better* memorize these words.	我們最好記住這些單字。
We'd better do the homework.	我們最好寫作業。
We'd better think of another idea.	我們最好再想想其它點子。
We'd better study hard if we want to make a good grade.	如果想取得好成績，我們最好努力學習。
We'd better get there early.	我們最好早點去那裡。

*「We'd better...」在口語時可省略 had，例如「We better go now.」。主詞是第二人稱時，had也可省略。此外，可以用 best 取代 better，「had best...」的語意一樣是「最好～」。

Dialogue

- T：Tomorrow we will have a vocabulary quiz. 　明天我們將進行單字測驗。
- S：**We'd better** memorize these words. 　我們最好記住這些單字。
- T：That's a good idea. 　好主意。
- S：There are so many of them! 　單字真的超多！

Dialogue

- T：The test will be worth half of your final grade. 　這測驗佔你們期末成績的 50%。
- S：**We'd better** study hard if we want to make a good grade. 　如果想取得好成績，我們最好努力學習。
- T：That's right. 　沒錯。
- S：I'm going straight to the library. 　我馬上去圖書館。

How about...? ～如何？

當您想要詢問對方意圖時,「What about...?」或「What do you think about...?」都是非常好用的表達句型。在學校裡有很多事情都需要徵求彼此的意見,所以掌握這類表達非常重要。尤其是在討論課堂上,都需要收集「我們的」想法,而不是「我的」想法。

How about Tuesday?	星期二如何?
How about you?	你呢?
How about this one?	這個如何?
How about writing it down?	寫下來如何?
How about another try?	再試一次如何?

Dialogue

S1 I'm really nervous about tomorrow's test. **How about** you?	關於明天的考試我很緊張,你呢?
S2 I'm not nervous.	我不緊張。
S1 Why not?	為什麼?
S2 Because I'm prepared!	因為我已經準備好了!

Dialogue

S1 I can't remember the past tense of 'go.'	我不記得「go」的過去式。
S2 It's 'went.'	是 went。
S1 Oh, that's right. Why can't I ever remember?	喔,對哦,我怎麼就是記不起來呢?
S2 **How about** another try?	再試一次如何?

📖 必須

I had no choice but... 我別無選擇，只能～／我不得不～

「have no choice but to＋原形動詞」的語意是「不得不做～」，描述除了（but～）某某事物之外別無選擇。當有人問您「為什麼這樣做？」時，您可以用這個句型來回應。類似的表達句型有「I can't help＋動名詞」和「I cannot but＋原形動詞」。

I had no choice but to do it.	我別無選擇，只能這麼做。
I had no choice but to look at my notes.	我別無選擇，只能看我的小抄。
I had no choice but to answer the question.	我別無選擇，只能回答這個問題。
I had no choice but to leave my homework at home.	我別無選擇，只能把作業留在家裡。
I had no choice but to come to class late.	我別無選擇，上課只能遲到了。

Dialogue

- **S1** Didn't you memorize your speech? 　你沒記住你的演講稿嗎？
- **S2** **I had no choice but** to look at my notes. 　我別無選擇，只能看我的小抄。
- **S1** Why? 　為什麼？
- **S2** I forgot everything that I was going to say. 　我把我要說的內容忘得一乾二淨。

Dialogue

- **T** Where is your assignment, Jeffery? 　Jeffery，你的作業在哪裡？
- **S** **I had no choice but** to leave my homework at home. 　我別無選擇，只能把作業留在家裡。
- **T** Why? 　為什麼？
- **S** I was going to miss the bus! 　我差點錯過公車！

We all need to... 我們都需要～

need to 的語意是「需要做～」或「必須得做～」。相反地,「不需要做～」可以用「don't need to」或「need not to」來表達,但 don't need to 更為常用。在跟英文母語人士對話時,經常會聽到諸如「We all...」或「you all...」之類的表達方式,此時的 all 是為了進一步強調所有人。

We all need to* study a little harder.	我們都需要更努力地學習。
We all need to clear off our desks for the test.	我們都需要清空桌面來進行考試。
We all need to be more careful.	我們都需要更加小心。
We all need to find a partner for this exercise.	我們都需要找一位夥伴來進行這個練習。
We all need to be quiet and listen.	我們都需要安靜傾聽。

*當老師對學生使用這個句型時,蘊含命令之意。當學生之間使用這個句型時,則給人一種必須去做的強烈建議。

Dialogue

T I wasn't very happy with the scores on the test.	我對你們的考試成績不太滿意。
S1 What should we do to improve?	我們要怎麼做才能提高成績呢?
S2 We all need to study a little harder.	我們都需要更努力地學習。
T That's a good idea.	好主意。

Dialogue

T You guys forgot to answer the last question.	你們忘記回答最後一個問題了。
S We all need to be more careful.	我們都需要更加小心。
T That's right. Every question is worth 10 points.	沒錯,每題 10 分。
S That's a lot!	這麼多啊!

📖 堅決與肯定

I won't... 我不會～

won't 是 will not 的縮寫。will 通常作為表示未來的助動詞，語意為「將做～」，但這裡與 I 連用，表示主詞的意願，語意為「我打算做～」。當老師責罵了學生之後，學生想表達：「我再也不會這麼做了」時，可以使用這個表達句型。除此之外，也能用來表明你做某件事的決心。

I won't do it again.	我不會再那樣做了。
I won't make that mistake again.	我不會再犯這樣的錯了。
I won't forget.	我不會忘記。
I won't fail.	我不會失敗。
I won't give up.	我不會放棄。

Dialogue

S What's wrong with my sentence?	我這句子有什麼問題嗎？
T You forgot to finish with a period.	你忘了加句號。
S **I won't** make that mistake again.	我不會再犯這樣的錯了。
T I hope not.	那就對了。

Dialogue

S1 Don't forget to bring your notebook tomorrow.	明天別忘了帶筆記本。
S2 Don't worry. **I won't** forget.	別擔心，我不會忘記。
S1 You'd better not. It's very important.	最好不要，這很重要。
S2 Okay, okay!	知道了啦！

I'm absolutely... 我絕對～／我真的～／我十分～

當被問及「Are you sure?（你確定嗎？）」時，可以回答「當然！」。除此之外，absolutely 也可用來修飾後面的形容詞，會帶有「真的」、「絕對」語意以加重語氣。這個句型意味著百分之百確信，所以不能隨便亂用。

I'm absolutely sure.	我當然很確定。
I'm absolutely confused.	我真的很困惑。
I'm absolutely certain.	我百分百確定。
I'm absolutely right.	我絕對是對的。
I'm absolutely pleased.	我真的很高興。

Dialogue

S1 What's the comparative form of 'happy'?	「happy」的比較級是什麼？
S2 It's 'happier.'	「happier」。
S1 Are you sure?	你確定嗎？
S2 I'm absolutely sure.	我百分百確定。

Dialogue

S1 You've made a mistake in this sentence.	你在這句犯了一個錯誤。
S2 No, I haven't. **I'm absolutely** right.	不，我沒犯錯，我絕對是對的。
S1 I'm afraid you're not. See? The verb is wrong.	恐怕不是喔，看到了吧？動詞錯了。
S2 Oh, I guess you're right. Sorry.	哦，我想你是對的，抱歉。

請求協助

Can you check...? 你能檢查一下～嗎？／你能看一下～嗎？

check 的語意是「確認、檢查」，這是當學生想請老師檢查他們的作業時可以使用的表達句型。當學生想問老師自己做的事是對還是錯時，請他們自信地舉手說「**Can you check** my work?」。

Can you check my work?	你能檢查一下我的作業嗎？
Can you check my essay?	你能看一下我的作文嗎？
Can you check this sentence?	你能看一下這個句子嗎？
Can you check the time?	你能告訴我現在幾點了嗎？
Can you check your dictionary?	你能查你的字典嗎？

Dialogue

S **Can you check** this sentence?	您能看一下這個句子嗎？
T Let me see. There's one mistake.	讓我瞧瞧，有一個地方錯了。
S What's wrong?	怎麼了？
T The verb is in the wrong place.	動詞放錯位置了。

Dialogue

S1 What does this word mean?	這個字是什麼意思？
S2 **Can you check** your dictionary?	你能查查你的字典嗎？
S1 Didn't you hear the teacher? No dictionaries are allowed!	你沒聽到老師說的嗎？不能用字典！
S2 Oh. I didn't know.	阿，我不知道嘛。

What is ... in English? ～用英語怎麼說？

當學生想表達一句話或某個單字，卻不知道如何用英語表達時，就可以使用這個表達句型。請把想詢問的中文用語放在 is 和 in 之間。舉例來說，當您想詢問「英語中的『字典』是什麼？」時，可以說「What is "字典" in English?」。相反地，當想問某個英文單字的中文是什麼時，就要改說「What is... in Chinese?」或「What is the meaning of this word?」。

What is this **in English**?	這個用英文怎麼說？
What is the most difficult word **in English**?	英文中最難的單字是什麼？
What is the way to say this **in English**?	這個用英文怎麼說？
What is your favorite word **in English**?	你最喜歡的英文單字是什麼？
What is that **in English**?	那個用英文怎麼說？

Dialogue

S1: What's the most difficult word **in English**?	英文中最難的單字是什麼？
S2: I think 'get' is very hard.	我覺得動詞「get」很難。
S1: Why? That's an easy word.	為什麼？這是一個簡單的字呀。
S2: But it means a thousand different things!	但它有許多不同的意義！

Dialogue

S1: **What is** that **in English**?	那個用英文怎麼說？
S2: This? It's an 'eraser.'	這個嗎？是 eraser。
S1: No, not the eraser, that other thing.	不，不是橡皮擦，是另一個。
S2: Oh. This is a 'pencil sharpener.'	哦，這個叫 pencil sharpener。

I'm looking for... 我正在找～

look for 是語意為「找～」的動詞片語，用於尋找特定的人事物，例如尋找弄丟的書。不過，請注意當您表達「在字典中查找單字」時，應該使用「look up」，而非「look for」。

I'm looking for a topic to write about.	我正在尋找寫作的主題。
I'm looking for the office.	我正在找辦公室。
I'm looking for my textbook.	我正在找我的課本。
I'm looking for Janice.	我在找 Janice。
I'm looking for a study partner.	我正在找一起學習的夥伴。

Dialogue

S1 **I'm looking for** a topic to write about.	我正在尋找寫作的主題。
S2 Have you tried looking in the newspaper?	你從報紙上找過了嗎？
S1 That sounds like a good idea.	這聽起來是個好主意。
S2 Current events can give us good topics.	時事會是很好的主題。

Dialogue

S1 Can I help you?	需要我幫你嗎？
S2 **I'm looking for** the office.	我正在找辦公室。
S1 Go to the end of the hall and turn right.	走廊走到底，然後右轉。
S2 Thank you!	謝謝！

We're out of... 我們～沒了。／我們～用完了。

be out of... 的語意是「用完～、用光～」，這是一種可以廣泛應用於多種情況的表達句型，例如當學習用品用完了，當考試時間不夠，或腦袋一片空白的情況下，都可以使用這個表達句型。介系詞 of 後面要接續名詞。

We're out of glue.	我們的膠水用完了。
We're out of time.	我們沒時間了。
We're out of patience.	我們的耐心見底了。
We're out of energy.	我們沒力氣了。
We're out of ideas.	我們沒想法了。

Dialogue

S1 Oh, no! **We're out of** time!	天啊！我們沒時間了！
S2 Yes, we are. Are you finished?	對阿，你完成了嗎？
S1 No, I still have two more questions to answer.	我還有兩題要寫。
S2 Sorry. You'll have to work faster next time.	很遺憾，下次你要寫快一點。

Dialogue

S1 What do you want to talk about next?	接下來你想要聊什麼？
S2 **We're out of** ideas.	我們沒想法了。
S1 Why don't we talk about phrasal verbs?	我們為什麼不談談動詞片語呢？
S2 That sounds fun!	聽起來很有趣！

There's no way... 沒辦法～／不可能～

P3_192

no way 是「no」的強調用語，蘊含了 never 之意。所以當有人說「There's no way...」時，意味著「沒有辦法～」或「～絕對不可能」。此外，這個句型也可以用來抱怨不可能的事、表達絕望的感覺或尋求建議。

There's no way I'll finish in time.	我不可能及時完成。
There's no way I'll ever understand this.	我永遠無法理解這個。
There's no way it's that easy.	絕不可能會那麼簡單。

There's no way to check our answers. 沒有辦法確認答案。
There's no way to know if we're right or not. 沒有辦法知道我們是否正確。

Dialogue

- **T** You have 30 minutes to write your essay. 你有 30 分鐘寫作文。
- **S** **There's no way** I'll finish in time. 我不可能及時完成。
- **T** Just try to write quickly. 儘量寫快一點。
- **S** That's easy to say, but not to do! 說來容易，做起來很難啊！

Dialogue

- **S1** Do you remember how to make the past tense in English? 你還記得英語的過去式是如何構成的嗎？
- **S2** Just add '-ed' to the verb. 只要在動詞後面加上「-ed」就行了。
- **S1** **There's no way** it's that easy. 絕不可能會這麼簡單。
- **S2** Well, there are some irregular verbs, too. 也有不規則動詞。

P3_193

Have you got...? 你有～嗎？

這是想詢問對方是否有某某東西時可以使用的表達句型，語意同「Do you have...?」。have got 的用法和語意與 have 相似，在口語中也會省略 have，只使用 got。但是，請記住 have got 不能用於祈使句中。

Have you got an extra pen? 你還有另一支筆嗎？
Have you got a moment? 您能給我一點時間嗎？
Have you got fifteen minutes? 你有 15 分鐘嗎？
Have you got some paper? 你有紙嗎？
Have you got the assignment? 你作業帶了嗎？

Dialogue

S1 We have to write a few sentences. 　　我們需要寫幾個句子。
S2 **Have you got** an extra pen? 　　你還有另一支筆嗎？
S1 Sure. Here you go. 　　當然，拿去吧。
S2 Thanks a lot! 　　感謝！

Dialogue

S Hi, Mr. Carter. 　　嗨，Carter 老師。
T Hi, Jake. 　　嗨，Jake。
S **Have you got** a moment? 　　您能給我一點時間嗎？
T Sure. What's up*? 　　當然，怎麼了嗎？

*在對話中，「What's up?」的語意是「發生了什麼事？」。在美國，「What's up?」通常作為問候語，此時語意跟「How are you?」和「How are you do?」相似。

All I need is... 我只要～就好。／我所需要的是～。

P3_194

這是用來表達一旦擁有了某樣東西，就不再需要其它東西的句型。這句型可以用來表達一種迫切感，或是僅有一個需求的簡單願望。All I need is 後面可接續一個名詞片語（即 be 動詞 is 的補語），名詞後面可再接 to 不定詞。

All I need is 5 more minutes. 　　再給我 5 分鐘就好。
All I need is 80 points. 　　我只要 80 分就好。
All I need is a chance to speak. 　　我只要有發言機會就好。
All I need is a look at my dictionary*. 　　我只要看一下字典就好。
All I need is time to think. 　　再給我一些時間思考。

*查字典的英文說法是「look up a dictionary」或「consult a dictionary」。

Dialogue

- T: All right, close your books.　　好，大家闔上書本。
- S: But I'm not finished!　　但我還沒念完！
- T: I'm sorry. Time is up.　　很遺憾，時間到了。
- S: **All I need is** 5 more minutes!　　再給我 5 分鐘就好。

Dialogue

- T: Please answer the question.　　請回答問題。
- S: Um...　　嗯…
- T: Now, please.　　趕快回答。
- S: **All I need is** time to think.　　再給我一些時間思考。

📖 感謝

Thank you for... 謝謝你～

眾所周知，Thank you...的語意是「謝謝」，這個句型是由「I would like to thank you」省略其中的「I would like to」而成。這是向老師或同學表達謝意時可以使用的表達句型，for 後面接續名詞或動名詞。

Thank you for your help.	謝謝你的幫忙。
Thank you for staying.	謝謝你的陪伴。
Thank you for keeping this confidential.	謝謝你幫我保守祕密。
Thank you for explaining it to me.	謝謝你向我解釋。
Thank you for being there.	謝謝你的到來。

P3_195

Dialogue

S1 I don't understand how to do this homework. 我不知道該怎麼做這個作業。
S2 Just write 5 sentences in the past tense. 寫 5 個過去式的句子。
S1 Oh, I see. **Thank you for** your help. 哦，我明白了，謝謝你的幫忙。
S2 No problem. 不客氣。

Dialogue

S1 I really appreciated your coming to my speech. 非常感謝您來參加我的演講。
S2 No problem. You gave a great speech. 不客氣，你的演講很精采。
S1 **Thank you for** being there. 謝謝你的到來。
S2 I wouldn't have missed it. 我當然不能錯過啦。

📖 同儕合作

Let me see if... 讓我看看是否～

see if 的語意是「看看是否～」，所以 Let me see if... 的語意是「讓我看看是否～」。當有學生請你幫忙或問你問題時，可以用這個句型來表達你無法立刻回答，需要考慮一下。

Let me see if it's correct.	讓我看看這是否正確。
Let me see if I can find it.	讓我看看能否找到。
Let me see if I can understand it.	讓我看看我能否理解。
Let me see if you did it right.	讓我看看你是否做對了。
Let me see if I can help.	讓我看看是否幫得上忙。

P3_196

Dialogue

S1 I wrote a sentence, but I'm not sure about it.　　我寫了一個句子，但不太確定對不對。
S2 **Let me see if** it's correct.　　讓我看看是否正確。
S1 What do you think?　　你覺得怎麼樣？
S2 I'm not sure. Let's ask the teacher.　　我也不確定，我們去問問老師吧。

Dialogue

S1 I can't understand this word.　　我無法理解這個詞。
S2 **Let me see if** I can help.　　讓我看看是否幫得上忙。
S1 Thanks!　　謝謝。
S2 No problem.　　不客氣。

📖 提出問題

P3_197

I don't understand why... 我不明白為何～

當您想指出或抱怨某些事情荒謬或不合理時，就可以使用這個表達句型。像是「我不明白」可以簡單地說「I don't understand.」，但使用「I don't understand why＋子句」可更具體地指出不明白之處。

I don't understand why we can't use our dictionaries.	我不明白我們為何不能使用字典。
I don't understand why this homework was so difficult.	我不懂這個作業為何會這麼難。
I don't understand why we have to do this exercise.	我不明白我們為何必須做這個練習題。
I don't understand why I'm doing so badly.	我不明白我為何做得那麼差。

> **Dialogue**

T It's time to start the exercise. 是時候開始做練習題了。
S **I don't understand why** we can't use our dictionaries. 我不明白我們為何不能使用字典。
T Because you rely on them too much. 因為你們太依賴字典了。
S That's because English is difficult! 那是因為英語太難了！

> **Dialogue**

T Please hand in your assignments. 請大家交作業。
S **I don't understand why** this homework was so difficult. 我不懂這個作業為何會這麼難。
T It's probably because you didn't pay attention yesterday. 可能是因為你們昨天沒有專心聽課。
S I guess you're right. 我想您說得對。

P3_198

I don't understand... 我不明白～

當你聽不懂老師的講解時，卻還是假裝有聽懂的話，那你可能永遠也無法聽懂。在這種情況下，你需要有勇氣說實話。I don't understand 後面可以接續名詞、疑問詞或「疑問詞＋to不定詞」等。

I don't understand your question. 我不明白你的問題。
I don't understand why we have to do this. 我不知道我們為什麼得這麼做。
I don't understand why you don't have your homework. 我不明白你為什麼沒帶作業。
I don't understand this exercise. 我不理解這個練習題。
I don't understand why I failed the test. 我不明白為什麼我考試不及格。

Dialogue

- **T** Okay, let's get started. 　　好，開始上課吧。
- **S** **I don't understand** this exercise. 　　我不理解這個練習題。
- **T** I'll explain it again. 　　我再解釋一遍。
- **S** Thank you, ma'am*. 　　謝謝老師。

Dialogue

- **T** Here is your score. 　　這是你的分數。
- **S** **I don't understand** why I failed the test. 　　我不明白為什麼我考試不及格。
- **T** Did you study? 　　你唸書了嗎？
- **S** Well... not really. 　　唔…其實沒有。
- **T** That's why. 　　這就是原因。

*美國的中小學老師最常見的稱謂是用如 Mr. 或 Ms.（如 Mr. Brown）的用語，有時也使用 ma'am、sir 等頭銜。如果關係友好的話，也可以直接用名字稱呼老師，例如 Sally 或 Tom。

How often should we...? 我們應該要多久～一次～？

「How often...?」的語意是「多常…?」或「多久…一次」。這是可以在多種情況下詢問頻率的句型，例如詢問每週有多少堂英語課，或者詢問每學期有多少次考試。這裡的 should 可以理解為義務，語意為「應該、必須」。

How often should we check our work?	我們應該要多久確認一次我們的學習？
How often should we show the teacher our journals?	我們應該要多久給老師看一次我們的日記？
How often should we practice speaking?	我們應該要多久練習一次口說？
How often should we keep a journal?	我們應該要多久寫一次日記？
How often should we practice?	我們應該要多久練習一次？

Dialogue

- S1 For this class we have to write in a journal. 我們這堂課要寫日記。
- S2 **How often should we** show the teacher our journals? 我們應該要多久給老師看一次我們的日記？
- S1 Once a week. 每週一次。
- S2 That doesn't sound too difficult. 這聽起來不太難。

Dialogue

- S1 We should work on our English over summer vacation. 我們在暑假期間要學習英語。
- S2 **How often should we** practice speaking? 我們應該要多久練習一次口說？
- S1 Every day! 每天都要！
- S2 That's a lot of work! 那可有得忙了！

Is there anything...? 有什麼～嗎？／有～的嗎？

當您需要某某東西或正在尋找什麼東西時，通常會使用「Is there anything...?」這個表達句型。在疑問句或否定句中，通常會用 anything，而不是 something，但當我們期望得到肯定回答或向對方推薦某事時，我們會使用 something。

Is there anything to memorize?	有什麼我需要記住的嗎？
Is there anything I can do?	有什麼我可以做的嗎？
Is there anything on the schedule?	時間表上有什麼嗎？
Is there anything else I need to do?	還有什麼其他我需要做的嗎？
Is there anything more difficult?	有再難一點的嗎？

> Dialogue

S Here is my homework.	這是我的作業。
T Thank you, Robert.	謝謝 Robert。
S **Is there anything** else I need to do?	還有什麼其他我需要做的嗎？
T Well, you need to write your name on it!	嗯，你需要在作業上寫下你的名字！
S Oops! I forgot!	哎呀！我忘了！

> Dialogue

S1 Let's do the exercise on page 74.	我們來做第 74 頁的練習題。
S2 It's seems easy. **Is there anything** more difficult?	看起來很簡單，有再難一點的嗎？
S1 This exercise isn't as easy as it looks.	這個練習題並不像看起來那麼簡單。
S2 All right. I'll try it.	好的，我試著寫寫看。

I'm not sure what... 我不確定～什麼

P3_201

「I'm not sure...」是跟「I'm sure...」語意相反的句型。not sure 的語意同 uncertain，表示無法確定或保證某事。換句話說，這是一種讓對方事先知道您無法 100% 確定自己所說的話的表達句型。此外，當有人問您「Are you sure...?」時，也可以使用這個句型來回應對方。

I'm not sure what* to do.	我不確定該做些什麼事。
I'm not sure what to bring.	我不確定該帶什麼。
I'm not sure what my responsibilities are.	我不確定我的職責是什麼。
I'm not sure what will happen.	我不確定會發生什麼事。
I'm not sure what he wants.	我不確定他想要什麼。

*除了 what 之外，也可以使用「疑問詞＋to 不定詞」來進行各種表達。舉例來說，「我不知道把這張椅子放在哪裡」的英文說法為「I'm not sure where to put this chair.」。

Dialogue

S1 Do you understand our assignment? 你明白我們的作業嗎？
S2 I'm not sure what to do. 我不確定該做些什麼事。
S1 I think we need to practice this dialogue. 我認為我們需要練習這個對話。
S2 Oh, that doesn't sound too difficult. 哦，這聽起來不太難。

Dialogue

S1 I hope we'll be able to make up the test. 我希望我們能夠補考。
S2 I'm not sure what will happen. 我不確定會發生什麼事。
S1 We had a good excuse for being absent. 我們有一個很好的缺課藉口。
S2 Yes, but it will be up to the teacher. 是的，但這取決於老師。

What was it like...? ～是什麼感覺？

老師上課時有時會分享自己念大學時期的故事，或是請學生分享假日去哪玩的經驗，此時可能會問起當時的經驗或感覺「當時是什麼感覺？」吧？此時可以使用的句型是「What was it like...?」。這是用來詢問對方對某事的經驗、感受或看法的表達句型。

What was it like* when you tried to speak to a native speaker? 試著跟母語人士說話是什麼感覺？

What was it like when you studied in New York? 在紐約念書是什麼感覺？

What was it like to live abroad? 在國外生活是什麼感覺？

What was it like to make such a high score? 拿到這麼高的分數是怎麼感覺？

*若What is/are 後面接人稱代名詞作為主詞，則可以用來表達「某人是怎樣的人」。舉例來說，「What is he like?」的語意就是「他是怎麼樣的人」。

Dialogue

- **S** **What was it like** when you studied in New York?
- **T** At first it was very difficult, but soon I understood everything.
- **S** It sounds scary.
- **T** It wasn't so bad.

在紐約念書是什麼感覺？
起初很困難，但很快什麼都懂了。
聽起來很可怕。
沒那麼糟。

Dialogue

- **S1** I got a perfect score on the TOEFL!
- **S2** **What was it like** to make such a high score?
- **S1** It felt fantastic!
- **S2** Well, you studied very hard for it. Good job!

我托福考了滿分！
拿到這麼高的分數是怎麼感覺？
棒呆了！
這都是你努力學習的成果，做得好！

What's the most efficient way...?
～最有效率的方法是什麼呢？

P3_203

efficient 可解釋為「有效率的」，意味著不浪費時間的「高效率」。後面既可接續 way、route、method等名詞，也可接續「way＋to不定詞」或「way of＋動名詞」，請一併記住。

What's the most efficient way to proceed from here?
從這裡開始最有效率的方法是什麼呢？

What's the most efficient way to learn English?
學英語最有效率的方法是什麼呢？

What's the most efficient way to speak English?
說英語最有效率的方式是什麼呢？

What's the most efficient way to approach this problem?
解決這個問題最有效率的方法是什麼呢？

> Dialogue

S1 **What's the most efficient way** to learn English?　　學習英語最有效的方法是什麼呢？

S2 Going to an English-speaking country is a fast way.　　快的方法就是去英語系國家。

S1 Why?　　為什麼？

S2 You have to speak English all the time.　　因為要一直說英語。

> Dialogue

S1 We have to agree on a theme for our project.　　我們必須敲定專案的主題。

S2 It will be hard to get this group to agree on anything.　　很難讓這組組員有一致的意見。

S1 **What's the most efficient way** to approach this problem?　　解決這個問題最有效的方法是什麼呢？

S2 I suggest we take a vote*.　　我建議我們進行投票。

*take a vote 的語意是「投票表決」，想表示「針對〜進行投票」時，要用介系詞 on。另外請注意，「多數表決制」的英文是 majority voting。

P3_204

What if...? 如果〜怎麼辦？

這是「What would happen if...?」的縮寫，語意為「如果…怎麼辦？」，if 後面接完整的子句。這是孩子們最喜歡使用的表達句型之一。

What if we don't understand?	如果我們不懂的話怎麼辦？
What if we fail?	如果我們考砸的話怎麼辦？
What if we can't find the answer?	如果我們找不到答案怎麼辦？
What if I don't know the word?	如果我不認識這個詞怎麼辦？
What if the test is too difficult?	如果考試太難怎麼辦？

Dialogue

- **T** Now I want you to read the story by yourselves.   現在我想讓你們自己讀這個故事。
- **S** **What if** we don't understand?   如果我們不懂的話怎麼辦？
- **T** You can ask questions if you need to.   有需要的話可以提問。
- **S** Good. I think I'll need to.   好，我想我會需要問。

Dialogue

- **S1** The test is tomorrow.   明天要考試。
- **S2** **What if** we fail?   如果我們考砸的話怎麼辦？
- **S1** We still have another chance in a few weeks.   幾週後我們還有一次機會。
- **S2** That's good because I'm not prepared.   太好了，因為我還沒準備好。

What I want to ask is... 我想問的（是）～

當您對某問題強烈質疑時，請不要拐彎抹角，直接明確地提問，此時只要利用這個表達句型就行了，這是在提問後用來總結問題的句型。What 的語意為「做～的某人事物」，是包含先行詞的關係代名詞。另外請注意，這裡的 what 是 is 的主詞。

What I want to ask is how to say this word.	我想問的是這個詞怎麼唸。
What I want to ask is very simple.	我想問的問題很簡單。
What I want to ask is what this word means.	我想問的是這個詞的意思。
What I want to ask is a difficult question.	我想問的是個很難的問題。
What I want to ask is a very silly question.	我想問一個很蠢的問題。

Dialogue

T Do you have a question about the grammar? 你對這個文法有什麼問題嗎？

S No. **What I want to ask is** how to say this word. 沒有，我想問的是這個詞怎麼唸。

T Okay. Which word is confusing? 好，哪個詞讓你感到困惑呢？

S 'Film.' 「Film」。

T Oh, that is a difficult word to pronounce. 哦，這個詞很難發音。

Dialogue

S1 **What I want to ask is** a very silly question. 我想問一個很蠢的問題。

S2 Okay, what is it? 好，是什麼呢？

S1 What is the opposite of 'small'? 「small」的反義詞是什麼？

S2 It's 'big' of course. 當然是「big」囉。

I don't know if... 我不知道～是否～

當您因情況不明確而無法掌握實際狀況時，就可以使用這個表達句型。句中的 if 可以替換成 whether，但有些時候只能用 whether。舉例來說，如 whether to 這樣後面接續不定詞時，或如 whether or not 這樣後面接續 or not 時，這兩種情況下都只能用 whether，不能用 if。

I don't know if this is the right answer. 我不知道這是不是正確答案。

I don't know if I did it correctly. 我不知道我做的對不對。

I don't know if he's coming. 我不知道他會不會來。

I don't know if this is working. 我不知道這是否正常運作。

I don't know if I can do it. 我不知道自己是否能做到。

Dialogue

S1 Did you do the homework?　　你寫作業了嗎？
S2 Yes, I did. Did you?　　嗯，我寫了，你呢？
S1 Yes, but **I don't know if** I did it correctly.　　我寫了，但我不知道我寫的對不對。
S2 I guess you'll find out soon!　　我想你很快就會知道的！

Dialogue

T I want you to lead the class today.　　我今天想請你帶這個班。
S **I don't know if** I can do it.　　我不知道自己是否能做到。
T Sure you can, I have faith in you.　　當然能做到，我相信你。
S Wow, thanks.　　哇，謝謝您。

How come...? 怎麼會～？／為什麼～？

P3_207

「How come...?」是「How did it come that...?」的縮寫。在句子中使用「How come...?」時，主要用來表示「到底是怎麼一回事？」，有時也用來表示「Why?」。這句型是 How did it come that...? 的縮寫，所以 How come 後面是接續省略 that 的子句。

How come this exercise is so long?	這練習題怎麼會那麼長呢？
How come you didn't do the homework?	你怎麼會沒寫作業呢？
How come it's too late?	怎麼會太遲了？
How come you failed the test?	你怎麼會考不及格呢？
How come nobody told us?	怎麼會沒人告訴我們呢？

Dialogue

S1 It's too late for us to get a good grade now.　　我們現在想取得好成績已經太遲了。

S2 How come it's too late?　　怎麼會太遲了？

S1 Our project still needs a lot of work.　　我們的作業仍有很多東西要做。

S2 Let's get started. We may be able to get it in on time.　　我們開始吧，說不定我們能準時完工。

Dialogue

T How come you failed the test?　　你怎麼會考不及格呢？

S It was too difficult.　　太難了。

T I think maybe you didn't study hard enough.　　我想或許是你努力不夠。

S I guess that's possible, too.　　也是有這個可能。

I have no idea... 我不知道～

這是當您想表示「我不知道」或「我不明白」時可用的表達句型。「I don't know.」、「I don't understand.」或「It isn't clear to me.」也可用於類似的情況。若「I have no idea...」後面接續「how＋to不定詞」或「how＋子句」的話，則語意為「我不知道該怎麼做～」，若接續「why＋子句」，則語意為「我不知道為什麼～」。

I have no idea what you're talking about.　　我不知道你在說什麼。

I have no idea what the answer is.　　我不知道答案是什麼。

I have no idea how to do it.　　我不知道該怎麼做。

I have no idea what's on the test.　　我不知道會考什麼。

I have no idea why he said that.　　我不知道他為什麼這麼說。

Dialogue

- **T** William, it's your turn.
- **S** **I have no idea** what the answer is.
- **T** Try looking in your book.
- **S** Oh, I see the answer now!

William,輪到你了。
我不知道答案是什麼。
試著在你的書裡找找看。
哦,我現在知道答案了!

Dialogue

- **S1** I'm worried.
- **S2** Why?
- **S1** **I have no idea** what's on the test.
- **S2** It covers chapter 4.
- **S1** Oh! That's not too difficult.

我很擔心。
為什麼?
我不知道會考什麼。
考試出自第 4 課。
哦!那就不會太難。

I wonder why... 我想知道為什麼～

無論在什麼情況下,只要有疑問都可以使用這個表達句型。若 wonder 後面接續以 why、what、whether 等開頭的子句或「疑問詞+to 不定詞」的話,語意為「我想知道為什麼/什麼/是否～」。舉例來說,「I wonder what happened.」的語意是「我想知道發生了什麼事」。

I wonder why no one passed the test.	我想知道為什麼沒有人及格。
I wonder why our experiment keeps failing.	我想知道為什麼實驗一直失敗。
I wonder why our teacher is absent.	我想知道老師為什麼沒來。
I wonder why Elizabeth has to stay after school.	我想知道為什麼 Elizabeth 放學後得留下來。
I wonder why everyone is outside.	我想知道為什麼大家都在外面。

> **Dialogue**

S1 Did you see the final grades? 　你看到期末成績了嗎？
S2 Yes. **I wonder why** no one passed the test. 　嗯，我想知道為什麼沒有人及格。
S1 It was too difficult. 　因為太難了。
S2 Perhaps it was. 　或許是的。

> **Dialogue**

S1 **I wonder why** our teacher is absent. 　我想知道老師為什麼沒來。
S2 Maybe she's sick. 　可能是她生病了。
S1 Maybe. Or she could be on vacation. 　或許吧，或者她可能正在度假。
S2 Yeah, she might be. 　對喔，可能是這樣。

📖 確認是否可以

Is it okay...? 可以～嗎？

這是想徵求同意時可以使用的表達句型，類似「Can I...?」或「May I...?」，okay 後面接續 if 子句或 to 不定詞。舉例來說，當學生在上課時間想去上廁所時，就可以說「Is it okay if I go to the bathroom?（我可以去廁所嗎？）」。

Is it okay if I look at my book? 　我可以看一下我的書嗎？
Is it okay if I open a window? 　我可以打開窗戶嗎？
Is it okay if I use my dictionary? 　我可以使用字典嗎？
Is it okay if I turn it in late? 　我可以晚點交嗎？
Is it okay if I go first? 　可以讓我先嗎？

Dialogue

T Can you summarize the story? 你能總結一下這個故事嗎?
S **Is it okay** if I look at my book? 我可以看一下我的書嗎?
T No. I want to see how well you remember it. 不行,我想看看你記得多少。
S This is going to be hard! 這樣會有點難耶!

Dialogue

S1 It's my turn to give a presentation. 輪到我做簡報了。
S2 **Is it okay** if I go first? I have to leave early today. 可以讓我先嗎?我今天必須早點離開。
S1 Sure! That gives me some more time! 當然!這樣我就有更多時間了!
S2 Yes, but you still have to give yours eventually. 好,但你最終還是得作簡報。

📖 做確認

Let me check... 讓我看一下/檢查～

請注意,當 check 作為及物動詞時,後面要接受詞,但在想表達「向～確認」的情況下,則要採用 check with someone 的形式。

Let me check your answers.	讓我檢查你寫的答案。
Let me check my dictionary.	讓我查一下字典。
Let me check my calendar.	讓我看一下我的行事曆。
Let me check your essay.	讓我看一下你寫的作文。
Let me check with the teacher.	讓我跟老師確認一下。

Dialogue

- **T** What does this word mean? 這個單字是什麼意思？
- **S** **Let me check** my dictionary. 讓我查一下字典。
- **T** No dictionaries are allowed on this exercise. 做這個練習題時不能使用字典。
- **S** Okay. I'll try to guess. 好吧，我試著猜猜看。

Dialogue

- **S1** Can we use our dictionaries on this exercise? 我們做這個練習題時可以使用字典嗎？
- **S2** **Let me check** with the teacher. Mr. Smith? 讓我跟老師確認一下。Smith 老師，我有問題！
- **T** Yes, Joey? Joey，怎麼了嗎？
- **S2** Can we use our dictionaries? 我們可以使用字典嗎？
- **T** I'm sorry, but no. 抱歉不可以。

There must be... 一定有～／肯定有～

P3_212

must 在這裡是助動詞，用來強烈表達肯定的猜測，所以當有人說「There must be...」，便帶有「一定有～」或「肯定會有～」的意味。舉例來說，「There must be a misunderstanding.」的語意是「肯定有誤會」。本句型的主詞位於 be 動詞後面，所以 be 動詞後面要接續名詞。

There must be an easier way to do this.	一定有更簡單的方法來做這件事。
There must be a thousand words to memorize.	肯定有一千個單字要背。
There must be something we can do to help.	一定有我們幫得上忙的地方。
There must be a better explanation.	一定有更好的解釋。
There must be some way to solve this problem.	一定有辦法解決這個問題。

Dialogue

🅣 Tonight's homework is to memorize this list of words.	今晚的作業就是背這個單字表。
🅢1 **There must be** a thousand words to memorize!	肯定有一千個單字要背。
🅢2 It's not that bad.	沒那麼多啦。
🅢1 Well, it's a lot.	唔,但還是很多。

Dialogue

🅣 Johnny won't be here this week because he's sick.	Johnny 生病了,所以這週不會來。
🅢 **There must be** something we can do to help.	一定有我們幫得上忙的地方。
🅣 Why don't we write him a get-well card*?	我們何不寫一張早日康復卡給他呢?
🅢 That's a great idea!	這主意不錯!

*get-well card 指的是祝福生病的人早日康復的「慰問卡」。

It sounds like... 聽起來(好像)～

P3_213

當您在聽完別人的故事後,想表達自己對這個故事的感受或想法時,就可以使用這個表達句型,此時 It sounds like 後面要接續子句。不過,It sounds like 後面也可接續名詞,例如「It sounds like a good idea.」,其語意為「這聽起來是個好主意」。

It sounds like we'll be studying a lot.	聽起來我們好像要學很多東西。
It sounds like the homework will be difficult.	聽起來作業好像會很難。
It sounds like you're going to get a high score.	聽起來你好像會取得高分。
It sounds like fun.	聽起來很有趣。
It sounds like a good idea.	聽起來是個好主意。

Dialogue

- **T** Don't forget that the homework will take a lot of time.　別忘了，作業會花很多時間。
- **S** It's only three questions!　只有三題而已！
- **T** Yes. But the questions are long.　是的，但題目很長。
- **S** **It sounds like** the homework will be difficult.　聽起來作業好像會很難。

Dialogue

- **S1** Tomorrow is our final exam.　我們明天期末考。
- **S2** I'm ready. I've been studying all day long.　我準備好了，我一整天都在念書。
- **S1** **It sounds like** you're going to get a high score.　聽起來你好像會取得高分。
- **S2** I'm sure I will.　我肯定會的。

I never thought... 我從沒想過～

P3_214

以中文來說，會用「我沒想到～」這句來描述一件自己從未想過的事。因此，當您想提及出乎意料之事時，就很適合使用這個表達句型。反之，當出現與您預期完全相反的結果時，可以用「I thought…」來表達「（儘管實際上不是，但）我以為…」。

I never thought I'd understand this.	我從沒想過我會明白這一點。
I never thought I'd be able to speak English.	我從沒想過我能說英語。
I never thought you'd get such a high score.	我從沒想過你會得到如此高分。
I never thought you'd get the right answer.	我從沒想過你會答對。
I never thought we'd finish this exercise.	我從沒想過我們會完成這練習題。

Dialogue

- **S** Wow! I got 95 points on the test! — 哇！我考試考 95 分！
- **T** **I never thought** you'd get such a high score. — 我從沒想過你會得到如此高分。
- **S** Neither did I! — 我也沒想過！
- **T** Good job! — 很好！

Dialogue

- **T** This is the last question. — 這是最後一題。
- **S** **I never thought** we'd finish this exercise. — 我從沒想過我們會完成這練習題。
- **T** It wasn't that long. — 沒那麼久。
- **S** It felt long. — 感覺很漫長。

Did you know…? 你知道～嗎？

「Do you know...?」的語意是「你知道～嗎？」，「Did you know...?」則是用來詢問「你之前知道～嗎？」的句型。當發生意想不到的事情時，或想詢問對方是否早就知道某件事時，都可以使用這個表達句型。及物動詞 know 後面可接續名詞或子句作為受詞，若後面接的是子句的話，則要使用連接詞 that，以「Did you know that...?」來表達，句中的 that 可以省略。

Did you know the quiz was today? — 你知道今天有小考嗎？
Did you know the answers? — 你知道答案嗎？
Did you know we have class today? — 你知道我們今天要上課嗎？
Did you know the class starts at 9:00? — 你知道 9 點開始上課嗎？
Did you know we had a substitute teacher? — 你知道我們有代課老師嗎？

Dialogue

S1 That test was very difficult. 　　　那次考試很難。
S2 Did you know the answers? 　　　答案你都知道嗎？
S1 Some, but not all of them. 　　　知道一些，不是全部。
S2 You probably did better than you think. 你考的可能比你想像的還要好。

Dialogue

S1 Who's that guy? 　　　那個人是誰？
S2 That's Mr. Wilkinson. 　　　那位是 Wilkinson 老師。
S1 Did you know we had a substitute teacher? 　　　你知道我們有代課老師嗎？
S2 Not until I walked through the door! 　　　我進來後才知道的！

P3_216

I have heard... 我聽說～

「I have heard...」的語意是「我聽說～」或「我聽過～」。「I have heard＋子句」是根據自己從別人那邊聽到的內容所轉述的內容，所以可解釋為「我聽說～」。若 I have heard 後面接的是名詞，則語意為「我聽過～」。

I have heard that this test is going to be hard. 　　　我聽說這次考試會很難。

I have heard that word before. 　　　我以前聽過這個詞。

I have heard you have a very good attitude in class. 　　　我聽說你們的上課態度很好。

I have heard that next semester will be even harder. 　　　我聽說下學期會更難。

I have heard you say that before. 　　　我之前聽你這麼說過。

Dialogue

- **T** Congratulations! The semester is over! 　恭喜！這學期終於結束了！
- **S** **I have heard** that next semester will be even harder. 　我聽說下學期會更難。
- **T** Don't worry. You're a good student. 　別擔心，你是很棒的學生。
- **S** I hope I'm good enough! 　希望我夠優秀！

Dialogue

- **T** Are you sure that's the right answer? 　你確定這是正確答案嗎？
- **S** Absolutely! I'm sure it's right. 　當然！我確信這是對的。
- **T** **I have heard** you say that before. 　我之前聽你這麼說過。
- **S** But I mean it this time! 　但這次是真的！

P3_217

I'm afraid, but... 我有點害怕，但～

「I'm afraid (that)...」的語意是「恐怕～」，與之類似卻略有不同的表達句型是「**I'm afraid, but...**」，其語意為「我害怕，但～」或「我很遺憾，但～」。當您需要去做一件重要卻令人感到緊張或害怕的事情時，就可以利用這個表達句型。

I'm afraid, but I'm going to speak anyway.	我有點害怕，但我還是要發表。
I'm afraid, but I think I can do it.	我有點害怕，但我認為我能做到。
I'm afraid, but he's not.	我有點害怕，但他不怕。
I'm afraid, but I'll try to do my best.	我有點害怕，但我會盡力而為。
I'm afraid, but there's nothing I can do about it.	我有點害怕，但我對此無能為力。

Dialogue

T Tomorrow you will all give your presentations. 明天你們都要作簡報。
S1 I'm nervous. How about you? 我很緊張,你呢?
S2 **I'm afraid, but** I think I can do it. 我有點害怕,但我認為我能做到。
S1 I hope I can be as brave as you. 希望我能像你一樣勇敢。

Dialogue

T Matthew, why is your partner doing all the speaking? Matthew,為什麼一直只有你的搭檔在發言?
S **I'm afraid, but** he's not. 我有點害怕,但他不怕。
T Why are you afraid? 你為什麼會害怕?
S I don't want to make any mistakes. 因為我不想犯錯。
T Don't worry. We all make mistakes. 別擔心,每個人都會犯錯。

It's easy to... 很容易~

P3_218

如果不常使用一門語言,就很容易忘記該語言,並對這語言不熟悉。當您面對一位口中說著「我已經聽很多遍了,但為什麼總是做錯?」且垂頭喪氣的學生,想對他／她說「如果你不繼續使用英語,就會很容易忘記」時,就可以使用這個表達句型。反之,當您想表達「某件事很難做到」時,只要用 difficult 或 hard 代替 easy 就行了。

It's easy to forget how to use this grammar.	很容易忘記如何使用這個文法。
It's easy to remember if you practice a little.	只要稍加練習,就能輕鬆記住。
It's easy to understand.	這很容易理解。
It's easy to say.	說起來容易。
It's easy to confuse these words.	這幾個單字很容易搞混。

Dialogue

- T: This exercise is easy.　　這個練習題很簡單。
- S: Yes, but I need the practice more.　　是的,但我需要再多練習幾次。
- T: Why?　　為什麼?
- S: **It's easy to** forget how to use this grammar.　　很容易忘記如何使用這個文法。

Dialogue

- S: I don't understand the difference between these words.　　我不明白這幾個單字有什麼差別。
- T: **It's easy to** confuse these words.　　這幾個單字很容易搞混。
- S: Can you explain them to me?　　您能解釋給我聽嗎?
- T: No problem.　　沒問題。

補充 Supplement

📖 學生提問

Can you repeat the instructions?	這段說明您可以再說一遍嗎?
Can we go over that problem again?	我們可以再討論一遍那個問題嗎?
I don't understand how you solved the problem.	我不太懂您是怎麼解這一題的。
How did you get that answer?	您是怎麼得出那個答案的?
I don't understand what you're talking about.	我不明白您在說什麼。

UNIT 10 下課或放學

📖 下課休息

When the bell rings, ... 打鐘時～

當要提醒學生遵守上課鐘響就要回座位坐好的規定時，就非常適合使用這個表達句型。這個句型用時間連接詞 when 來提醒某情況或條件，當 when 子句出現在句首時，請注意副詞子句後面要加上逗號 (,)。

When the bell rings, take your seats.	打鐘時就請入座。
When the bell rings, we will begin.	打鐘時我們就開始。
When the bell rings, class is dismissed.	打鐘時就下課。
When the bell rings, you can go home.	打鐘時你們就可以回家了。
When the bell rings, it's time for recess.	打鐘時就可以休息了。

Dialogue

🅣 You look tired, Jimmy.	Jimmy，你看起來很累。
🅢 When can we go home, Ms. Wilson?	Wilson 老師，我們何時可以回家？
🅣 **When the bell rings,** you can go home.	打鐘時你們就可以回家了。
🅢 How soon will that be?	那還要多久？

Dialogue

🅣 Sit still, children.	孩子們，請安靜地坐好。
🅢 We want to go outside.	我們想去外面。
🅣 **When the bell rings,** it's time for recess.	打鐘時就可以休息了。
🅢 Can we wait by the door?	我們可以在門口等嗎？

Let's take a break... ～我們休息一下吧！

P3_220

take a break 是指停下手邊正在做的事並「稍微休息一下」。雖然 break 本身有「短暫休息」的意思，但也可以加上 short 或 quick 修飾，即 take a short [quick] break。或是 take a ten-minute break 這樣，提到具體的時間。通常在句首會加上 Let's（我們來休息一下），但也可以用 Why don't we take a break?（我們何不休息一下呢？），兩者意思是相同的。

Let's take a break after this.	做完這個，我們就休息一下吧！
Let's take a break for a minute.	我們休息一會兒吧！
Let's take a break at the cafeteria.	我們在餐廳休息一下吧！
Let's take a break at lunch time.	午餐時間時，我們休息一下吧！
Let's take a break from studying.	我們停下手邊的學習，休息一下吧！

Dialogue

S This activity is really hard.	這個活動真的很難。
T I can see that you're getting tired.	我看得出來你累了。
S **Let's take a break** after this.	做完這個，我們就休息一下吧！
T Sounds good.	好的。

Dialogue

S1 **Let's take a break** from studying.	我們停下手邊的學習，休息一下吧！
S2 We need to finish this exercise first.	我們要先完成這個練習題。
S1 But I'm so tired.	但是我很累。
S2 Don't worry. We're almost finished.	別擔心，就快完成了。

📖 待在原位

Stay seated... 請待在座位上，～

這是要孩子們安靜坐好的表達句型。這個句型大多會搭配以 until 或 while 連接的子句，**Stay seated until...** 表示「請留在座位直到～」。stay 的語意是「維持～的狀態」，後面緊接著一個描述該主詞的形容詞，其相似詞為 remain。

Stay seated until the bell rings.	請坐在座位上，直到打鐘。
Stay seated until I collect your papers.	請待在座位上，直到我收齊你們的考卷。
Stay seated until class is over.	請坐在座位上，直到下課。
Stay seated until the test is over.	請待在座位上，直到考試結束。
Stay seated until I call your name.	請待在座位上，直到我叫到你們的名字。

Dialogue

- 🇹 Your homework tonight is page 55.　你們今晚的作業是第 55 頁。
- 🇸 Okay. Let's go home!　知道了，我們回家吧！
- 🇹 Please **stay seated** until class is over.　請坐在座位上，直到下課。
- 🇸 I'm sorry.　抱歉。

Dialogue

- 🇹 Now you will all take turns giving your presentations.　現在你們輪流進行口頭報告。
- 🇸 I'm nervous.　我好緊張。
- 🇹 Please **stay seated** until I call your name.　請待在座位上，直到我叫到你們的名字。
- 🇸 I hope I'm not first!　希望我不是第一個！

📖 放學前提醒

By the way, ... 順帶一提，～

這是聊到一半想轉換話題時可以使用的表達句型。在口語中，Now 也跟 by the way 一樣，經常被用來轉換談話的主題。

By the way, what topic did you choose?	順帶一提，你選了什麼主題？
By the way, I read your essay yesterday.	順帶一提，我昨天讀了你寫的作文。
By the way, do you remember the meaning of this word?	順帶一提，你記得這個詞的意思嗎？
By the way, are you finished with your essay?	順帶一提，你的作文寫完了嗎？
By the way, when do you think you'll be finished?	順帶一提，你覺得什麼時候能寫完呢？

Dialogue

- 🇹 When you write your essay, you should organize your ideas. 　寫文章時應該要整理好思緒。
- 🇸 I think I understand how to do that. 　我想我知道該怎麼做了。
- 🇹 **By the way,** what topic did you choose? 　順帶一提，你選了什麼主題？
- 🇸 I'm going to write about my hometown. 　我打算寫我的家鄉。

Dialogue

- 🇹 Do you have your homework? 　你有帶作業嗎？
- 🇸 Yes. Here it is. 　有的，在這裡。
- 🇹 **By the way,** are you finished with your essay? 　順帶一提，你的作文寫完了嗎？
- 🇸 Not yet. I'll be finished by tomorrow. 　還沒，我打算明天完成。

Like I said before, ... 正如我之前所說，~

有時，某些話只說一遍而已，沒有幾個孩子真的會聽進去的。Like I said before 是用來重述之前說過的內容的表達句型。這句型中的 like 是連接詞，語意與 as 相近。Like 可用作動詞或介系詞，但在美國口語中有時用 like 代替 as。類似的表達句型是 As I told you before。

Like I said before, the test will be on Monday.	正如我之前所說，考試將於週一進行。
Like I said before, it's important to practice pronunciation.	正如我之前所說，發音練習很重要。
Like I said before, learning English takes patience.	正如我之前所說，學習英語需要耐心。
Like I said before, the homework is on page 87.	正如我之前所說，作業在第 87 頁。

Dialogue

- S When is the test?
  考試是什麼時候？
- T **Like I said before,** the test will be on Monday.
  正如我之前所說，考試將於週一進行。
- S What time?
  幾點考呢？
- T Again, it will be at the beginning of class.
  我再說一次，一上課就開始考。

Dialogue

- S What are we supposed to do tonight?
  今晚我們要做什麼呢？
- T **Like I said before,** the homework is on page 87.
  正如我之前所說，作業在第 87 頁。
- S Oh, I'm sorry I forgot.
  哦，對不起，我忘了。
- T No problem. Just don't forget to do your homework.
  沒關係，別忘了寫作業。

Remember to... 要記得～

這是在下課前，想叮嚀學生們不要忘了帶重要物品、作業時，可以使用的表達句型，類似的表達句型有 Don't forget~。當你想叮嚀容易忘東忘西的學生不要忘記時，就可以使用這個表達句型。

Remember to do your homework. 　　要記得寫作業。
Remember to bring a pen. 　　要記得帶筆。
Remember to write down the new words. 　　要記得寫下新單字。
Remember to study for the test. 　　要記得念書準備考試。
Remember to read chapter 9. 　　要記得讀第 9 課。

Dialogue

S Hurray! Time to go home! 　　耶！可以回家了！
T **Remember to** do your homework. 　　要記得寫作業。
S What page is it? 　　是哪一頁呢？
T Page 73. 　　第 73 頁。

Dialogue

S See you tomorrow, Mr. Smith. 　　Smith 老師，明天見。
T **Remember to** read chapter 9. 　　要記得讀第 9 課。
S All of it? 　　全部嗎？
T Yes, all of it. 　　對，全部。

Remember to bring... 要記得帶～

這是想告訴學生不要忘記帶重要物品時可以使用的表達句型，語意跟「Don't forget to bring...」相似，所以您可以自行選擇要用的句型。

Remember to bring* a note from your parents.	記得要帶有父母簽名的假單。
Remember to bring your textbook.	記得要帶課本。
Remember to bring a notebook.	記得要帶筆記本。
Remember to bring your homework.	記得要帶作業。
Remember to bring red pens.	記得要帶紅筆。

* bring 的語意是「拿來、帶來」，take 的語意是從一個地方「帶到、拿到」另一個地方。因此，當媽媽告訴孩子上學不要忘記帶傘時，應該要用 take，不是 bring，也就是「Don't forget to take an umbrella.」。

Dialogue

S I won't be in class this Friday for the test.	我無法參加這個星期五的考試。
T That's okay. You can take it next week.	沒關係，你可以參加下週的考試。
S Great. I have a dentist appointment on Friday.	太好了，星期五我要去看牙醫。
T **Remember to bring** a note from your parents.	記得要帶有父母簽名的假單。

Dialogue

S Can you help me after class, Mr. Johnson?	Johnson 老師，下課後您能幫我一下嗎？
T Sure.	當然。
S Terrific. I don't understand how to solve this question.	太棒了，我不懂該如何解這一題。
T No problem. **Remember to bring** your textbook.	沒問題，記得要帶課本。

Be sure to study... 務必要好好學習～

「Be sure to...」是用來提醒學生不要忘記某件事的表達句型。在課堂上，老師很常提到「務必要好好複習～」，所以「Be sure to study...」應該是較常用的句型，請牢記在心。

Be sure to study for the quiz.	務必要好好準備小考。
Be sure to study chapter 11.	務必要好好念第 11 課。
Be sure to study the glossary.	務必要好好研讀單字表。
Be sure to study this week.	這週務必要好好學習。
Be sure to study with a friend.	務必和朋友一起學習。

Dialogue

T Have a good weekend, Charlie.	Charlie，祝你週末愉快。
S Thanks Mrs. Benson!	謝謝 Benson 老師！
T **Be sure to study** for the quiz.	務必要好好準備小考。
S I'm planning on it.	正有此打算。

Dialogue

T Oral exams are on Friday.	口試是在星期五。
S What will they cover?	考試的範圍是？
T Verbs. **Be sure to study** chapter 11.	動詞。務必要好好念第 11 課。
S I'll write that down so I don't forget.	我會把寫下來，以免忘記。

📖 放學道別

We'll meet again... 我們～再見。

這是結束課程前的表達句型。除此之外，還可以用意味著「今天先到這裡」的「Let's call it a day」或「That's all for today.」，或者「星期～見」意義的「See you on...」。

We'll meet again next week.	我們下週見。
We'll meet again next time.	我們下次見。
We'll meet again after the vacation.	我們假期結束後見。
We'll meet again on Friday.	我們星期五見。
We'll meet again after lunch.	我們午餐後見。

Dialogue

- 🅣 Do you have any more questions? 還有其它問題嗎？
- 🅢 No. I think I understand everything. 沒有了，我想我都懂了。
- 🅣 Good. **We'll meet again** next week. 好的，我們下週見。
- 🅢 Okay. See you then! 好的，再見！

Dialogue

- 🅣 Are you having any problems with your homework? 你作業有遇到什麼問題嗎？
- 🅢 Yes. I'm a little confused about the topic. 有，我對這個主題有點不太懂。
- 🅣 **We'll meet again** after lunch. 我們午餐後見。
- 🅢 Okay. I'll ask you some questions then. 好的，我有幾個問題想問您。

Have a terrific... 祝你有個愉快的～

這是一個非常實用的問候表達，能讓您跟對方道別。在下課後或宣布開始放假時，可以使用這個表達句型來向大家道別。句型中的 terrific 的意思是「極好的」，也可用 wonderful、nice、good 等來替換。「Have a terrific...」後面基本上是接 time、day、evening、weekend 等跟時間有關的名詞，但也可以接 trip、flight、vacation、meal 等。

Have a terrific day.	祝你有美好的一天。
Have a terrific vacation.	祝你假期愉快。
Have a terrific time.	祝你玩得開心。
Have a terrific evening.	祝你有個美好的夜晚。
Have a terrific weekend.	祝你週末愉快。

Dialogue

T I heard you're going on a trip.	聽說你要去旅行。
S Yes, I'm so excited.	對啊，我真的很興奮。
T **Have a terrific** time.	祝你玩得開心。
S I plan to!	我會的！

Dialogue

T You should all be proud of your final grades.	你們都應該為自己的期末成績感到驕傲。
S Trust us, we are!	我們也是這麼覺得！
T **Have a terrific** weekend.	祝你們週末愉快。
S You, too, Mrs. Walker.	Walker 老師您也是。

補充 Supplement

📖 下課

That's it for today.	今天就到這裡。
That's all we'll be covering today.	這就是我們今天的所有內容。
Does anyone have any questions?	有人有問題嗎？
We're finished for today.	我們今天的課上完了。
We'll go over more tomorrow.	明天我們再繼續。

📖 作業

◎ Homework (Assignment) 作業

You'll do the assignment on page 38.	你們要做第 38 頁的作業。
I'll pass out a worksheet for your homework.	我會把一張練習題發下去給你們，當作你們的作業。
Your homework today is to read chapter 12.	你們今天的作業是讀第 12 章。
Please read the story and answer the questions for your homework.	你們的作業是，請讀這篇故事並回答問題。
Does anyone have questions about the assignment?	有人對作業有問題的嗎？

◎ Deadline 繳交期限

This is due tomorrow.	這份作業明天截止。
Your essay is due next Monday.	你們的作文下週一要交。
You have two days to work on this.	你們有兩天的時間完成這作業。
I'll give you another day to finish up the homework.	我會多給你們一天時間完成作業。
The assignment is due on Wednesday.	作業星期三前要繳交。

📖 考試

◎ Quiz and test 小考與考試

We'll have a test on chapter 6 next week.	我們下週要考第 6 章。
Our next test will be on Monday.	我們下次的測驗時間是在星期一。
Please study for the quiz tomorrow!	請好好為明天的小考做準備！
We'll be having a pop quiz in math today.	今天我們會有一個數學的臨時小考。
Our final test is in one week.	一週後就是我們的期末考。

◎ Put away the textbooks 請學生把課本收起來

Please put everything away.	請把所有東西都收起來。
Clear off your desk.	清空你們的桌面。
All you need is a pencil.	你只需要一支鉛筆。
Put all your books away.	把所有的書本都收起來。
Please put your iPads and textbooks away.	請把你們的 iPad 和課本收起來。

◎ Pass the test sheets 請學生發考卷

Please take one and pass the rest back.	請拿一份，其餘的往後傳。
Can you pass out the tests?	你可以幫我發考卷嗎？
Everyone needs one of these.	每個人都需要一份這個。
Can someone pass these out for me?	有人可以幫我發這些嗎？
Take one and pass them along.	請拿一份，並傳下去。

◎ Receive the test paper 確認是否都拿到考卷

Does everyone have a copy of the test?	每個人都有拿到考卷嗎？
Everyone should have two pages.	每個人都應該會有兩頁。

Raise your hand if you didn't get a test.	沒有拿到考卷的話,請舉手。
Did you get one?	你有拿到嗎?
Anyone need a copy of the test?	有人需要考卷嗎?

◎ **Time is up 請學生停筆**

Time is up!	時間到!
Please put your pencil down.	請放下鉛筆。
Pencils down!	把鉛筆放下!
Turn over your tests, please.	請把考卷翻過去。
Everyone stop writing, time is up!	每個人都停筆,時間到了!

MEMO

PART 4

各科目上課基本用語

Classroom English
Expressions for
different subjects

■■■

UNIT 01 幼兒園教師基本用語

📖 日常對話

How are you today?	你今天好嗎？
Do you want me to help you?	你要我幫你嗎？
How are you feeling today?	你今天覺得怎麼樣？
Let's have some snacks.	我們來吃點點心。
It's time to have lunch.	午餐時間到了。
Wash your hands with soap.	要用肥皂洗手。
Brush your teeth thoroughly.	牙齒要好好刷喔。
Never run around in the classroom.	不要在教室裡跑來跑去。

📖 熱身與帶動唱

Sing along with me!	跟著我一起唱！
Can you sing this song with me?	你們能跟我一起唱這首歌嗎？
Let's take a dance break!	我們來跳個舞動一動吧！
Clap your hands with me!	跟我一起拍手吧！

📖 課堂互動

Who wants to try this?	誰想試試看這個？
Who wants to answer?	誰要來回答？
Any volunteers?	有誰要自願嗎？
Time is up.	時間到。

Let's sit down for story time.	我們坐下來聽故事吧。
I'm going to read you a story.	我要為你們唸個故事。
Who has heard this story before?	誰之前聽過這個故事？
What's your favorite book?	你們最喜歡的書是什麼？
Do you like Dr. Seuss books?	你們喜歡蘇斯博士的書嗎？
Let's say the alphabet.	我們來唸字母吧。
Today we're going to learn about the letter B.	今天我們要學習字母 B。
Does the word "book" start with B?	「book」這個單字是以 B 開頭的嗎？
Show me how to write an A.	請示範怎麼寫 A。
What letter is this?	這是什麼字母？
Who can help me spell "cat"?	誰能幫我拼出「cat」？
Let's review our weekly words.	我們來復習我們的每週單字吧。
Who knows what this says?	誰知道這是什麼意思？
Who knows this word?	誰知道這個詞？
Can you tell me what this says?	你們能告訴我這是什麼意思嗎？

UNIT 02 國小各科教師基本用語

📖 數學課

◎ 數字

Today we will study even and odd numbers.	今天我們要學習偶數和奇數。
Is number 2 an even number?	2 是偶數嗎？
What number comes after 8?	8 後面是什麼數字？
Who can tell me what number this is?	誰能告訴我這個數字是多少？
Let's count out loud.	我們來大聲數數吧。
Try counting on when adding numbers.	請試著繼續往下加下去。
Can you count by tens?	你能以 10 為單位來數嗎？
Which number is greater?	哪個數字比較大？
Is 10 greater than 8?	10 大於 8 嗎？
Is 40 greater than 30?	40 大於 30 嗎？

◎ 加減乘除

Today we're reviewing addition.	今天我們要複習加法。
What is 2 more than 3?	3 加 2 是多少？
What is 2 less than 3?	3 減 2 是多少？
What do you get if you take 2 away from 6?	6 減 2 等於多少？
3 plus 4 equals 7.	3 加 4 等於 7。
What is 10 more than 25?	25 加 10 是多少？
What does it equal?	它等於多少？
What number is double 4?	4 的兩倍是多少？
We will study multiplication in 3rd grade.	我們三年級時會學乘法。

P4_002

◎ 教學與解題

Please look at question 2.	請看第 2 題。
We'll be reviewing chapter 3 today.	今天我們要複習第 3 章。
Turn to lesson 4 in your math textbook.	翻到數學課本的第 4 課。
Always use a pencil in math class.	在數學課上一定要用鉛筆。
Please take a worksheet.	請拿一份練習題試卷。
Please turn to the next lesson.	請翻到下一課。
Do you have a question?	你們有問題嗎？
We will have a test on this tomorrow.	明天我們要考這部分。
We have a pop quiz today.	今天我們有個臨時小考。
Can someone tell me the answer to number 6?	誰能告訴我第 6 題的答案？
Watch as I solve the problem on the blackboard.	看我如何在黑板上解這題吧。
Watch me do it first.	先看我做一遍。
Who can solve the problem on the board?	誰能解黑板上的題目？
Did you get the right answer?	你有得出正確答案嗎？
Can you write out the problem?	你能把問題寫出來嗎？
Make sure you show your work!	務必把你的解題過程寫出來！
Try this problem again.	再試一次這道題。
Talk through what you did.	說說你是怎麼做的。
How did you get this answer?	你是怎麼得出這個答案的？
Can you make a graph?	你能做一個圖表嗎？
Use a pie chart to show your answer.	用圓餅圖來呈現你的答案。
Where did you get that number?	你從哪裡得出了這個數字？
How much is a dime and 2 nickels worth?	一枚一角硬幣和兩枚五分硬幣加起來一共是多少？
If you have 3 apples and I take one away, how many are left?	如果你有 3 個蘋果，我拿走 1 個，還剩幾個？

What fraction is this? 這分數是什麼？
What is half of 8? 8 的一半是多少？
How much is a quarter worth? 四分之一是多少？

◎ 時間

What time does the clock say? 時鐘現在是幾點？
Is it half past twelve? 現在是十二點半嗎？
Show me where the clock's hands should go. 告訴我時鐘的指針指在哪裡。

補充單字

addition 加法	**oval** 橢圓形
subtraction 減法	**cube** 立方體
multiplication 乘法	**sphere** 球體
division 除法	**cone** 圓錐體
one half 二分之一	**cylinder** 圓柱體
one quarter 四分之一	**pyramid** 三角錐
shape 形狀	**centimeter** 公分
square 正方形	**meter** 公尺
circle 圓形	**gram** 公克
triangle 三角形	**kilogram** 公斤
rectangle 長方形	

自然科學課

◎ 動植物

P4_003

Today we will be learning about plants. 今天我們將學習植物。
This is a plant's stem. 這是植物的莖。
Here is a picture of the roots. 這是植物根部的圖片。

We will learn the difference between living and non-living things.	我們將學習生物與非生物的差異。
Is a sunflower living or non-living?	向日葵是生物還是非生物？
Will a seed grow if it's left in the dark?	如果種子被放在黑暗中，它會生長嗎？
We're going to plant seeds today.	今天我們要播種。
Do you think it will grow?	你認為它會生長嗎？
Can you label the parts of the plant?	你能標註植物的各部分嗎？
What happens when a flower dies?	當花枯萎時會發生什麼事？
Our next lesson is on animal life cycles.	下一課我們要學習動物的生命週期。
Your homework is about the food chain.	你的家庭作業是關於食物鏈。

◎ 人體

This chapter is about the human body.	這一章是關於人體。
Where is the brain?	大腦在哪裡？
The heart pumps blood.	心臟負責輸血。
You taste with your tongue.	舌頭用來品嚐。
The nose is for smelling.	鼻子負責嗅覺。

補充單字

head 頭
face 臉
hair 頭髮
eye(s) 眼睛
ear(s) 耳朵
nose 鼻子
mouth 嘴
tongue 舌頭

teeth/tooth 牙齒
shoulder(s) 肩膀
neck 脖子
hand(s) 手
finger(s) 手指
arm(s) 手臂
leg(s) 腿
toe(s) 腳趾

◎ 氣候與天氣

Who can tell me the four seasons?	誰能告訴我四個季節？
Winter is my favorite season.	冬天是我最喜歡的季節。
Flowers bloom in the spring.	花朵在春天盛開。
It is hot and sunny in the summer.	夏天會熱且晴朗。
Tell me about the weather.	跟我聊聊天氣。
It's going to rain today.	今天會下雨。

補充單字

sunny 晴天的，艷陽高照的	cold 冷的
cloudy 多雲的	hot 熱的
windy 有風的	spring 春天
rainy 下雨的	summer 夏天
misty 有霧的	fall (autumn) 秋天
foggy 起霧的	winter 冬天

◎ 地球科學

Why is it important to recycle?	為什麼回收很重要？
Can you recycle paper?	你能回收紙張嗎？
We get coal from the Earth.	地球有煤炭。
Gravity pulls objects towards the Earth.	重力將物體拉向地球。
How do magnets work?	磁鐵是如何運作的？
This is a volcano.	這是一座火山。
Lava comes out of a volcano.	熔岩從火山噴出。
We live on the planet Earth.	我們居住在地球上。
Can you see electricity?	你能看見電嗎？
Is there gravity on the moon?	月球上有重力嗎？
What is the largest planet?	最大的行星是哪顆？

Which planet is closest to the sun?	哪顆行星離太陽最近？
What phase is the moon in today?	今天的月亮處於什麼階段？
We'll have a full moon tonight.	今晚會有滿月。

◎ 物理化學

Who knows the three states of matter?	誰知道物質的三態是哪三態？
Is helium a gas or solid?	氦是氣體還是固體？
Water is a liquid.	水是液體。
A rock is a solid.	石頭是固體。
Give an example of precipitation.	舉一個降水的例子。
Is snow precipitation?	雪是降水的一種嗎？
How is rain made?	雨是如何形成的？
What is your hypothesis?	你的假設是什麼？
Today we will be doing an experiment.	今天我們要做一個實驗。
Put on your safety glasses.	戴上你的護目鏡。
What did you observe?	你觀察到了什麼？

體育課

P4_004

◎ 暖身

Let's warm up by running a few laps.	我們先跑個幾圈來熱身吧。
Everyone needs to stretch.	每個人都需要伸展一下。
Let's stretch sideways.	我們來向兩側做伸展動作
Stand up straight with your arms up.	身體站直，把雙手舉高高。

◎ 籃球

Today, we're going to play basketball.	今天我們要打籃球。
Use your right hand to dribble the ball.	用你的右手運球。
Practice your left-hand dribble.	練習用左手運球。
Let's practice free throws.	我們來練習罰球吧。

295

Shoot the ball!	投籃！
You made it!	你投進了！

◎ 足球

Kick the ball.	踢球。
Aim for the cones.	瞄準三角錐。
Try to kick it into the goal.	試著踢進球門。
Block the ball!	把球擋下來！
You scored!	你得分了！

◎ 棒球

Can you catch the ball?	你能接住球嗎？
Find a partner and play catch.	找搭檔一起傳接球。
Swing the bat.	揮棒。
Keep your eye on the ball.	注意看球。
Homerun!	全壘打！
Run to first base!	跑一壘！
You're a great pitcher.	你是一位很棒的投手。
Can someone show us how to swing the bat?	誰能示範一下如何揮棒？

◎ 網球

Grab a tennis racket.	拿支網球拍吧。
Hit it over the net.	把球打過網。
Show me how you hit a backhand.	示範一下如何用反手擊球。
Practice your serve for a bit.	練習一下你的發球。
Can you pick up the balls?	你能幫忙去撿球嗎？

◎ 游泳

We're going to swim in gym class next week.	下週體育課我們要游泳。

Everyone in the pool!	所有人都下水！
Let's practice treading water.	我們來練習踩水吧。
Float on your back.	來仰漂吧。
Let's try the backstroke.	我們試試仰式。
Kick with your legs.	用腿踢水。
Who wants to jump off the diving board?	誰想跳水？

◎ 體操

We'll use the mats for tumbling class.	我們會用墊子來上翻滾課。
That was a great somersault!	那是個很棒的翻筋斗！
Try to keep your arms straight when doing a handstand.	倒立時試著把手臂伸直。
Let's do a forward roll.	我們來做前滾翻。
Let's do sit-ups.	我們來做仰臥起坐。

◎ 田徑

Today we're running for gym class.	今天的體育課我們要跑步。
Slow down just a little bit.	慢一點。
Give me one more lap.	再跑一圈。
Don't give up!	不要放棄！
Who can show me how to jump a hurdle?	誰能示範一下如何跳欄？
Hold the ball like this.	像這樣拿著球。
Try to step with your left foot.	試著用左腳跨步。
Step and throw!	跨步並投擲！
Catch it with both hands.	用雙手接住它。

📖 音樂課

◎ 節拍與韻律

P4_005

Clap along with me.	跟著我一起拍手。
Clap to the beat.	跟著節奏拍手。
Stomp your feet!	踏步！
Do you hear that rhythm?	你聽到這個韻律了嗎？
Listen to the song.	聽這首歌。
I'll play the song again.	我會再播放一遍這首歌。
Let's warm up with scales.	我們用音階來熱身吧。
This is a high pitch.	這是一個高音。
We'll learn the difference between high and low.	我們會學習高音和低音的區別。
This lesson is about fast and slow beat.	這堂課是關於快的拍子和慢的拍子。
Is this a slow beat?	這是慢的拍子嗎？
I'll play it faster.	我會彈快一點。
Sing up high, sing down low.	唱高音，再唱低音。
High and low, and fast and slow are opposites.	高與低，快與慢，這些都是相反的。
Can you hear the difference?	你能聽出差異嗎？
Can you play the scales again?	你能再彈一次音階嗎？
Clap a steady beat with me.	跟著我穩定打節拍。
Do you hear the tempo change?	你有聽到節奏的變化嗎？

◎ 音符

Look at these notes.	看看這些音符。
Do you know what note this is?	你知道這音符是什麼嗎？
There are seven musical notes.	有七個音符。
What note is this?	這音符是什麼嗎？
We'll have a test on notes on Tuesday.	我們週二會有音符的測驗。

補充單字：節奏與音符（rhythm, notes）

rhythm 節奏	quarter note 四分音符
scale 音階	eighth note; quaver 八分音符
interval 音程	sixteenth note; semiquaver 十六分音符
pitch 音高	
Range 音域	thirty-second note; demisemiquaver 三十二分音符
colour 音色	
beat 拍子	dotted note 附點音符
downbeat 強拍	rest 休止符
upbeat 弱拍	semitone / half step 半音
tied note 減時音符	whole tone / whole step 全音
chord 和弦	sharp (#) 升記號
whole note; semibreve 全音符	flat (♭) 降記號
half note; minim 二分音符	natural (♮) 還原記號

◎ 歌曲

Can you sing along with me?	你能跟我一起唱嗎？
Repeat after me.	跟著我複誦。
I'll sing it first, and you echo back to me.	我唱一遍，接著你們跟著唱一遍。
This month we'll be singing Christmas songs.	這個月我們會唱聖誕歌曲。
We're getting ready for a concert.	我們正準備一場音樂會。
Our Christmas concert is next week.	我們的聖誕音樂會在下週。
Do you know this song?	你們知道這首歌嗎？
What genre is this?	這是什麼音樂類型？
This is a jazz piece.	這是爵士樂。
Let's sing a lullaby.	我們來唱搖籃曲吧。
It's a folk song.	這是一首民謠。
Listen to the lyrics of the song.	聽聽這首歌的歌詞。

◎ 表演與樂器

We'll have a talent show next month.	下個月我們會有才藝表演。
Here's audition information.	這裡是試鏡資訊。
We'll watch the band concert together.	我們會一起觀看樂隊演奏會。
Today we're going to play instruments!	今天我們要演奏樂器！
An instrument plays music.	樂器是用來演奏音樂的。
What are the 4 types of instruments?	有哪四種樂器類型？
The four types of instruments are percussion, brass, woodwind, and string.	這四種樂器類型，包含打擊樂器、銅管樂器、木管樂器和弦樂器。
This is a tambourine.	這是一個鈴鼓。
Can you play the bells?	你們會敲鐘琴嗎？
I'll show you how to play it.	我會示範怎麼演奏。
This is a steady beat.	這是個穩定的拍子。
A guitar is an example of a string instrument.	吉他是典型的一種弦樂器。
What type of instrument is the violin?	小提琴是哪一類樂器？
Is a piano a string instrument?	鋼琴是弦樂器嗎？

補充單字：樂器 (musical instruments)

piano 鋼琴	french horn 法國號
guitar 吉他	trumpet 小號
flute 長笛	trombone 長號
piccolo 短笛	tuba 大號
violin 小提琴	xylophone 木琴
viola 中提琴	accordion 手風琴
cello 大提琴	drums 鼓
double bass 低音提琴	triangle 三角鐵
ukulele 烏克麗麗	woodblock 木魚
harmonica 口琴	maracas 沙鈴
saxophone 薩克斯風	

📖 視覺藝術課

◎ 色相環

We're starting our lesson on the color wheel.	我們現在開始學習色相環。
This is a color wheel.	這是色相環。
The primary colors are red, yellow, and blue.	原色也就是紅色、黃色和藍色。
What are the primary colors?	原色是什麼？
Is this a primary or secondary color?	這是原色還是二次色？
What are secondary colors?	二次色是什麼？
Is purple a secondary color?	紫色是二次色嗎？

◎ 色調

Let's talk about warm and cool colors.	我們來談談暖色調和冷色調。
Is red a warm color?	紅色是暖色調嗎？
Blue is a cool color.	藍色是冷色調。

◎ 調色

You can mix colors together.	你們可以把顏色混合在一起。
What do yellow and blue make if you mix them?	黃色和藍色混合在一起會變成什麼顏色？
Can you mix the red and blue paint?	你們能把紅色和藍色的顏料混在一起嗎？
Try mixing it.	試著調色一下。
What happens if you mix white paint with the red?	如果把白色顏料和紅色混在一起會怎樣？

◎ 繪畫

Is this smooth?	這線條滑順嗎？
Show me what texture is.	示範一下有手感的效果。
Does this drawing have texture?	這幅畫很有手感嗎？

Feel the dry paint.	摸摸乾的顏料。
Can you create a pattern?	你能設計一個圖案嗎？
Let's make a shape pattern together.	我們一起製作出形狀圖案吧。
We're going to be painting today.	今天我們要畫畫（油畫之類）。
Can you get out your markers?	你可以拿出你的彩色筆嗎？
Let's use colored pencils for this.	我們用色鉛筆來畫這個吧。
What are you painting?	你在畫什麼（油畫之類）？
What are you drawing?	你在畫什麼（素描之類）？
I want you to sketch a picture of an animal.	我希望你們畫動物的素描。
Try using light and dark pencils.	試著使用淺色和深色鉛筆。
Push harder to make the pencil darker.	下筆用力點，讓鉛筆畫得更深。
Can you blend that more?	你能混合得更均勻點嗎？
How does the painting make you feel?	這幅畫你感覺怎麼樣？
The artist was trying to make you happy with the painting.	藝術家試圖用這幅畫讓你有快樂的感受。
What type of scene is that?	這是什麼類型的場景？
I want you to draw a self-portrait for homework.	回家作業我希望你畫一幅自畫像。
Is that a landscape or portrait?	那是風景畫還是肖像畫？
We'll be using clay for our next lesson.	我們下一堂課會使用黏土。
Everyone should be molding their clay.	每個人都應該要塑造自己的黏土。
Once your sculpture is done, I will bake it.	你們的雕塑都完成後，我再來烘乾。
Baking clay makes it hard.	烘乾黏土會讓它變硬。
Do you want to paint your sculpture?	你想將你的雕塑上色嗎？
What are you making?	你在做什麼呢？
I love your drawing!	我喜歡你的畫！
We will learn how to draw 3D images this year.	今年我們會學習如何畫 3D 畫。

Let's use watercolor paints for this project.
我們用水彩顏料來完成這作品吧。

I want you to trace over your picture.
我希望你描你的這張圖。

Today we will be making fingerprint trees.
今天我們會用蓋手印的方式來畫樹。

We'll do finger-paint this year.
今年我們會用手指來作畫。

Put on a smock so you don't get paint on your clothes.
穿上圍裙，以免顏料弄到衣服上。

Make sure you rinse the brush.
畫筆務必要沖洗乾淨。

Don't spill the paint!
別把顏料灑出來！

補充單字：顏色 (basic colors)

black 黑色	light red 淡紅色
white 白色	dark blue 深藍色
red 紅色	light blue 淡藍色
orange 橙色	indigo 靛藍色
yellow 黃色	teal 青綠色
green 綠色	olive 橄欖綠
blue 藍色	light green 淺綠色
purple 紫色	lemon yellow 鵝黃色
pink 粉色	beige 米色
silver 銀色	coffee color 咖啡色
gold 金色	ivory 象牙白
gray 灰色	light gray 淺灰色
brown 棕色	dark gray 深灰色
dark red 深紅色	rose 玫瑰色

台灣廣廈 國際出版集團
Taiwan Mansion International Group

國家圖書館出版品預行編目（CIP）資料

套用、替換、零失誤！老師天天在用雙語教學萬用句 /
白善燁著 . -- 初版 . -- 新北市：國際學村, 2025.02
　面；　公分
ISBN 978-986-454-405-9（平裝）
1.CST: 英語　2.CST: 語言學習

805.1　　　　　　　　　　　　　　　　113018542

國際學村

套用、替換、零失誤！老師天天在用雙語教學萬用句

作　　　者／白善燁	編輯中心編輯長／伍峻宏・**編輯**／古竣元
譯　　　者／許竹瑩	封面設計／何偉凱・**內頁排版**／菩薩蠻數位文化有限公司
	製版・印刷・裝訂／東豪・紘億・弼聖・秉成

行企研發中心總監／陳冠蒨　　　線上學習中心總監／陳冠蒨
媒體公關組／陳柔彣　　　　　　企劃開發組／江季珊、張哲剛
綜合業務組／何欣穎

發　行　人／江媛珍
法律顧問／第一國際法律事務所 余淑杏律師・北辰著作權事務所 蕭雄淋律師
出　　　版／國際學村
發　　　行／台灣廣廈有聲圖書有限公司
　　　　　　地址：新北市235中和區中山路二段359巷7號2樓
　　　　　　電話：（886）2-2225-5777・傳真：（886）2-2225-8052

讀者服務信箱／cs@booknews.com.tw

代理印務・全球總經銷／知遠文化事業有限公司
　　　　　　地址：新北市222深坑區北深路三段155巷25號5樓
　　　　　　電話：（886）2-2664-8800・傳真：（886）2-2664-8801
郵政劃撥／劃撥帳號：18836722
　　　　　　劃撥戶名：知遠文化事業有限公司（※單次購書金額未達1000元，請另付70元郵資。）

■出版日期：2025年02月　　ISBN：978-986-454-405-9
　　　　　　　　　　　　　版權所有，未經同意不得重製、轉載、翻印。

교실영어 핵심패턴 233
All rights reserved.
Original Korean edition published by Baek, Seon Yeob
Chinese Translation rights arranged with Baek, Seon Yeob
Chinese Translation Copyright ©2025 by Taiwan Mansion Publishing Co., Ltd.
through M.J. Agency, in Taipei.